Tyne O'Connell was born in Brisbane, Australia.
Educated by Catholic nuns, she studied gemmology and
for several years bought and sold gemstones around the
world. She has lived in Cairo where she traded in
antiquities.

She now lives in London in a converted Victorian ware-
house and writes full time. This is her first novel.

Sex, Lies
& Litigation

Tyne O'Connell

review

First published in 1996
by HEADLINE BOOK PUBLISHING

First published in paperback in 1997
by HEADLINE BOOK PUBLISHING

A REVIEW paperback

10 9 8 7 6 5 4 3 2 1

ISBN 0 7472 5613 6

Typeset by
Letterpart Ltd, Reigate, Surrey

Printed and bound in Great Britain by
Cox & Wyman Ltd, Reading, Berks

HEADLINE BOOK PUBLISHING
A division of Hodder Headline PLC
338 Euston Road
London NW1 3BH

For Eric, S.P., Cordelia, Zad and Kajj

Acknowledgements

To the brilliant women and men of the Bar and Bench who gave up their valuable time answering my questions, lending their archbolds, taking me to dinners, checking my manuscript and taking my calls when they were in a hurry for court or late for a conference. Especially to Colin Aylot, Martin Gibson, Robert Silberberg. Also to R.H., T.D., N.W., B.H., and Judge G.

Of course my thanks must also go to their long-suffering and brilliant clerks, chambers administrators and secretaries.

Chapter 1

Only your girlfriends can tell you you've got lipstick on your teeth!

I had just broken the heel of my new two-hundred-pound Manolo Blahnik stilettos – the first two hundred pounds I hadn't made yet! I climbed out of the heat of the black cab and felt the other heel sink into the hot tar of the square in Notting Hill. For a minute I thought I'd just walked onto a Merchant Ivory set. A mixture of crisp white Georgiana circled a garden of some six or seven acres suffocating on roses. I was *so* nervous.

I was due to start Bar school next week with an overdraft at Natwest that made me want to sign up for the French Foreign Legion and I had nowhere to live. And that was just the start of it. The only person I knew in this city was my ex-boyfriend, Giles the super-bastard.

You know the sort! Gorgeous, successful, vowels to die for and genetically programmed to break hearts. He used to lick *crème fraîche* off my belly. I had even toyed with the idea of marriage, but that was in the days before I found out that I wasn't the only one with an anatomical dessert bowl!

I rang the buzzer with my broken heel. A female Cockney twang answered.

'Yeah?' Laughter and muffled voices crackled over the intercom.

'I'm here about the room?' I called out.

I heard another burst of giggling as the door buzzed and I pushed it open onto a high-ceilinged lobby with mosaic tiles. It smelled of stale champagne and vodka and something musty, vaguely redolent of backstage at the ballet.

The ad I'd pulled from the notice board at the Temple library read, 'Two professional women looking for one other to share large flat in Notting Hill – must be open minded.' That was me I'd told myself – my mind is an abyss.

But even I – whose idea of housework is to flap my duvet around my pillows – wasn't prepared for the *Home Alone* mess of designer shopping bags, shoes, magazines, clothes, underwear, jewellery and make-up which were strewn over every surface. It was as if two hundred well-heeled women had been asked to empty their handbags for market research.

Gaultier perfume kissed my senses and Elastica's lyrics wrapped around me like a Lycra body suit. The evidence was clear – this flat screamed GIRLS!

Since walking in on Goldilocks in my boyfriend's bed, I'd been clinging to an anti-man stance like a Zimmer frame. *Get real!* I'd tell myself everyday as I woke up with my heart in my throat and tears stinging my eyes. *They all cheat, they all lie, they're all selfish and they all leave the seat up in the loo. You are over men,* I would insist whenever my groin stirred from its coma. From now on in, this sister is doing it for herself!

'Take a seat,' urged Charles, suggesting a Mae West lips' sofa choking on magazines and shoes. She sat opposite on one of the two red velvet chairs by EDRA that looked like vulvas. She had a no-nonsense plummy voice like Princess Anne's – somewhat at odds with her bleached-blonde crop and tiny black satin shorts. She also had those few extra inches that give a girl a stomping edge in life – mile-high stilettos.

'Yeah take your shoes off,' insisted Sam, the voice I'd heard on the intercom.

'Excuse the mess but we had a—' Charles started.

'We had a cleaner but she walked out,' broke in Sam. *'Oh you so messy mizzes – I not clean your shit no more,'* she mimicked in Cockney cum Portuguese.

Sam was small and shapely with short neat hair. She wore jeans with the knees frayed away and a T-shirt and she talked at a thousand miles a minute with languid interruptions from Charles.

'So if cleanliness is your thing, Evelyn,' she chatted away like

Lois Lane meets Tank Girl, 'seriously – this is *not* the flat for you. We've seen cleaners come and go but mostly they go. I blame all those middle-class matrons that clean up everything before the dailies arrive. Like your mother, eh, Charles? "Charlotte! The cleaner is coming today – don't forget to clean up your mess in the bathroom!" '

We seemed to be getting through the preliminary stuff pretty well I thought to myself hopefully as I relaxed into the sofa, trying to strike a pose that showed I belonged. I liked Charles' measured assurance plus the fact that she was a barrister four years called. That had to be an asset.

Sam, on the other hand, was more like a one-woman army mowing through conversations like a Panzer division gone AWOL and I was slightly terrified of ending up under her tracks. She had one of those viciously sharp wits that come at you like an automatic weapon and take no prisoners.

Charles and I shared Temple gossip while Sam made tea. She was telling me how she'd been asked for sex to secure her tenancy but that, as luck would have it, she'd accidentally walked in on her pupil master being ridden around his room by Anita the receptionist. As Charles put it, 'He was riding the smooth with the rough.'

Sam called out from the kitchen. 'If you want serious scandal you should try the bond market. We get the real sickos!' she promised, as if we should be humbled by the bond markets superiority over the more moderate sickos of the Bar.

Later, as we sat cross-legged amongst the paraphernalia sipping a concoction called Red Zinger with a welcome breeze blowing through the French doors from the square, I was thinking, *Yeah I can handle this.* Everything was going swimmingly, which was great because God knows I needed this room! Then out of the blue, Sam asked *that* question.

'So, Evelyn, do you have a man in your life?'

I spluttered into my cup as the aperture of my mind snapped shut. Despite a voice inside telling me to stay calm, I couldn't. I manifestly lost it actually. Finding out the man you've had up on a pedestal – the man you let eat his dessert off your belly – is cheating on you kind of warps your self-control I guess.

My contempt for the male gene pool started pouring out of me like bile from the possessed. I told them that not only was there no man in my life, but that if one of those missing-ribbed bastards tried to cross the threshold of my temple, they'd be doing it without genitals!

I'd been doing a lot of reading about ancient female rituals concerning that very matter – the castration of men's bits. Thing was, I didn't see anything strange about it at the time. Gran always insisted that only your girlfriends can tell you if you've got lipstick on your teeth.

Charles and Sam looked at me as if realising for the first time that I hadn't walked through a metal detector on my way in – while I held forth on the virtues of genital desecration. What's more I couldn't stop myself going into details about how some ancient matriarchal societies had these rituals where they'd string men out on mountain tops with herbal ointment smeared on their organs of lust – so that birds of prey might be encouraged to swoop down and peck off their . . .

'OK already. Chill out,' yelled Sam. 'We're all girls here all right?'

Somehow I managed to get a grip. I tried to smile up at her insouciantly from the ditch I'd just dug for myself. What the hell was I thinking – running around like a radical wimmin's separatist? They were looking for someone to share the bills, a bit of washing-up and the odd joke. Who was going to open up their flat to a feminist Pol Pot?

'Well, maybe you feel even more strongly than us, Evelyn. It's not that we hate men you see,' Charles explained calmly. 'It's just well . . . the reason I asked is . . .'

'We're lesbians,' added Sam, walking over to the balcony.

'That's right,' Charles agreed, going over and putting her arms around her – just in case I wasn't familiar with the term.

'And, well, as you can imagine,' she went on, 'men um . . . well, because we're lesbians. I mean it's not that we're . . . um . . . separatists or anything mad like that. Not that we don't like separatists or anything. Well gosh, I'm running around a PC minefield here aren't I? But look, the point is, we've got nothing against men or their . . . um whatsits and well it's just that they—'

'Don't have a lot of place in our lives!' Sam interrupted, rolling a knot around the midriff of her Calvin Klein T-shirt, exposing a navel-ring.

'Exactly. I mean, especially their um . . . um . . .' Charles struggled for the word, scraping back her blonde crop for inspiration. 'Genitals,' Sam explained.

Sitting there watching those red velvet vulvas yawning at me, I decided that this was just what I needed. What better way to avoid men than living with lesbians? After all, living with single girls usually means a stream of men running through the living room like a river. And I loved the flat – the atmosphere. OK it was a mess, but it was the sort of mess I liked.

But that was when I had the fit. I'd slurped a mouthful of tea on top of a biscuit which must have gone down the wrong way and I went into this frenzied coughing spasm. God it was *so* embarrassing. I must have looked like some sort of puritanical vicar's wife choking on her sense of decency. I mean it's not as if I was shocked or anything. You don't spend twelve years in a convent school and not discover the mysteries of the clit-club for God's sake. But I could tell by their faces that they thought I disapproved of them.

Charles ran off to get me a drink of water while Sam looked down on me with undisclosed hatred.

'God, I'm so sorry,' I struggled to explain. 'Look, I hope you don't think I was shocked or anything . . . you know by what you said. It was just the biscuit . . .' I floundered.

She looked at me in sad disgust like a farmer looking at a calf with BSE. 'Oh no. Not a bit. We get that reaction all the time,' she reassured me sarcastically.

'Well you're wrong,' I insisted feeling braver. I was a bit hot under the collar actually. We Horntons don't like being misjudged. It's the last thing you need as a Catholic. 'The truth is, I've just broken up with my boyfriend. That's why I was mouthing off just then. Look, I'm not trying to patronise you honestly. To tell the truth, living with women is just what I need at the moment. I mean you probably guessed, men aren't exactly flavour of the month with me.'

Charles passed me the water. I felt reassured by the way they looked at one another, like two nurses agreeing that it was time to unstrap the straightjacket.

That was two years ago. I got the room – and I'm still in it.

Chapter 2

She was gagging on her ovaries!

There's a lot to be said for living with lesbians. Apart from make-up, cocktails and clothes, Charles, Sam and I shared the same sense of humour. I call it Salome humour because it usually means some poor bloke's head ends up on the comedy platter.

The fact was we meshed. We were the same but different. Charles was brought up in Gloucestershire and Sam in Essex. Charles went to Roedean, Sam went to Billericay Comprehensive and I went to a convent school in Sydney.

They would tell me about life as lesbians in provincial England and I would shock them with my fearsome Aussie stories of swimming amongst six foot sharks (the two-legged variety) and what it felt like to have sex with the sort of man whose only other body contact was with surfboards. We were exotic in one another's eyes.

While I trudged through exams and pupillage and finally into a tenancy at 17 Pump Court, the girls were there to remind me that there was more to life than reality. I doubt I would have got through it all without them feeding me intravenous backup the way only girlfriends can.

Since I moved in I had gone on and on about how inept and gross and treacherous men were and they had nodded like they understood. What I needed was serious counselling probably – or an exorcist even.

They were usually still in bed on Sundays when I took myself off to Brompton Oratory for a spot of Latin mass. I enjoy my religion more when I can't understand what the priest's trying to say and I *lurv* all that trippy incense bit. One of my hang-ups is that I didn't get to be an altar boy. But my biggest hang-up of all – bigger than altar boys, or men, or orange lipstick even – is guilt. It's a truly momentous thing with me – seismic actually.

After mass I'd come home practically drunk from all the worship and repentance to find the girls eating one of the RBs – Recovery Breakfasts – muesli, fresh fruit, yoghurt and vitamin capsules. Crouched over their picnic on the floor, they'd look up at me through their Ray-Bans like they couldn't remember who I was and were wondering what the fuck I was doing in their flat before deciding, what the hell, and offering me a vitamin drink.

These RBs were a ritual with them. A detoxifying nutrition blitz, to wash away the sins of Friday and Saturday nights. I don't want to imply that they had a drug problem or anything. They were your average girls living on London's knife edge of career-driven stress and in-your-face leisure.

It was just that while I was doing serious class-A guilt, they were doing drugs! Ecstasy and coke mostly – every weekend. They had their own dealer. Which as a fashion accessory in London ranks about even with a personal trainer I guess. But come Sundays the chemicals went away and the two-piece suits came back from the cleaners and the all day recovery breakfast took over the flat.

So there we were in the living room on one of those long Sundays after a typical RB. Sam and Charles were recovering from the weekend – I was still getting over my birth, my gender, Catholicism and, well, everything basically.

I was lying stretched out on *the lips*. I'd just painted my toenails a really neat fuchsia colour that matched the new Manolo Blahnik slingbacks with steel heels I'd gone into overdraft for. I was contentedly reading *Vogue*'s guide to the snootiest shop assistants on Bond Street, trying to pretend I wasn't going to go into the office tomorrow and have the usual brawl in the clerk's room about work. As in why don't they give me any?

The girls – as per normal – were lying on the vulva chairs which had been pushed closer together so they could plug their bare limbs into one another like ac/dc adapters. Sometimes I felt jealous watching their easy physicality with one another. It wasn't grossly sexual or anything – more like a sensual ease with one another from which I felt excluded.

I never said anything. But sometimes – usually during one of my fortnightly bouts of PMT – watching them slotting into one another like Russian dolls, I'd get this sinking jealous feeling, like someone was doing keyhole surgery on my chest.

The best thing about our relationship was that they were really supportive of my decision to be a man-hating hetero-sexual. They never pushed the issue.

Up until that night.

It was Sam who opened the Pandora's box – childlike in white Calvin Klein knickers and DKNY T-shirt. She looked decep-tively innocent. What really bugged me at the time was that she hadn't even had the decency to take off her Walkman while she dropped her napalm.

'So, Evelyn, when are you going to start seeing, you know . . . men again?' You've probably gathered that subtlety suits Sam about as much as stilettos suit the average diesel-dyke.

I rolled my eyes at Charles. We were on the same wavelength Charles and I. After all, it was Charles who'd saved my butt during exams in those all night-study blitzes where she'd drum in the practice of evidence and procedure and the liberty of the subject till I recited them in my sleep – in biblical tongues.

At three in the morning during my exams, Sam would stagger out and ask, 'Are you coming to bed, Charles, or what?' And we'd jump on her for poor negotiating skills. It was Charles who'd taken me to Ede & Ravenscroft to buy my wig. It was Charles who went to kick-boxing classes in Bethnal Green with me and covered my back on the way home on the tube. And it was Charles I trusted more than anyone else not to bring up *that* subject. So naturally I turned to her now.

But this was an attack from all sides. Her brutality set alarm bells ringing.

'Yeah. You'll grow over with cobwebs, girl!' she agreed.

What was going on here? They knew the first command-ments. Don't mention the M word to Evelyn, etc.

I looked into their Ray-Bans and gave them both a cold, hard stare. They'd made an agreement when I moved in not to hassle me about my sex life – or lack thereof. Besides, it wasn't as if it was a big sacrifice for them – men weren't exactly their subject either.

Sam loathes them the way most women loath cervical smear tests. And even Charles, the more liberal of the two, referred to men's gropingly inept bedside manners as bed-pan manners.

So what was going on? Summer had arrived with a Mediterranean passion, but I felt a sudden chill in the air.

'Is it us that puts you off them – you know, puts you off . . . um . . . men?' Charles enquired nonchalantly. She was avoiding my eyes – smoothing the creases on her new Liza Bruce shift she'd bought with the proceeds of her first murder trial – blood money she called it.

'Yeah, you've got to face them again sometime,' Sam warned.

'Face them?' I exclaimed. 'You make men sound like a crime I'm trying to run away from.'

She took off the Walkman and went over to leaf through our CD collection – the one haven of organisation in the chaos of our flat.

I looked from one to the other. It was obvious this was a pre-planned attack.

'Yeah, it's not as if you've found a substitute for them,' Sam taunted as she stretched out on the floor and commenced painting her nails.

I watched as a drop of plum red polish fell from the brush onto her T-shirt.

My patience was draining from me like blood from a haemophiliac. 'Fuck off!' I snapped.

'Evelyn!' Charles said my name like the priest used to say it in confession before he gave me six-thousand Hail Marys for my penance. 'Don't let the bastards get you down, girl.'

I folded my arms and tried to remember whether my horoscope had warned me of treachery from close friends.

'Don't let the bastards get me down?' I repeated while my eyebrows jostled with my hairline for room. Oh this was brilliant! 'Sounds like that's precisely what you're proposing! And besides, it's really none of your business what I do or don't do with men. Well is it?' I quipped acidly, throwing my lanky legs over the side of the sofa. Then I buried my head in the AAA rating awarded to YSL for arrogant staff.

After half an hour of conspiratorial whispering in the kitchen, they came back with herbal tea to resume the attack. 'Evelyn!' they meowed.

Charles came and sat on the sofa and spoke in a kinder, more conciliatory way. 'Look, Evvy, we just think it's time for you to kind of . . . get . . . well, maybe the time has come to . . .' She picked at the velvet vulva beside her while Sinead O'Connor added her Celtic vowels to the argument.

'Get back in the ring!' Sam added, admiring her talons which were now glistening in plum gloss.

'That's right. Back in the ring,' Charles agreed. 'Where you belong. I mean, be reasonable, Evelyn. It's not as if you're gay or anything – so why not face what you are? Put the past behind you.'

Sam came over and crouched by me. 'Yeah live a little! Giles was a super-bastard – we know that but . . . But . . . well, come on, Evvy.'

She blew on her nails again and then I realised it was *my* new DKNY T-shirt she was wearing – and splattering in polish. 'Face it, Evvy, they can't all be bastards!' she reasoned looking through her Ray-Bans earnestly.

But I refused to be pried from my obdurate resistance to men that easily. I raised my eyes heavenward as one who's being given the facts of life by a pair of infants. 'And what would *you* know?' I challenged. 'I wouldn't think either of you were in a position to judge. I mean you're hardly in the ring yourselves are you? Well, darlings? Come on then? Tell me why you're so keen for me to get in there all of a sudden?' I demanded, keen to press home my advantage.

'*Palease!*' snapped Sam. 'At least *we* know where *we* stand.'

'So do I!' I shrieked. 'And it's in *my* fifty quid T-shirt!'

The girls went silent. Sinead carried on her heartfelt soliloquy. Clearly there was another agenda here. We were discussing something other than what we appeared to be discussing. And that was when I realised that this conversation was just a front. Like those bars that say the word 'escort' instead of 'prostitute'.

The thing was the girls had their own problems these days. Sperm problems. And I had a sneaking suspicion that when they talked about *men* and me getting back in the ring, they were using a code. For men read sperm. For get back in the ring read find me a donor.

Charles and Sam wanted a kid.

The truth was they were sick of the sex, drugs and rave lifestyle and now they wanted to move on to night-feeds, nappies, and nannies. Sam was especially clucky. It was a natural progression I guess. Lots of lesbian couples go through this. Lots of hetero couples do too come to think of it. It's a pretty ubiquitous urge – to propagate yourself. Hell, think of Abraham.

They had been together for over five years, they made plenty of money, they owned this flat and now they wanted to get going on the 2.4 bit. Problem was – there wasn't a spermatozoa to rub between them. Not that Sam was discouraged – she was already suffering phantom morning sickness. I had also noticed a steady rise in the number of little cuddly toys making their way in with the shopping each week. Face it – the girl was practically gagging on her ovaries.

They'd started searching for a donor a few weeks back without the slightest success. Sperm is not the most readily available of commodities. You would have thought mankind was swimming in the stuff – but the truth is, it's harder to come by than heroin in Notting Hill.

Like a fool I'd presumed it was just a phase that would pass in time, like the time she declared she was a Buddhist – a fad that lasted about as long as it took her to realise that orange wasn't her colour. But I was deluding myself.

'This is all about you two wanting a sprog isn't it? I mean it's nothing to do with me hating men is it? You just want to use me as a sperm collector? Well don't you?' I raged.

They blinked at me flirtatiously.

'Can't you ask someone at work?' I suggested, my voice suffused with sarcasm. 'Why are you hassling me to do your *dirty work*?'

I felt lousy as soon as I said it. 'Dirty work' isn't exactly the politically correct term for doing your friends a favour after all. Even if it is a favour that involves handling men's ejaculations.

'Sure, Evelyn. *Brilliant!*' Charles snapped as she threw a teddy she'd been idly toying with into the air. 'I mean it's not as if you're our best friend or anything. It's not as if you're the only hetero friend we've got. I mean how could we even *dream* of asking you – our *best friend* – to do us a favour?'

Teddy had landed face up in last night's Sainsbury's watercress and cardamom soup.

Charles carried on. 'I know, why don't I approach my head of chambers?' she sneered with more out-of-character sarcasm. I'd never seen her like this. But she was bloody good at it actually – making me feel bad.

'Or maybe you'd like me to bring it up at the next chambers' management meeting? 'Thing is, chaps, I'm a bit stuck for sperm right at the moment, so if any of you feel disposed to pop a bit of what comes readily to you in a jar, I'd be most obliged?' Yeah I'm sure that'll go down about as well as a vasectomy with the blokes.

'I'm sorry to have asked, Evelyn, but the fact is we want a baby and as lesbians we're forced to rely on our *friends* doing our *dirty work*.' She glared at me the way I glare at blokes who drool at me on the tube.

'But why can't you do it yourselves? I mean you do have your own vaginas,' I reminded them.

They looked at one another nervously. 'Well it's not as if we haven't thought of that ourselves. But we just can't do it, Evvy. I mean think about it. You're used to sex with men – you've even enjoyed it before. But when I contemplate sex with a man . . .' Charles shivered – as if coupling with a man was one down from drinking urine. Then she slumped into a vulva. 'I just can't.'

This left Sam alone in the middle of the floor.

'Well don't look at me!' she pleaded.

We both looked at her.

'Uh ah,' she said, shaking her head.

'If you think for a minute that I'm going to have some bond trader pumping my body . . .? Besides there's no way I'll bear the fruit of one of those City-hog's loins!' she declared, firmly folding her arms across her chest. 'Think about it. It would probably be born with a mobile phone grafted to its ear.'

'Well what about me?' I asked. 'What's good for the goose and so on?'

'That's different. It's a different thing altogether. You're a hetero!'

'So what if I am a hetero?' I shouted. I didn't like the way she made *hetero* sound like *bimbo*.

'Well you're . . . you know . . . that's what you do.' She jilted her pelvis at me in a disgusting manner. 'Oh, you know what I mean, Evv. It's different for you. I mean before Giles and everything that's the sort of thing you did. You used to do it for fun, for Christ's sake!'

'What's that got to do with it?' I demanded. But I knew where we were heading. This was one idea that wasn't going to sink into the soup. It was one of those ideas that bob up and down on the horizon like a piece of glow-in-the-dark Styrofoam.

I walked over to the sink and ran teddy under the tap.

'You don't seriously want to bring a baby into *this* kitchen do you?' I exclaimed. But I guess some things don't have to be said between friends. I knew what I was in for by the way they came and cuddled me round the waist and said, 'Oh, Evvy! You wouldn't have to do anything much. Just find someone nice and run the used condoms into us when you're finished.'

So that was how it all began. I guess that's fate – one minute I was a celibate manhater whose only challenge in life was avoiding chippy shop staff on Bond Street. The next minute I was agreeing to become a vessel for sperm donations. Where would it all end?

But what else could I do? I reasoned as I tossed and turned in bed that night. I couldn't just turn my back on them in their hour of need. I was their link to reproduction – I was their link to men – to the zygote. I couldn't exactly deny them that – could I? Not with my Catholic guilt.

Christ it was practically a spiritual quest. I felt a bit like Arthur must have felt on his quest for the Holy Grail, or Noah on his search for two of each. These past two years Sam and Charles had become like sisters to me, they were the closest thing I had to family in England after all. Now they wanted me to help them have a kid. What would that make me – a sperm mother?

I have a lot on my plate at the moment, I wrote to my parents in Australia that night (without going into details). I mean, it wasn't as if my last few letters – detailing my dreary cases at Snaresbrook Crown Court and the woeful weather in London – had prepared them for anything close to this.

I couldn't even face my prayers. What was I supposed to say? Dear Lord, come to me in my hour of need. The thing is, God, I ... um ... er ... um ... need to find some semen for my girlfriends.

This was going to take more than an Our Father and three Hail Marys.

Chapter 3

The bad-lipstick day

Two weeks later I was having what we girls call a Bad-Lipstick Day – a BLD.

'Never take drugs before marmalade,' Charles warned me as she spread it all over her toast. Even behind her Ray-Bans the weekend's excesses were obvious. 'They send you mad,' she insisted, not looking entirely clear-headed herself.

It sounded like a truism my grandmother might have told me as a child. Gran was big on marmalade, big on truisms, big on drugs come to think of it. She was always upsetting our family doctor by referring to him publicly as her *pusher*.

Why hadn't I listened to her?

It all started the night before – when Sam and Charles had their dealer over for a last visit.

'Now we've decided to do this parent thing,' they explained to him as if they were dismissing an employee, 'we're really sorry but we won't be able to use you anymore. The thing is we're giving up all this chemical shit – so we can get pregnant.'

Albert took it philosophically. He just turned his attentions to me – Miss Goody Two Shoes who thought it was excessive to take two paracetamol at a time. 'So what about you, Evelyn – are you trying to get pregnant as well?' he had teased.

OK, so I was a bit stupid to take ecstasy before my first trial at the Old Bailey. But what's a girl to do when a black Adonis falls into her kitchen while she's having a fit of nerves, selling

17

something he says will 'make you feel mellow'? Buy up like the Japanese in Duty Free, that's what.

The problem started when I dropped the stuff. If only I'd taken Bill Clinton's advice and not swallowed!

Anyway, Charles went off to Snaresbrook Crown Court in full charge of her faculties, leaving me in no doubt that I was classifiably insane. Instead of getting myself together for the Bailey, I proved my mental ill health by setting about on a mad attempt at washing up the pile of dishes that had been accumulating in the sink since the Portuguese cleaner left two years ago.

Me who never washes up? Now that was definitely one of Gran's sayings – 'show me a woman with dishwater hands and I'll show you a man with a mistress.' I took it to heart. I may have sworn off men – but that doesn't mean I've got to spend my life at the kitchen sink does it? This was a serious case of genetics gone wrong! *Me* in an apron with my hands draped into a tub of Fairy Liquid?

That years of feminism should lead to this! Gran would have turned in her grave – if we hadn't had her cremated.

Five minutes later my hands looked like swollen pig's bladders that had just been cut open. And excuse me, I thought, reading the label, this stuff's meant to be *good* for your hands? The radio was belting out one of those pop dirges about the desperation of the millennia. What the hell was I doing? I was due to defend a GBH in an hour – and three hours before I'd accidentally taken ecstasy!

I confronted the clock and realised I had no more than half an hour to spare! The memory of that tab came oozing back into my consciousness like blood going up a syringe bulb. And I started to realise that this whole ecstasy thing might have been a bad career move.

In acknowledgement of my circumstances I opted for a quiet little Dolca Gabanna two-piece. Very court-like, I thought – using every point of my IQ just to make sure I was putting it on the right way round. I didn't want to look more of a jerk than I felt. I could just see it . . . 'If Your Lordship would mind waiting two minutes while I invert my gown?'

Five minutes later I was still trying to find the armholes and then when I did I realised that the jacket was inside out. Then I tried to remember what this case was about. Who was I defending anyway? Had I ever met this suspected bastard? Had I even received a brief? But my brain was on pause at that stage.

The *Go To* command was jammed with a garbled arena of instructions: my father insisting I eat a hearty breakfast before a case (significantly there'd been no mention of ecstasy); my mother's warning me to get a good night's sleep (I'd been at The Ministry of Sound most of last night); my instructing solicitor insisting that I arrive half an hour before the trial in order to have a *con* with my client – (I was running half an hour late).

And last but not least, Albert, the black drug dealer with his ring-of-confidence smile, assuring me the Es were so mild I'd have to take at least two just to get *sorted*! I was going to sue the bastard for breach of promise.

Later on in the cab on the way through the bumper-to-bumper traffic, I had this preternatural sense that something dreadful was about to happen – like that feeling mystics get just before they get on a lift that plummets to its doom. But I wasn't psychic – I wasn't even intuitive, but I had a creeping feeling I was on *that* lift.

My cabby wasn't helping. He was one of those cab drivers carefully trained in the knowledge of wind-up. He had his ear up against the radio relaying the traffic reports so he could make a bee-line for every point of congestion in the city. Talk about the knowledge – this guy threw the A-Z at me. From Kensington High Street to Marble Arch to Kings Cross, there wasn't a traffic jam in London that morning we didn't do.

He waved warmly to bus drivers who swerved out in front of us. He stalled at pedestrian crossings even when there was no one nearby. He smoked a cigar and laughed immoderately at his own inner comedy. I mean, I only took a cab because I was too paranoid to take the tube. But now even eye-ball knifers of the Central Line were preferable to watching my entire legal-aid budget spin round on the meter. I offered to tip him if he ran a few red lights. He shut the adjoining window.

By the time a punk courier with a jumble sale of earrings through his face pulled up beside us as the lights turned green at Holborn and asked for directions to Gray's Inn Road, self-control was a thing of the past. My driver pulled over and gave explicit and mind-numbingly detailed instructions until the lights changed to red.

This wasn't happening. I started climbing the walls of the cab. I searched for distraction in the ashtray – opening and closing it, thinking about how I could use it as a weapon on one of us. Watching it gape open like a slobbering orifice with dusty gums and buck teeth, I suddenly regretted not smoking.

Only criminals and housewives smoke, Gran used to insist. In her mind there wasn't a lot to choose between the two groups – she had it in for both of them. That's why she'd started her legal dynasty. It was all a plan to rid her part of the world of housewives and criminals.

She had married a barrister in London in 1935 and promptly gave birth in rapid succession to four girls and one boy – all born with wigs on their heads. And then out of the blue she decided to emigrate to Sydney with the youngest – my father. Her explanation was that England was dead – and I had to concur. She loved the sun, the sea and the yachts bobbing in the harbour – and so did I. I wanted to go home.

That was when I remembered it! The GBH I was meant to be defending was a Mr Keith Conan of Shepherds Bush. And on top of the racing mind and the paranoia I started to feel sick.

The pre-trial hearing came back to me like a first period as I remembered Keith calling the magistrate a wanker and threatening to castrate the clerk. I sat in the shadow of his solicitor, hiding in my gown, hoping no one would require my services – especially Keith. Give me a break here – I was just on my legal training wheels – I was too young for GBH. This was all Candida's fault.

So where was *she* now? My money was on the hair salon. You don't get hair like Candida's hanging around the Old Bailey. 'The case is a walkover, darling. Poor Mr Conan was severely provoked. A clever counsel will demonstrate that!' she had insisted as she *returned* the brief.

He was severely provoked? I marvelled. I was the one being bloody provoked. You only had to take one look at Keith of Shepherds Bush to see he was a man with his charm on inside out – and definitely not a man to be handled on ecstasy. Keith didn't just have 'form', the man was a walking crime bureaucracy. Let's get real – I needed defending from him!

This was worse than I thought. This was a Section 18 of a BLD. We are talking Orange Frost!

I knew then – this was going to the sort of day that came off on my teeth.

Chapter 4

Ours is not to question why. Ours is to defend, prosecute, litigate and die!

As the cab approached the Old Bailey, I pulled the wig out of my briefcase and placed it on my head like a halo. It was my grandfather's wig – the wig that had launched thousands of the most litigious divorces of Mayfair, weighed with a suitable sense of ancestral veneration and redolent of all his triumphant cases.

My DNA swelled with pride before squirming – as I dutifully tried to fabricate a case for my head-butting client. Why did it have to be GBH? When I went to the Bar it was because I wanted to bring bastard landlords to justice or fight for the rights of fragile pensioners caught stealing sausages from Marks and Spencers for their cat. I could hear Gran's voice, clear with the resonance of St Mary's, Ascot: 'Ours is not to question why, Evelyn, ours is to defend, prosecute, litigate and die!'

Was this the scenario my whole life had been elaborately preparing me for? Had my parents actually paid good money for this? From the Loreto nuns in Kirribilli? From Oxford? To Bar school?

I wanted to phone fate on my mobile and plead for an adjournment on life – to explain how I wasn't really ready – how I wasn't certain I was cut out for a career at the Bar – how recently I'd started having cravings for cigarettes and washing-up – how I'd inadvertently taken ecstasy a few hours ago – and how I honestly thought that Keith Conan, the head-butter, deserved a better brief than a man-hater wearing Orange Frost with her gown on inside out!

I threw myself out of the taxi with no more than ten minutes to spare. While I was paying the fare, Our Golden Lady of Justice looked down on me from above the dome of the Central Criminal Court. Tall and statuesque – here was a woman made to wear Lacroix! In her classical robe she was the Donatella of Versace, the Loulou de la Falaise of Yves Saint Laurent, the muse of the justice system. She was weighing up my chances, and as a fellow woman she knew they were halved by this lipstick shade.

Tearing into the court building I felt like someone who'd taken speed not ecstasy! And even drugged I knew I lacked dignity. Sister Conchilio wouldn't have been surprised. My mark in deportment was the lowest ever recorded at the Loreto College for Gentlewomen. My final report read, 'She has the gait of an animal of prey.'

My predatory stride was halted by the patient, shuffling queue at the metal-detection booth. When it came to my turn the guard identified me as the sort of stuck-up young female barrister he lived to humiliate. I was told to empty my pockets.

Time and time again I walked through with all beeps squealing until I had shed my watch, my rings, my keys and my spare change. In the end we decided it was the wire supports in my bra that were making the machine whirr like a car alarm. You can't buy this kind of humiliation – even in Japan. I prayed for death.

It was only my ancestry – which traced itself back to the Tyburn martyrs – that carried me on.

Once in the marble sanctum, my gait parted cells of witnesses huddled around, sedated by their awe of the surroundings. Solicitors talked to barristers clutching ubiquitous volumes of Archbold with yellow Post-it notes marking relevant pages. They spoke with the insouciance of professionals about murders and armed robberies.

Police and Securicor guards mingled and moped around the edges, waiting hopefully for a suicide bomber or a Care-in-the-Community patient off medication to break the boredom.

The problem now facing me, I realised as I searched the heads of the crowd, was how was I going to find my solicitor? It was a problem made all the harder by the fact that I didn't know what he looked like. Mr Dobbs, the sweet old chap I'd been dealing with up to now had upped and died last week. An omen of major proportions. A neon sign lighting up my future blinking – GO BACK YOU ARE GOING THE WRONG WAY!

I was meant to meet his replacement twenty minutes ago at the metal-detection booth, but I guess he had moved on. I decided to use the advantage of my six foot two (in heels) to scan the crowd. Failing that, I dived into the sea of pinstripes hoping he would pick me out by my desperation.

At first I thought it was my urgency that was making everyone stare, but then I saw the truth as a small plait fell into my eye. Oh Christ, my bloody wig was on back to front.

I was gripping my brief under my armpit to rearrange it when I spotted him down the back of the lobby, veiled in plumes of other people's smoke, holding his papers against his charcoal Armani suit. The sexiest-looking man I'd ever seen in my life.

Now let me assure you – Armani suits at the Bailey look about as absurd as Americans in deerstalkers on Baker Street. This is the sartorial home of pinstripes and handcuffs, uniforms and guns. But he had the sort of face that could get away with wearing a John Paul Gaultier micro-kilt if he wanted.

Words like gorgeous and G-spot and swoon sprang to my mind. He was tall with foppish blond hair he had tried, with limited success, to tame with gel – speaking euphemistically this man was genetically superb. As Sam would say – prime donor material!

I couldn't take my eyes off him – far more worrying though was that he couldn't take his off me. He seemed to have fixated on me. Questions kamakazied into one another in my brain. What could he possibly want? What should I do? Apart from the odd fantasy and marble statue in Florence I'd never seen this man before in my life.

Next thing I knew he was grinning at me like a Care-in-the-Community patient off his medication, waving at me frantically. He started coming towards me. That's me – guaranteed to attract the loonies.

I said a quick novena while he shuffled through the crowd and the fog of a thousand Marlboros. His gaze remained fixed on me. He flicked his hair from his eyes so he could get a better view. I looked around hopelessly for help. Maybe he was just a particularly gorgeous serial killer. Where are the Securicor guards when you need them?

Was it my lipstick, my gown, my bands that had him so excited? *Oh I get it,* I thought, *maybe he's the Old Bailey style council coming to charge me with sartorial ineptitude. I know it looks bad but it is a Dolca Gabanna,* I wanted to cry out. I was on the verge of showing him the label. Thank God I stopped myself. Had I actually paid unearned money to feel like this?

I felt my armpits moisten. I felt my left tit slip underneath the rim of my bra and last of all I felt my brief tumble from its pink ribbon and fall, taking my self-confidence with it.

The papers fluttered everywhere. I stood quivering while the eyes of every creature of the judicial system condemned me as a fool.

I crouched amongst a sea of pinstriped legs and harvested my fallen brief madly. Looking at my hands as they grabbed around other people's shoes, I half expected stigmata to appear. I was being martyred to the *fin de siècle.*

And then realisation hit me like a contraction. It was my solicitor – Julian Summers!

'Evelyn! God, I was starting to panic!' he cried out as I grabbed the last page of my brief and stood to face him. *He* was starting to panic? Talk about men having lower panic thresholds. But God he was edible! My jaw opened and closed for a bit before the sound came out. When it did, it was all sort of squeaky and ineffectual like I'd swallowed my rape alarm or something.

'Julian? Shit – I'm sorry. I've been . . . well . . . it's my stomach actually. Nerves, well, an ulcer basically.' I rubbed my stomach and tried to look as adorably worthy of forgiveness as a girl can in a venerable wig.

From his phone voice, I'd envisaged a spotty kid from South London – straight out of university, wet behind the ears. Not this catwalk god. Not this sex-on-legs. I started having retrospective orgasms – like I'd been having phone sex all along.

'Love the suit! Armani is it?' I enquired. But I already knew I'd broken the back of his irritation with me.

He put his head back and laughed – a throaty laugh, self-aware and sexy as hell.

My out-of-condition libido started flexing its muscles.

Chapter 5

The romantic nature

Criminal defence, who'd do it? Certainly not a fledgling barrister with ecstasy in her system if she had a choice. But that was my point, I had no choice. We girls have been throwing ourselves in front of horses, burning our bras and signing petitions for a century for a little choice. So why were my choices so hellishly minimal? To go to work, or not go to work... and starve?

Give me a break – is that worth throwing yourself in front of a horse for? I felt like fishing my bra out of the charred ashes and going home for a bit of domestic drudgery.

Julian walked off. 'Let's head on down,' he suggested and I followed him like a chattel.

Downstairs in the cells, a Securicor guard in a pea-green uniform picked his nose and peered through the Dickensian ledger for Mr Keith Conan. If I was about to swerve from my loathing of mankind, here was the bloke to put me back on the straight and narrow. His name was embroidered on his pocket, which says a lot about a man I guess.

While we waited for Tom-*get-a-hygiene-code*-Betts to find our client in the book, I gave myself a mental update of the case and mused on the implications of entering a not-guilty plea on a Section 18 when there were three credible witnesses out there – one of them a priest – and all of them prepared to swear on the Bible, the Koran, the Torah and their Social Security Giro that they saw the defendant approach the victim and, without provocation of any kind, head butt him into a three-week coma.

What was it Candida had said about this case being a walkover? This was a walkover all right, I could already see the footprints on my gown.

Finally we were led through a series of bars to our assigned room. The guard scrawled Keith Conan on the door and clanked off down to the cells to find our man – he who would pay for my lipstick and nail polish for the next few weeks.

Julian and I waited, grim faced and anxious, while the smells and sounds of the cells gave all my orifices a police body search. It's times like this that I wish I had a hobby – one that doesn't damage my nails as much as biting them. *Focus*, I told myself. *You are a professional woman with a responsibility to your client.*

I looked at Julian. He smiled a full-calorie cream smile in the direction of my legs. Normally I'd kick a bloke in the groin for a look like that.

I used to do that sort of stuff all the time – hit blokes like Julian in the groin. It was when I first started kick-boxing and I figured it was my duty as a modern woman to redress the balance of thousands of years of male harassment. It worked like this – some bloke would do a line on me, or some creep on the Underground would figure my bottom looked like it needed a squeeze and WHAM into the gonads flew the heel of my six-inch stiletto.

The thought of Julian's groin made me bite my lip. I tried to distract myself by reading a few lines of graffiti about Man U(nited) and the obscene bodily functions assigned to their enemies.

'You get used to the smell I s'pose,' Julian suggested, referring to the stench of villains and their hygiene crimes, penned into small spaces. But all I could notice was that he had clear green eyes flecked with brown and eyelashes that curled up at the ends, beckoning to me like Siamese fingernails.

I nodded agreeably, thinking about all the men in my life at the moment – blokes in chambers and the man who came to read the gas meter mostly. I couldn't think what colour any of their eyes were. Certainly none of them had eyelashes that curled up like Siamese fingernails.

Julian began pacing the unpaceable. Our conference room

was about six foot by six foot and hopelessly claustrophobic even with the glass partition. I had another one of those premonition thingamees – a homicide coming on maybe?

But as Keith was finally led in I had a surge of adrenaline. He was just as I remembered – hunched of shoulder and mean of face. This was the sort of bloke that made a girl wish she'd worn her bicycle helmet. His, I would wager, was not a romantic nature. In fact if I was head-hunting head-butters – Keith would be my man.

I'd heard rumours of thugs having steel plates inserted into their skulls to give their head butts more punch. The patch above my nose felt suddenly soft. I tried to move my eyes up in their sockets in order to get a look at it.

Keith and Julian looked on, troubled at my rendition of an epileptic fit. 'Ah,' I said sagely to offset any concern. 'You came, Mr Conan.'

'Give me a chance, luv, I only just got here,' Keith joked, thumping Julian in the ribs with his elbow.

Julian fell forward and grimaced. I tossed up the idea of running out now while I still had the chance and throwing my wig and gown in a bin on the Strand. Who was I kidding? I wasn't cut out for this. This isn't what Sister Conchilio meant when she spoke dreamily of *vocations*.

Somehow I managed to effect the necessary introductions. And, as I explained Mr Dodds' replacement, I realised that there was a light at the end of the tunnel after all. Not strictly a light, more of a wet match, but I tried to strike it anyway.

I suggested to Keith that if he was dissatisfied with the unscheduled change of solicitor – if he thought it prejudiced his case, for example – he could apply for an adjournment and ask for another solicitor. I repeated the point again seeing the obvious advantage of the judge putting the case off for a few weeks – or a lifetime even.

Julian looked on stunned. This wasn't strictly the case. I could see he was trying to calculate how much beef I might have consumed over a lifetime. His cheeks went a bright orange making him look like more of a Ken doll than ever.

'Nah, fuck that,' Keith sneered. 'I'm not going to rot in 'ere while they find me another poxy lawyer.'

I thought Julian was going to cry. Putting on his Armani suit

29

this morning, he probably thought he had taken every precaution possible to avoid jibes like *poxy*. But there it was. You have to take the rough with the smooth in law. He recovered himself quickly and offered his hand.

'Mr Conan.'

His overture was rejected with disdain.

'Fuck off all right! I don't have to tell you nothing all right!'

Then he pointed at Julian with his index and little fingers – the way vampires do when you go at them with a wooden crucifix. Turning to me he gave a warm, toothless grin.

'Do we 'ave to have this jerk in here or what?'

I smiled my best bad-lipstick-day smile and shrugged.

Julian cowered in the corner like a scolded child and pretended to arrange his notes.

In hindsight I can see that I was going the right way about making an enemy, but I was too 'mellow' to know. Stuck for words I decided it was time for a bonding prop. 'Cigarette, Keith?'

I offered the packet of Marlboros Charles had made me bring. Sizing Keith up as a fan of daytime television, I was making the most of my accent. Hamming up those Aussie inflections at the ends of my sentences for all they were worth.

'Thanks, mate – you're all right you know.' He grinned fondly. Something told me we were bonding beautifully as I lit his cigarette and embarked on my pre-trial pep talk. Listening to my voice jumping around the walls, I was surprised at how in command it sounded.

'Now, Keith, on this plea of not guilty?'

'Not guilty – that's right, man. You're brilliant ya know that? Hey, Julie, the judge is goin' to love 'er, eh?' He nudged Julian in the ribs hard.

'Pretty good case they've got unfortunately, Keith,' I warned severely. I didn't want to let this bonding thing get out of hand.

'Eh, Julie – the judge is going to be droolin' when he sees 'er or what?' he asked excitedly.

I ignored him. 'They've got three credible witnesses, Keith. One of them a priest,' I reminded him sternly. 'While we number relatively few witnesses of our own. Well ... er ... none, basically!'

I crossed my legs. Keith's head started rocking, but I ploughed on.

'Now I know you've entered a plea of not guilty. I don't suppose you've, um, any inclination of changing that to a guilty. I mean, you do realise that were you to plead guilty, the judge would be obliged to give you a reduced sentence?' I was still holding out an iota of hope that he'd change his plea and make my job easier. But then again I was on drugs!

Keith said nothing but his eyes had transfixed themselves at my chest.

'I think Mr Dobbs, who's sadly no longer with us, may have mentioned I'm a profound mitigator!' I went on, lying through my teeth. I couldn't have mitigated myself out of a paper bag the way I felt now.

'Fuck off, man. He fucking took a kick at me dog,' Keith yelled. Punching a fist into his hand for emphasis. They were big, angry, frustrated hands looking for something to do – with the words HATE and KILL tattooed on the knuckles.

I flurried my papers, searching for evidence of dog kicking. Just the word dog would have been a relief. Julian looked warily at Keith. The case instructions I'd received swam across the page like worms in a jar of water. I couldn't see the word dog anywhere. The whole thing seemed to be written in a Gaelic script. The room was a canister of nicotine.

I looked up. Julian was plucking at the seam of his jacket as if looking for fleas. He was taking what's known as passive revenge on me for trying to have him knocked off the case earlier.

Keith was sitting quietly, staring at me, flicking his ear.

Between them they offered a solid argument for the annihilation of their sex. If I could just get Tom Betts from the front desk in here the evidence would be insurmountable. We sat immersed in our own thoughts like this until, overwhelmed by my surroundings, I finally convinced myself that I was hyperventilating and that the only solution was to find a pocket of air.

I imagined there was just such a pocket caught between my hair and my wig. The dilemma confronting me now was how Keith might construe his barrister tearing off her wig and sucking on it?

He ground his cigarette into the cement of the floor with his fingers. Hope was spitting me out like old chewing gum.

I pressed my wig tightly onto the crown of my skull as I tried to remove all sense of panic from my voice and ploughed on. 'You haven't mentioned the dog before, Keith?' I squeaked.

Julian moved in his seat as if he might lay an egg.

Keith stood over me – something was brewing behind those bloodshot eyes. I was sure of it.

Then I heard myself make a strained squeaking sound like I'd just swallowed my rape alarm again. Julian had started squeezing his legs together as if he was in some kind of geriatric exercise class. He held my Archbold tightly to his lap. Meanwhile my lymph glands took the opportunity to drop a lifetime of toxins into my armpits.

We were in trouble, I thought, as Keith started unbuttoning his flies with a grim determination. We were turbo-blasting our way into a realm of criminality far beyond the scope of textbook law.

I hoped that I was just having one of those drug-induced hallucination thingammies – maybe my brain had swelled? The thought of falling into a coma seemed vaguely seductive compared to this. Julian gazed with terror at Keith. He didn't look much in the mood for egg-laying now.

Keith grunted.

Oh Lord Jesus help us, I thought. *He's going to crap.*

I should be so lucky. A nanosecond later a massive penis with a foreskin like a drainpipe was directed towards my face. What the hell did he want – a blow job?

I'm not what you'd call a deep throater at the best of times – with the best of men. Men who take baths even! I threw my head backwards and then to the side, the way chooks do when they see an axe coming. The indefatigable penis – as if equipped with an electronic honing device – moved ever closer.

I felt as if I had a part in one of those porno-thriller-snuff movies and I was playing the part of the one that wasn't going to live to see my pay cheque. Where were the censors now? This whole event belonged on the cutting-room floor!

As the foreskin arrived at my nose it stopped and it was peeled back to reveal a small moist square which looked suspiciously like the tab of ecstasy I'd taken four hours ago. I watched the penis, hanging sadly outside the flies like a drunk Securior guard at his post, while Keith unwrapped the square of paper and passed it to me.

It would have been churlish to refuse so I grabbed it eagerly and tried to focus. I was hoping it would read I HATE BLOW JOBS! But it didn't.

I held it at arm's length and tried to ignore its malodorous smell. It was a picture of a pit bull terrier.

I didn't need a law degree for this shit! I needed tranquillisers. I needed months' worth of Prozac. I pleaded to the Virgin Mary to let me disappear into the osteopathic hell of my plastic chair. A lousy tab of ecstasy? I was meant to be experiencing *mellow* for Christ's sake? Well if this was mellow I wanted a stress attack. A lobotomy would be preferable to this!

'Me dog, Vomit!' Keith announced like a proud father.

Julian leaned in to take a look.

Keith showed no enthusiasm for putting away his penis. It was huge. He could have been a porn star if he wanted. He needed an agent not a barrister.

I went back to the photograph.

Vomit looked and smelled like he'd been up Keith's foreskin for quite some time. I thought of my parents sitting down to enjoy the view on their terrace overlooking the harbour.

Looking out on the yachts sipping their Hunter Valley claret, my father would be thinking of me, trying to envisage me at the Old Bailey, asking my mother how she thought I was getting on. And I could bet my overdraft she wasn't replying, 'Oh she's probably just getting a better look at her client's penis now, dear.' The sun was already going down on the horizon in Sydney. Here in London the day from hell was just beginning to dig in.

I held the wilting snapshot in one hand while I pressed my other hand against the vulnerable area above my nose. It looked a lot like Keith's penis – before it had shown such worrying signs of erection.

Keith laughed warmly as his penis became a turgid weapon. 'Brilliant dog, man.'

I looked up. 'Fuck, Keith, I don't know if this will help.' But even I realised this was not the time for counsel. It was like thirty years too late for Keith. So I took my wig off and sucked on it for all it was worth.

Julian pretended to be unfazed and carried on on my behalf. 'You see, Keith, it's a bit late for you to produce more evidence – unless it was previously unavailable and even then it should have been mentioned.'

Keith's penis began to deflate. He grabbed the photograph haughtily and set about meticulously refolding it and replacing it under the foreskin of his now collapsing erection. I felt guilty. Maybe we'd offended him?

But I had underestimated his resilience – he was a man of philosophical bent. He shrugged his shoulder. 'Yeah well . . . I just thought. Worth a try, know what I mean?'

I nodded vigorously. 'Sure! No, absolutely. Always a good idea. And Vomit looks like a fine animal, Keith. Have you thought of showing him? (I was really losing it big time). No? Well let's say we take our chances on the not-guilty plea? We'll give them the stuff that you've been unemployed for a while . . . well . . . er . . . forever basically. You were under a lot of pressure and you genuinely misconstrued events and felt yourself to be under attack.'

I could feel Julian beaming at me.

'Sure, man, you're the boss,' Keith agreed. 'Let's kick arse then!'

He likes me, I thought. At times like this, when friendship is thin on the ground, a girl takes what she can get. I'd all but forgotten what life outside this cell was like by now. I'd kind of relaxed within the cosiness of these cold walls. It was a simple world with simple rules. I knew my way around. *You're over the worst*, I told myself.

But then Keith went over to the door and shouted with all his might – something that no barrister wants to hear once she's planned how she's going to spend her fee.

'GET ME ANOTHER BRIEF!'

Guards came running from everywhere. Meanwhile I collapsed into a pile of black rags on the floor. If Dolce Gabanna only knew where this suit was going to end up as they lovingly draped the cloth over models in their studio they would have sacked their marketing team.

Keith looked down on me and smiled. 'Just kidding, mate,' he explained as they cuffed him and led him away.

Julian pulled me from my heap of designer despair on the floor. His hair brushed against my face and Armani Pour Homme (what else?) in all its spicy sharpness cauterised my intelligence. Underneath all the creases of his suit I sensed there were pectorals worth getting the specimen jar out for.

I guess it was a chemical reaction to the ecstasy or something. Or maybe Sam and Charles had put a spell on me? But as I reached out and took his hand I realised that one way or another this guy was going to play havoc with my biorhythms.

Lust had me by the fallopians.

But was this what I wanted? No! Dear reader, I want you to understand this point above all others. This was not what I wanted. I wanted to mitigate against my fate – I was over men remember? I was vulnerable – swooning under the influence of a class-A drug – my client having unravelled the secrets of his foreskin to me. And then there were my girlfriends – talking about nothing but sperm for the last month.

This had to be a setup.

Chapter 6

Courting Disaster!

The public gallery of Court Three was already full. The noises, the smells and the polished dark wood of this legal edifice tingled all my nerve endings and tranquillised my fears. I mean hell, I was here. At the Old Bailey! Sure I'd been to crown court before and I'd been here with my pupil master, but this was the Bailey and the wig was on my head now. I could hardly suppress my excitement. There was nothing I wanted to do more than punch my fist into the hallowed court air and say YES!

The Crown Prosecution Service (CPS) clerk was looking his nerdy best – it's a job that has nerdyness written into the job description. Beside him the prosecution council shuffled papers with assurance. Didn't I recognise him? I thought. That perfect complexion that screamed 'I've never been to Benidorm', those sexy eyes emphasised by the thick-rimmed glasses he kept pushing up that handsome aristocratic nose? Or was I hallucinating again? I was crossing the boundaries between reality and panic like an Olympic hurdler. I sucked hard on one of my tonsils.

'Are you OK?' Julian looked at me, all concern. There was a tiny black hair waiting to burst from his left nostril. I wanted to bite it off. After two years on the celibacy rack I think I might have misplaced the manual for sexual attraction.

'I think I might need a drink of water,' I explained.

'You do look a bit peakish,' he agreed as he poured me a glass of cloudy water from the jug. 'Poor thing.'

Peakish? Did he mean he was recognising in my visage a hint of my urge to nip at his nasal follicles? I felt my face for evidence of peakishness. It felt like rubber. I took a gulp of the cloudy water. It tasted like a viral infection. There was a lump in my throat and I couldn't swallow. I turned terrified towards Julian.

'Are you OK?' he asked again, now bug-eyed with fear. I could tell he wasn't in the mood for his brief to collapse.

The water sloshed about my mouth as in a toilet that wouldn't flush. Then the prosecuting counsel waved. Was this a mirage or did I have a serious case of madness on my hands? Get a grip, girl! A small stream of water trickled from the side of my mouth. Barristers do not wave to one another in court – I mean it's not a written rule or anything but it's lore. Then the familiar-looking counsel for the *persecution* smiled, raised his eyebrows and for nanosecond I thought he winked at me?

I took another sharp intake of breath – the water went down.

'Are you OK?' Julian asked again, now looking about him for assistance. 'Do you need to go outside?'

'Just feeling a bit... um... peakish. I'll be all right in a moment.' I tried to reassure him by smiling bravely. God he was gorgeous. *Hang on a minute*, I thought, *was I seriously considering becoming a walking sperm bank for my lesbian housemates?*

'All you'd need to do is collect the condoms when it's over and run them into our room,' they had said. Oh brilliant! Just what every fucked-up Catholic girl wants to hear when she's toying with the possibility of sex for the first time in two years. And, anyway, was Julian the sort of bloke who wanted to see his spermatozoon make whoopee with a lesbian's egg via a turkey baster?

I didn't care. All I wanted to do was to tear off his Yves St Laurent shirt and rub my hands all over his muscles. If I was endowed with a penis, it would be embarrassing me now. But why – we were strangers to one another's phenotype? I mean, let's get this much straight – I go for vulnerable men (preferably in glasses). I go for skinny fragile men that look like lead singers in British pop bands. It's written into my genes – *thou shalt not date men who can fend for themselves.*

And, any way you looked at it, Julian had a body that made Robocop look like a kitchen appliance.

But my train of thought was halted when Keith was led in by four guards. He was wearing handcuffs at the front – jiggling and juggling about as if his skin was loose. The guards manhandled him into the dock. He took a swipe at one with his shoulder and then the other guard did something to him that looked like a Heimlich manoeuvre so that he lolled pathetically into the chair.

I looked at Julian – he was gritting his teeth. There was a little nerve twitching in his cheek. God how I wanted to kiss it.

'All rise,' bellowed the clerk of the court suddenly. I recognised her from the Lesbo bar in Soho that Charles had taken me to last week. She was topless the last time I saw her with pierced nipples with little gold rings through the centre. I was finding it hard to concentrate.

'Hear yea, hear yea, hear yea,' she cried before rambling on with a little chant about 'all being upstanding' and the like – I was waiting for her to whip out a stick with bells stuck on and start a Morris dance. This is the sort of showmanship you get if your crime is serious enough to make it to the Old Bailey, I thought to myself – very tempting.

Court proceedings got under way according to protocol but I pretty soon sensed that the equilibrium wasn't going to last. I was about to be derailed from my confidence in terra firma by the changing expressions on Keith's face. As the prosecution counsel rose to present his case, a bag of nausea split in my stomach.

I wasn't coping. I should have paid an analyst to *sort me* not a drug dealer. Despite my earlier delusions that the ecstasy might be wearing off, I knew now I was wrong. It was just coming on. I clenched my hands as a marmalade chunk marinated in bile travelled up my oesophagus.

As counsel for the prosecution struggled to seduce the jury with his opening speech it was impossible to ignore the fact that Keith was becoming increasingly agitated about something or someone up in the public gallery. At first this agitation took the form of shoulders hunching and unhunching in the way fighters warm up before a fight, but pretty soon he became more verbally bellicose, urging whoever it was to come down and 'be had'.

'Com'n then, com'n. Yeah com'n, I'll have yer. I'll have yer, COME ON! Yeah that's right, I'll have yer. I'll have yer! HERE – NOW!' he bellowed.

Keith was an eloquent communicator. No one was in any doubt as to his meaning – we just couldn't hear or find his would-be assailant. Everyone craned their necks looking up into the public gallery. I heard something go crunch in my spinal column. I made a mental note to ask Lee if I could charge my gay osteopath's bill to my legal-aid fee.

Judge Camp looked bored and irritated in turns. He looked at his watch and advised me to advise my client that restraint would be in his best interests. I remonstrated with Keith, waving him to sit down and be still. When this had no effect the judge cast a frozen look of contempt over Julian and myself and threatened contempt of court. But Keith was determined to have it out with his invisible tormentor in the public gallery.

The four Securicor guards flanking Keith seemed equally happy to let him have his say. They reminded me of mothers with screaming children in shopping centres who want the world to know the full enormity of a mother's lot. They stood impassively, exchanging raised eyebrows with one another, showing no enthusiasm for the Heimlich manoeuvres of old.

Something told me my time had come. Now was the time for all good women etc. etc. to understate the obvious.

I rose to my feet. By now my legs felt like jelly, I had a cramp in my stomach and another in my left shoulder which conspired to present me to the Bar as a parody of Richard III.

Miraculously though I managed to stay upright. 'Your Lordship,' I said with all the bravado of a fox at a hunt-meet. 'I think now might be a good time to take an adjournment so that I may have a conference with my client.'

Judge Camp looked about the court, allowing his gaze to fall like sour cream on the guards who were now disposed to press restraint on Keith. Two of them wrestled him into a head lock, another two twisted his arms behind his back while three or four others scrambled about on the floor trying to contain his thrashing legs. This was my client – this demented lunatic it was taking seven trained Securicor guards to hold down! Embarrassed is not the word.

The Honourable Mr Justice Camp looked at his watch again.

Then he looked at the jury. They blinked back like rabbits do while you align them in your gun sights.

The judge looked down on me disconsolately. I prayed he was in the mood for a cup of tea.

'An adjournment you think?' His eyes crinkled up – I couldn't tell if he was in pain or just thrilled to see me.

My mouth had seized up again so I let my head loll around a bit like Gandhi did before he mobilised millions.

'I *will* allow you half an hour with your client, Miss Hornton, but I strongly advise you to bring the full force of your powers of persuasion to bear on him. We don't want to waste any more of the taxpayer's money or the jury's time than absolutely necessary do we?' He cast a stern eye about the court as if looking for taxpayer's money wasters. 'Do I make myself clear? Court will resume in half an hour.'

I took another gulp of water while the 'hear yea, hear yea, hear yeas' were administered. The counsel for the prosecution looked over to me – the way attendants at Harrods look at me while they try and decide whether I'm a shoplifter or the wife of an Arab sheikh.

Then he raised his eyebrows and winked.

Winked? Was I being patronised here? OK so my client had lost it but that wasn't a reflection on me – it's the luck of the draw in crime. I began to fume. Who the hell did he think he was?

And suddenly it hit me like a hot mud pack. This was no trick of the drug, no mad paranoia, no hysterical mood fluctuation of my menstrual cycle. The man who couldn't keep his eyebrows to himself – disguised as counsel for the *persecution* was none other than my ex. The super-bastard *extraordinaire*. Giles Billington-Frith.

Chapter 7

These ecstasy things should come with an embarrassment warning

Down in the cells Keith's mood had not lightened. Julian and I waited in our conference room, listening to him making noises like a surfer being taken by a shark while the guard went to get him. His howls communicated all our dread of this case.

We didn't speak – I thought about Giles. It was like opening Pandora's Box II. Although we were both in chambers in the Temple, I hadn't actually seen him since the night I'd discovered Goldilocks in his bed two years ago. I was meant to be moving in with him for Christ's sake – and there she was under the duvet we'd bought together!

We had met five years ago during my first month at Oxford. I was still adjusting to life in England, let alone university. I was the only Australian in my college. Supposedly, Oxford has a great history of antipodeans, but it wasn't wearing it on its sleeve that night at The Turl. Luckily I sub-majored in self-defence. The cliché of Australians as uncouth savages had little place in Loreto College for Gentlewomen – but try telling that to the best and finest of England when they're in their cups.

I took their preconceptions of me on the chin for the most part – unless they involved my virtue, in which case they took my stiletto in the testicles. That was how we met. Giles was about to defend my honour when I got in first with a side kick that ended up in his solar plexus. He took it like a man and fell into a whimpering heap.

At the time I thought there was something adorable about his foetal form lying at my feet. But from that moment on, all the subjugation was done by me. It was as if the Women's Movement had never happened. The suffragettes had died in vain. Germaine Greer had wasted her ink. I mean here we were at the end of the millennium and I was walking around with 'chattel' written all over me. As Gran used to warn us kids – if you want to be kicked just bend over. And, girl, did Giles get the boot in that night.

Now he was back. They say revenge is sweeter served cold.

Well, what about putrid and rotting?

Julian put his hand on one of mine and gave it a reassuring squeeze. I looked up at him. Was he really worth giving up my man-fast for? I asked myself earnestly. *After all*, I told myself, *you've just got over the last bastard. You've just won back your independence.* Get real, this guy had a face worth giving up breathing for!

His hair was framing his pale face like a halo of straw. He reminded me of the infant Jesus in a nativity scene at school. It was made of wax. One Christmas, the chapel had become so hot during the service that the baby melted and his face had spread out amongst the straw of his crib.

Before I had time to dwell on the Freudian implications, Keith was bundled into the room in handcuffs, bleeding heavily from the nose, cheeks and neck. He was still yelling and throwing his body about and the stench of fresh haemoglobin was sickeningly thick.

'He's had a go at himself,' explained the guard.

I muttered doubtfully about prison brutality.

'With this!' he insisted, pressing a glob of something into one of my hands.

Keith elaborated on his mood, bobbing and weaving like a rugby player on his way to score a goal. ''E was fuckin' goin' for me up there! Did you see 'im didja – didja? Fuckin' cunt! I'll fuckin' have him I will. I would 'ave 'ad him in there. They should o' let me.'

The guard shook his head. 'He was in the toilet. We have to let them go – we're not nurses you know!'

The shorter of the two guards nodded gravely. They both had their names embroidered on their pockets like staff at McDonald's. It was hard to take anything they said seriously.

'Didja see 'im?' interrupted Keith, the blood spreading out like a grotesque red stocking over his features. "E was fuckin' eggin' me on from up there. Didja see him . . . didja?'

Julian looked at me with one eyebrow cocked – I concurred with a nod. 'Can't we have a doctor?' I asked, still flummoxed by the inscrutable glump in my hand and the copious amounts of blood on Keith. I didn't like the cavalier attitude of the Securicor men one bit.

'What, for him?' The guard laughed nastily, pointing at Keith. 'He's OK. Just needs a splash with water. He did it with a bloody button – broke it in half with his teeth. Look!'

Everyone looked doubtfully at the contents of Keith's mouth.

'Well his gums then. Anyway, he's just scratched himself. Look at it,' he persisted, pushing the stigmata-like chip about the palm of my hand with his finger. He was right, it did appear to be half a shirt button.

Julian clenched his jaw.

"E was up there goin' like this,' Keith interjected, bobbing around in a re-enactment of his enemy in the public gallery, mouthing the words, com'on then.'

'A fucking button,' repeated the Securicor guard, turning to leave. 'Gees, I've seen it all now. Tried to top himself with a bloody button.'

He wandered out as the other guard brought in a wet towel.

'These are desperate times,' he added darkly, wrapping it about Keith's face.

Left alone, we attempted to resuscitate the case. While Keith sat leaning back in the orange plastic of the chair, I tried valiantly to talk him up.

'Remember what we're here for, Keith. After all this is your big day in court. You can't let some jerk in the gallery fuck it up for you.' I decided to avoid mentioning the point that this jerk was a figment of his imagination. 'That's what they want to do – get you riled.'

I paced the cell, relaxed by the sound of my voice pawing at the walls.

'You've got to keep your head, Keith. Keep your eyes on the judge and jury – stay calm . . .'

Keith pulled the towel from his face and looked up at me. At that moment he bore a striking resemblance to Vomit – the pit bull. I looked nervously at the remaining buttons on his blood-stained shirt.

'You callin' me paranoid or wot?' he asked.

I wanted to explain that I would be the last person in the world to cast that stone. 'Not at all. Not at all. You know what I mean, Keith.'

Keith didn't look convinced. 'Don't fuckin' tell me what I know! RIGHT? I don't like to be TOLD. Right?'

Julian was looking at his feet – or more pointedly his shoes. He was still on his passive revenge rampage. Obviously that remark about poxy lawyers was still smarting. But I felt enough was enough. All right, it was insensitive and unprofessional of me to suggest to Keith that Julian might prejudice his hearing. So maybe I deserved a stern look, or a ticking off, but now was not the time to be taking passive anything. This situation called for action – all hands on deck and stuff. I mean look at what this Keith maniac had managed to do to himself with half a button?

On the other hand maybe it wasn't passive revenge. Maybe Julian had taken the rumours that the age of chivalry is dead seriously or something.

Sometimes I feel that feminism has got its priorities wrong. For instance, I think the first battle the Women's Movement should have tackled is the battle of the loo seat. Don't get me wrong, I'm not whingeing about having the vote. I like the equal opportunity bit and earning my own living – and I'm on for opening my own doors and paying my own bills and halving the cost of child care with the government.

It's the details that I don't like – like going without a seat on public transport while members of the non-stiletto wearing public sit. And the way men still wolf-whistle at us from up on building sites when they know we are too far away to slug them. Sometimes I think all we've done is make *their* life easier. OK fine, I know it's no longer women and children first – but *please* we're talking serious headcase with half a dozen buttons still left on his shirt. I don't think it's too much to ask that Julian at least look sympathetic?

'I'm on your side remember, Keith,' I pleaded unconvincingly. 'I want to win this case as much as you do. But fuck, (I thought the odd obscenity was permissible under the circs), we've got a lot going against us here. They've got a lot of ammunition. We've got to keep our cool and show the jury that we're not thrown by that bunch of wankers out there.'

I eyed Julian, who was nodding sagely (at his shoe). I was going to slam the heel of my stiletto into it soon if he didn't look up. But my pep talk seemed to be working. After a few more soothing words, Keith retreated back under his towel – as happy as a sunbather. But the damage was already done. It had been a harrowing moment. I took another look at the broken button squelching in my hand!

A clammy, pearly, bloodstained chip that had reduced a head-butting maniac into a stigmartyred anti-saint. The smell of gore made me crease in the middle like a suicide note. What I needed was to get rid of the smell. I pulled out the trusty packet of fags. 'Cigarette, Keith?'

Keith popped his head out from under the towel. Apart from a few scratches he looked fine now. 'Cheers, man. I'll just take one for later if you don't mind?'

I didn't really feel it was my place to mind. I smiled generously as he took the best part of the packet with his cuffed hands. 'Go right ahead,' I urged.

Then I passed the pack to Julian.

'Cigarette, Julian?'

He looked at me as if I was mad. But at least he was noticing me.

I pushed the cigarettes closer. 'Go on,' I goaded, getting a little bit of that passive revenge stuff of my own.

Julian edged further back in his seat as if I'd offered him an infected syringe.

'Thank you, but I don't smoke, Evelyn.'

'Don't let that stop you. Look I'm having one?'

To prove this I took a cigarette from the packet and placed it in my mouth as if it was the most natural thing in the world. Gran's voice was in my ears – only housewives and criminals smoke. But I played deaf.

I lit Keith's cigarette and offered the pack to Julian once more. He shook his head, his eyes bountiful with incomprehension. I lit my own and shook the pack in his direction again.

'Sure?' I egged.

'Yeah! Go on.' Keith joined in. He was a man animated in crisis.

I know I should have stopped hassling then, but I couldn't. Events just took me over. Maybe it was a power thing. Whatever it was, it was compelling stuff. Julian's shoes couldn't be further from his mind now. 'See – it's great!' I dragged heavily and smiled. No smoke came out. I must have forgotten to exhale. I went a pale shade of Securicor-guard-uniform green.

'Yeah, try it. For Christ's sake it's not going to kill you, man!' Keith bullied. He seemed to be taking the matter a bit too seriously.

'Yeah, live a little.' I choked, trying to be light-hearted while the smoke was winding its way through a maze of passageways within me, discovering my anatomy as I never had.

I shook the cigarettes at Julian again.

Keith grabbed my wrist with his cuffed hands and shook the packet harder – aggressively even. I began to get worried.

He began shouting. 'Com'on, man. Just try it. For fuck's sake what are you afraid of? Shit, I've been smoking since I was nine! Never did me any harm.'

Harm was not a matter that either Julian or I wanted to take up with Keith. I took a deep drag of smoke. Now I knew how Italian women felt – blowing their smoke into the faces of prospective paramours. I blew my smoke at Julian. His mind was not on love though. He looked about, wildly uncomfortable. And looking at it from his point of view he was right to be a little scared. What could I have been thinking of?

I put the cigarettes away. Julian started to breathe out. Looking at Keith, spread out on the orange chair – the words HATE and KILL emblazoned across his knuckles, the towel wrapped about his face leaving a small gap for the cigarette to poke through – I decided he wasn't a bad bloke really. After all he loved his dog didn't he? What was its name? Vomit?'

That was what did it. Suddenly I was curling up around the edges. My stomach wanted out! I banged on the window. 'HELP! Let me out.'

A dozen guards burst into the smoke capsule but I was out and down the corridor before they had time to assess the situation.

★ ★ ★

In the loo, cleaning myself up I asked my reflection for advice. 'You've blown it,' she told me. 'Julian must think you're a first-rate maniac. Barking – that's how he'll describe you to his colleagues.' She was right of course. I blamed Giles. It was obvious that seeing him had really shaken me up.

What was I thinking of? Harassing the first man I'd got close enough to see his eye colour to smoke? What kind of a chat-up line was that? OK, I know drugs kill but these ecstasy things should come with an embarrassment warning.

Chapter 8

Learning to tell the difference between a hormonal imbalance and a religion

Back in court, events transpired like a mugging on Oxford Street. Julian was solicitous and friendly which made me feel even worse. *He hates me,* I thought. *He's patronising me,* I thought. *He doesn't think you're up to it,* I thought. And he was right.

Drugs cause brain damage. A police unit had come to school armed with videos and pamphlets to warn me of that. Memory is particularly prone to being dissolved by chemical intrusion they'd warned.

In our salad days, crisp with the cynicism of youth we had laughed at our elders and their crude attempts to talk us out of our harmless fun. But they had been telling the truth. All my days at Bar school, all those days I'd spent wasting away, poring over the liberty of the subject and Archbold in The Temple library were now no more than a black hole in my synapse.

I put my head in my hands. The golden rule of the wigged set is never, ever, ever, look defeated – especially in defeat! Julian asked me again if I was OK.

'Sure,' I said without much conviction as I tried to sit up and face him. 'I'm sorry about what took place down there – you know with the cigarettes. I was just extremely nervous. I don't know what came over me.'

'Sure,' he responded insincerely.

Despite myself I looked over at the prosecuting counsel. That was a big mistake. I would have been better looking at the eyes of Medusa because Giles gave me a concerned nod which brought back a hundred memories I'd done my best to eradicate. Memories that reminded me of how I'd loved a two-faced bastard above all else.

The first commandment is thou shalt not take false gods against me. Well, Giles was my golden calf – fêted and petted and carried aloft. Gran had always warned me as a kid to keep men in perspective. 'Evelyn,' she used to say in the middle of the rosary or something, 'the hardest thing about love is learning to tell the difference between a hormonal imbalance and a religion.'

I know you're going to think I'm, like, totally backward ... but I thought Giles was going to be different. I mean, try and get a handle on what I was up against. He had bones to die for. Cheekbones, jaw bones and all the other bones that define beauty. Not only was he over six foot, suave and sophisticated, with the body of a consumptive god and vowels to die for, but he had the kind of hair that no woman with her womb still intact can resist – bedroom hair.

I gave up everything for that man. Suddenly it was as if nothing in my life was worth anything before Giles Billington-Frith came into it. I stopped calling up my girlfriends to see what they were doing. I stopped asking myself what *I* wanted to do. And the worst humiliation of all – I started waiting for him to ring.

Was I possessed or what? I should have asked a responsible adult to get me to an exorcist. Instead I wrote poetry and stuff comparing his eyes to a Greek island. The man wore horn-rimmed glasses for God's sake ! Nana Mouskouri would have been more like it. But love's like that. That's why it's called a virus because no matter what you do to avoid it, no matter what feminist vitamins and victim immunisations you take, it always floors you.

Love is the great leveller, Gran always said. And I was plastered down to a smooth self-sacrificial finish. You know that bit about from dust you have come and to dust you shall go? Well that's my love life. One minute I was a statue of Venus – fecund with the strength of womanhood – the next WHAM, I'm trodden underfoot by a nerdy bloke in glasses who has cheating written into his DNA.

Putting it simply Giles is what's known as a SNAB – Sensitive New-Age Bastard. That means he'd done a crash course in what makes women tick and he knows what buttons to press to make them explode. The strange thing was, everyone who knew me said how lucky I was. Everyone told me what a sweetheart he was – what a lamb. Well, let's get this much straight, lambs don't make their girlfriends sleep on the wet patch!

I shot him my most poisonous look. This was war. I might be losing the battle to win the heart of Julian, but I was damn well going to win the war against Giles.

Back in the dock, Keith was at it again. This time the enemy was within – within the bricks and mortar and wood panelling of the court. He started shadow-boxing and throwing himself dementedly at the dock.

My remonstrations went unheeded. He was threatened with contempt. The judge urged me to restrain my client. The Securicor guards – all eight of them huddled in the dock with Keith – cleaned dirt from under their nails while he went berserk.

Time seemed to be strung out like toffee, but in fact it was all over within minutes. After failing to convince the wood panelling of his urge to do battle, he contented himself with head-butting the dock and rendering himself unconscious – to the loud applause of the public gallery.

The judge looked at me disconsolately. He was balding as I watched. What had this venerable old Edwardian gentleman done to deserve this? I asked myself. I was young, I could take a knock, but this poor judge deserved better. He held his glasses in his hand, waving them loosely as one who has seen enough of life and feels it's time for that holiday in the Bahamas.

Looking at Keith being carried out, looking at the judge looking at his watch – and looking at Julian staring at his shoes – I felt like eating my three volumes of Archbold. Our vain hopes and undiluted trust in the legal system were a thing of the past. We were living in new and as yet judicially uncharted times.

Then Julian looked into my eyes and gave me a reassuring smile – a smile that said I know you're up against it, but I'm relying on you to save the day.

I hatched my plan to kill two birds with one stone. I would

seduce Julian with my legal acumen. I would stun him with my influence over Judge Camp. And I'd make Giles wish he'd been a solicitor. I rose nonchalantly and addressed the judge, suggesting that it might be prudent for a doctor to take a look at my client.

The judge sighed and looked down on me as if I were the cause of his piles. Then he replaced his glasses on the end of his nose and sighed again.

'What exactly appears to be the matter with your client *this time*, Miss Hornton?'

I hesitated suggesting it was a bad tattoo day. Now that I was actually putting my bold plan into action I started having grave doubts about the viability of its execution. What if the judge requested a personal word with me and the counsel for the prosecution? If that happened I would be locked in a confined space with a man I was dying to give an on-the-spot vasectomy. Would I be able to control myself? What would Judge Camp do if I didn't?

'I really couldn't say, my lord,' I answered with oratory skills even the unconscious Keith could probably have mustered.

Giles was now giving me one of those smirking 'I know what you're thinking but you don't know what I'm thinking' looks of his. But I did. You don't go down on a man for three years without knowing every cortex of his brain. I knew what he was thinking better than he did.

The judge pushed his glasses up his nose and looked at me closely as my father had looked at me twenty years ago when I had written my name in lipstick on his new set of encyclopaedias.

'Perhaps you might like to hazard a guess just the same, Miss Hornton? I'm sure the jury are keen to get back to their lives with the satisfaction that they've witnessed this great institution of law and order working with the efficiency of a well-oiled machine. Perhaps you and Mr Billington-Frith would care to have a word with me in chambers?'

Then he took his glasses off and I realised we'd just been rehearsing my worst fears. The curtain was only now going up and I knew as never before the despair of a Vietnamese refugee sent back to Saigon after three months in a leaky junk.

Summoning my legs to walk, I looked pleadingly at the grey-faced, blinking rabbits of the jury. Their noses twitched, but they didn't smile – they looked like they wanted their lunch.

Watching Giles as he gave the jury a compassionate nod and smiled inanely at me, I wanted him dead. I wanted him strung up on a mountain top with herbal ointment smeared across his genitalia. Vultures would feast on this bloke's sweetmeats and I gave him a look that made that clear!

In the judge's chamber – with his glasses once more perched on the end of his nose – Judge Camp turned to face Giles and me. At a manly six foot six I knew I was in the presence of one who wouldn't cower from a head-butter in a button-up shirt. He dealt with me gently, speaking to me like a priest to a child who's just admitted to not knowing the difference between right and wrong.

'Now, Miss Hornton, I hope I don't have to remind you that your client is your responsibility? Mmm?' He looked at me over his glasses as if he did.

'You must press on him that he would do well to temper his exuberance with a little sober contemplation about what he's here for?'

'Yes, Judge, but if you'd just bear with me, I'm sure he's just a little . . . um . . . nervous.'

It was a regrettable adjective. Mice are nervous. Hamsters are nervous. Even the unconscious Keith would have trouble passing himself off as a hamster.

Giles glared with undisclosed irritation. 'Hardly nervous,' he spluttered.

I kept my eyes on the judge. 'What I mean is . . .' I explained sweetly, 'perhaps he needs medical attention – for the . . . er . . . bump?'

'If I might say something here, Judge?' Giles interjected. 'I think it's obvious that the accused's antics are nothing more than a performance designed to waste the court's time.'

My lord didn't look impressed by this ejaculation. In fact I recognised in those kindly features an ally.

'Obvious?' He growled. 'Nothing is obvious. If it was obvious, Mr Billington-Frith, none of us would be here.'

I swam into my advantage with a strong overarm. 'I can see how my client's behaviour could be construed, Judge, but honestly, I don't believe there's any malice of forethought. He's mixed up, nervous – paranoid. All I'm suggesting is that a doctor takes a look at him in case he requires a stitch or medication.'

'What sort of medical attention did you have in mind exactly?' the judge asked while I said a quick prayer that his mind was on the cod, waiting in its tarragon sauce at Hall.

Giles mouthed the word cyanide.

I felt sick with memories again. He had used our secret way of communicating. So correct and polite, Giles never stooped to showing his irritation with rude waiters or arrogant staff – but he'd mouth parallel conversations with me about them behind their backs. Sometimes I couldn't help myself. I'd have to break down and laugh. But I didn't break down now.

I explained that I thought the defendant may have given himself concussion. 'To err on the side of prudence, Judge, I'd like a doctor to take a look at him this afternoon. Just to satisfy all parties that he is fit to stand trial.'

Giles rolled his eyes. He used to roll his eyes if the phone rang while we were kissing. But he'd always go to answer it I bitterly remembered.

Judge Camp looked down on me once again. I had the feeling I'd connected with him on the *prudence* issue. 'Well, Miss Hornton, I will consent to come under your influence on this occasion. I've decided, all things considered, Mr Billington-Frith, to grant Miss Hornton's request. But only on condition, Miss Hornton, you make it clear to your client that any further bouts of vigour will be treated as contempt of court – regardless of the state of his nerves. We'll resume tomorrow.'

I refrained from kissing his feet. 'Of course, Judge. I'm sure I can make him understand,' I lied. But then, I reasoned, none of us was in a mood for the truth.

Giles snorted. This man who has laid back while my lips carried him to heaven, this man who had moaned and snored while I tossed and turned on the wet patch, actually *snorted*! My legs were itching to lash out in his general direction, but instead I smiled sweetly.

He'd keep.

Chapter 9

Give unto Caesar what is Caesar's

As we left the court, Julian and I briefly discussed the plan of attack for the next day. It wasn't that he exactly said he regretted the day he took my head clerk's counsel and hired me. But by the way he backed away from me as I tried to shake his hand, I could tell he thought it.

He gave me a light pat on the shoulder instead. So much body contact on our first meeting! I was worried he'd hear my clitoris moaning. I briefly tortured the idea of inviting him for a drink at Chez Gerard or Benjamin Stillingfleet's, but I decided there'd be plenty of time for that once we had Keith firmly attached to the lobotomy table. The first thing was to impress him with my legal finesse – I could demonstrate my irresistible charms later.

As I turned to leave, I spotted Giles coming out of the lifts. It was time to run for it. He had confrontation written in bold across his kick-me-in-the-gonad countenance and I was not tempted to stop and rake over the corpse of our dead relationship in front of Julian while a hundred crooks and their briefs watched on.

He followed me outside the Bailey, calling my name, but I was gratefully devoured by a throng of pedestrians. Just the same, hearing my name called so piteously felt like heart surgery. I remembered a time when that voice could make my womb leap – a time when the concept of speaking in the first

person singular was anathema. Hello! Earth to lunar module –
this girl was in pre-Women's Rights orbit.

All through Oxford we had spoken of the future as if it were
the next course. Even momentary separation was unthinkable –
I used to ache for him to come back from making coffee. I would
call out his name just as he called mine now and he would
appear with the coffees on a tray – stark-naked.

My heart throbbed in my throat at this image. Turning down
Fleet Street, memories were charging through my brain like a
marauding army. I mean, it wasn't as if he was especially func-
tional as a romantic or anything. He was your usual male clone –
which is to say he couldn't recite *ba-ba-black-sheep* when he was
sober whereas when he was drunk sixteen cantos of Byron's Don
Juan was par for the course. But the truth was it didn't matter
much what he said or did. I lived for him to probe my inner self.

All in all there was no limit to my utterly sick-making belief
in this bloke as icon. I genuinely believed that only he could
make me whole – it was as if I'd never read *The Female Eunuch*.

Giles is different, I wrote to my parents, who'd seen their
letter quota plummet since he'd arrived on the scene. What I
meant was the omens were good – even his family seemed to
like me. Well . . . at least they hadn't offered him money to never
see me again. This is it! I assured the world as it watched on
dumbfounded. Trust me I know what I'm doing. That's what
Eva Braun probably told her parents too.

I tried to block out the screamings of my humiliated
X-chromosomes by pounding down the cobbled squares and
tunnels of the Temple. I was one of those walking wounded you
see on the streets of big cities. Everyone who passed me must
have known something was wrong. I suppose I should have felt
alienated by the way they stepped aside to let me pass, but I
was grateful.

This might be a city boasting over twelve million people, but
the Inns of Court are a legal microcosm and there was a good
chance I was going to have to stand against or with some of
these people stepping aside for me.

My eyes were burning with tears which I tried to deal with as
I turned into Pump Court and saw the Georgian terrace that
nursed my chambers appear on the horizon like an eighteenth-
century refuge. That's when I first realised what it was I needed

more than anything else – another century.

Far from the crowds and scaffolding of Fleet Street, 17 Pump Court was still and silent. There were no telltale signs of the millennia here, no cars, no people, just cobbled streets and dark medieval tunnels that had survived the attacks of Zeppelins, Luftwaffe and Semtex. I gathered myself together. I was going to be OK, I told myself. Life goes on.

The ecstasy had done its worst and I was coming down. Down to what though was the big question? How far down was I going to go? The reality was I was sinking faster than the pizza I'd grabbed from a fast-food shop on the way.

While I fumbled with the code on the glass security doors, our junior clerk, Lee, lifted his head, saw who it was and went back to the football pages of the *Sun*. He was sprawled out all over Gabby's reception desk, sporting a new haircut that had first made itself popular around Snaresbrook Crown Court.

I couldn't remember the code. Lee was immersed in Cantona's latest triumph. I looked hopefully inside for a saviour. I didn't want to divulge myself to Lee as an airhead of a woman who couldn't remember her own code. So I plugged in ad hoc number arrangements.

The Nazis had a song which roughly translates as 'Tomorrow belongs to me'. It could have been written for Lee. This was his age, he was repeatedly reminding anyone who'd listen. 'Fink about it,' he'd say. 'Look around you. It's the age of the common man innit? I mean I could 'ave been a barrister if I'd have wanted to. Just didn't feel like it. Doesn't mean I deserve less respect though. Or less money,' he'd reason. 'The class system's dead. Even *The Times* says so!'

I punched in another permutation on my birth date. English Law Reports lined the walls from floor to ceiling. Everything looked civilised and calming. Except *that* carpet. The grey carpet with a corporate maroon stripe through the centre was a big sore point. God, the battles that had been fought at management meetings over that carpet.

It was at head clerk Warren's insistence that we'd just spent a fortune on our refurbishments, but we had drawn the line at corporate carpet. In the end Warren had all but wept till we capitulated and opened up our purse strings. I felt like a demented data inputer as I punched in the numbers to no avail. Lee turned pages lackadaisically.

'Go OK?' he asked dubiously when I finally broke in.

'Part heard,' I explained, slumping exhausted into the soft old leather of the sofa. 'He went berserk in court. It's a long story, but first he cut himself up in the cells with a button and then he head-butted the dock and knocked himself unconscious. So the judge agreed that a doctor should take a look at him this afternoon. We'll resume tomorrow.'

Lee went back to reading the sporting pages. Clearly head-butters trying to top themselves with buttons and slam dancing into docks were an everyday occurrence where he came from. I felt slightly miffed.

'Uha,' he said after a minute had elapsed. 'Sure.' He closed the paper and deigned to notice me. 'Miss Raphael wants to see you. She's got an arson up for trial in Hove and she's double booked,' he announced.

I felt the blood drain away from my face. Candida was returning another brief.

'She's got an appeal on at the Royal Courts of Justice so she needs you go down to Hove for the trial. Anyway, she says it's a walkover.'

Another walkover? I balked. I was starting to feel like the weak one at the front of the crowds at the Christmas sales. Was someone getting this on tape or what? I swivelled my head around on its axis looking for the camera.

'Listen, Miss Hornton, you're not after a cheap mobile are you?' Lee asked suddenly.

'Sorry?'

'A mobile? I can get you one really cheap.'

I fumbled with the hem of my skirt. I was not in the mental disk drive for this question. Let's face it, I wasn't in the mood for my own anatomy right this moment. 'I bought a mobile on your instruction last month,' I explained, rising to leave.

'From me?' he persisted.

'Well no as it happens. From a man who makes it his life's work to sell mobile phones. Why?'

. 'Nothing. I can just get 'em cheap off a mate o' mine.'

'I'll keep that in mind, Lee, but I thought it was insurance you were selling?' I reminded him stupidly.

The thing about Lee was that he lived above his means, he had big income problems that he was certain members of chambers could solve if only they'd try. He was always selling something. His haircut may cry out for arrest, his freckled features may cry out for a slap, but as a fledgling barrister finding my wings, I relied on Lee for a flight path. In other words it was incumbent on me to suck up.

Just as I had been genetically programmed to fall for the wrong men, Lee had been programmed to look after barristers. His father had been a clerk and his father's father before him, not to mention uncles, cousins and brothers.

'Give unto Caesar what is Caesar's and to your clerk ten percent of all you earn', was my family motto.

I had foolishly got his hopes up now. His freckles were glowing with excitement as he asked, 'You want some insurance then do you, Miss Hornton?'

'Not just at the minute, Lee. I thought you were selling it that's all. Maybe when I earn enough to pay London's cabstabulary I'll look into it. But I'd better get going and see what this arson's about now.'

I was babbling incoherently – backing out towards the door. 'Hove you say?' I muttered in retreat.

'So your grievous bodily 'arm's still going on then? I fort it would've pleaded?' he persevered.

'No, tomorrow now.' I looked at my watch for effect. 'Oh gosh, is that the time?'

It felt as if my body was beginning to lose consciousness. I wondered if I could get away with crawling to my room.

Lee got up to help me. 'Are you all right, Miss Hornton? You're not ill are you? Only you look like you're about to collapse. Which reminds me I've got a couple of chairs back 'ere want doin' up – I could let you 'ave them cheap. You know, spruce your room up a bit?' He made sprucing gestures with his hands – like a farmer shovelling manure onto his crop.

By the time I escaped into my room, I had to breathe into a paper bag to stop myself hyperventilating. The piles of briefs wrapped up in pink ribbons soothed me to some degree as, incredible as it is to think, there were people out there who actually needed me – who were relying on my services!

This was sobering stuff. I sat down and tried to do a yoga exercise I'd seen demonstrated on one of Sam's Exercises For Motherhood videos. But no sooner had I got my left leg around my right shoulder than Candida swept in, floating on a rug of Diorissimo. The perfume of the forties she called it. I never knew if she meant her age or the era.

If I were to be charitable, I would have to admit that she wasn't a bad recommendation for her age, notwithstanding her gold jewels and big black hair. But Candida is not a woman in need of charity. She is the bane of my existence.

Perhaps I should explain a few things about her before we go on. Explain how this middle-aged woman, although a good foot shorter than me, had made my time at 17 Pump Court a living hell from day one. I mean where do I start? I think the fly was in the ointment the day I was born a girl.

Don't wear your gender on your sleeve, Gran used to warn us as kids. But no one told Candida. Most of the time she wore it all over her body. She got where she was today by using every female wile she had to cut down any other woman in her path. She was what we Loreto girls called an anti-girlfriend. Her goal in life was to poison the confidence and reputation of every other woman who was called to the Bar. She was known by other women as the Lucrezia Borgia of the Temple.

As the only other woman in chambers beside our receptionist, I bore the full force of her anti-girlfriend crusade. I'd heard whispers that she was beside herself with anguish when chambers discussed taking me on. Rumour had it that she cried openly when she realised she was beaten. 'The fact is, women are good business, Candida. And I dare say you'll enjoy the company,' announced our head of chambers – Mark Sidcup QC. But Candida had never sought company – she was a one-woman act.

It wasn't that she made any outward show of hostility towards me. If anything she was the ultimate in chumminess. Giving me tips, popping in for girly chats, generously passing on cases. But I knew and she knew that where she really wanted me was strung up on Tyburn Hill. I braced myself for battle.

I imagined she'd come in to check up on the case. But my intuition was way out of whack today.

'No woman can feel safe in the Temple while that dreadful

Gabby girl is on the street giving men the wrong idea!' she cried
as she slammed the door.

I supposed she was referring to the low-cut, high-skirted
ensembles that Gabby minced about in – not to mention the
dark mysteries of her rumoured pierced navel.

I wanted to admit that Gabby was a liability, but not because
she wore short skirts and pierced her bellybutton. Gabby lost
files like butterflies, ate cream buns at her desk and smeared
surviving files with sticky globs. She filed her nails when the
phone was ringing and she was always kissing Lee in the
kitchen when I wanted to make a cup of coffee. So you see, it
was an indictment on my feelings for Candida that I rushed to
Gabby's defence now. I may as well have rushed at a herd of
stampeding vandals.

'I really don't see how you can defend her, Evelyn – not with
your situation,' she argued, as she slid her corseted bottom over
the side of my desk. She was always referring darkly to *my
situation*. I was still in the dark as to what *my situation* actually
was, but I didn't have the nerve to ask. Just the same it was
there – an unspoken handicap I carried around with me. Like
halitosis or a visible panty line.

She leaned over towards me conspiratorially. 'But enough of
that. I hear you were seen in court today with Julian Summers?'
She raised her eyebrows suggestively. 'Max saw you there! And
I think I might just know something about dear Julian that
you'll be interested in . . .'

'I'm rather busy just at the moment Candida,' I explained,
shuffling briefs about. I wasn't in the mood to discuss Julian
now – especially not with this gold-dipped Thatcher.

'You have time for what I'm about to tell you!' she insisted,
flicking through the mail on my desk. 'He's quite a dish – as I'm
sure you noticed, but there's something rather dark about dear
Julian. I'm surprised you haven't heard the latest.'

'Mmm,' I sighed, unable to disguise my curiosity. She must
have noticed my ears were panting for more.

'Not that I approve of rumours, but I suppose I should warn
you – as your friend. Woman to woman,' she whispered, the
way we used to whisper about heavy petting in the changing
rooms at gym.

I nodded despite my doubts. Woman to woman was my kind

of language. I tensed as she leaned in so close I could smell the stilton and Chablis on her breath.

'Warn me?' I pressed, as my day came rolling up my oesophagus like a pizza-flavoured bowling ball.

'Don't breathe a word of this. Definitely don't mention that you heard it from me. It's only gossip after all. But well, we are in the same set and perhaps it's my duty as a girlfriend,' she meowed without a hint of duplicity in her voice. 'And you'll only hear it from someone else anyway. He's got a . . . well, a reputation. The word around the Temple is that . . . well, apparently Julian had a . . .'

But I didn't get to hear the rest – I had to charge off down the corridor in search of what our American cousins refer to as the rest room.

Chapter 10

The only place to love a man or fight a man is below the belt

By the time I left chambers, I was close to feeling human. I'd tried to find Candida again to get the dirt on Julian, but she was in conference – which meant she'd clocked off. The Bar was just an alternative hair salon to Candida – a place to collect interesting discourse for the next dinner party. She was at the real salon now getting puffed and preened by Stefan in preparation for the evening.

So what was it she was trying to tell me? That Julian was a Lothario, a criminal on the run, a hunt saboteur, a philanderer, only after one thing, or the son of a travelling salesman? Or was it something more serious like Aids? More likely she had it in for him for some imagined slight I told myself. Anyway I tried to put it from my mind.

It was six o'clock and the days were beginning to stretch themselves into the evenings. I was standing outside chambers, looking up at the windows where others still toiled, feeling a twinge of guilt about leaving before seven, when I felt a hand on my shoulder.

I knew it was Giles without turning around by the way his arm touched mine – firmly with the certainty of a man that has never been refused. I flicked it away like a cockroach and gave him the full force of my 'why don't you just shrivel up and die look' and walked off.

'Evelyn, we have to talk,' he pleaded when he caught up.

'Giles, I don't have to do anything with you – apart from tear your case apart.'

He was scraping his hair back, looking desperately confused and angry – and, yes I'll admit it, deliciously assailable. I was torn by conflicting urges to give him an on-the-spot vasectomy and fall into his arms and kiss all those miscreant hair tentacles.

'Evelyn, what happened?' he pleaded. 'You just disappeared. I wrote, I phoned, I searched one end of Oxford to the other. Don't you think I deserved better than that?'

It was my turn to look incredulous. I was no longer confused by contradictory impulses. I ground my stiletto heels to sharpen them.

'Look, Giles, I don't know what you were brought up to think of as your just deserts, but let me urge you not to ask *me* to give them to you. Believe me, I am not the woman to turn to. You don't want what *I* think you deserve!'

I turned around and walked off – feeling justifiably proud of both my eloquence and self-control. As far as I was concerned, Giles should be singing hallelujah that his manhood was still intact. But no, by the sound of his feet scuttling along behind me, I could tell he wanted to take this confrontation thing further.

'I just can't believe you!' he persisted. 'After everything we went through? What's with you? All right. OK it's over! I accept that. I accepted that two years ago – six weeks after looking for you all over Oxford. Did you know I rang your parents? And your mother said Giles who? Or was that meant to be funny? I was meant to be having Christmas with your family! What happened? Can you just tell me that?'

What happened? This guy was unreal. What did he mean – what happened? He sounded like Mussolini after the mobs tore him limb from limb. You pissed people off, mate – tortured and oppressed them! Until they'd had enough!

This was a bloke who should be counting his limbs and praising the Lord that I didn't have a mob at my disposal.

'Jesus give me strength!' I prayed as I strode towards the tube. Giles trotted behind me three or four paces. I pretended to ignore him. The gas man was lighting the streetlamps above us. In the Michaelmas term we were doing away with all that – the Temple was going electric.

It was a sentimental expense we couldn't justify according to Candida and her vanguard. Well, Giles was an emotional expense I couldn't justify. The Temple was over gas and I was over Giles.

But he wasn't about to let me get over anything that easily. We had come to Temple Tube, but I didn't want him following me down there and risk being tagged home so I decided to walk down Embankment and find a cab. Giles caught up with me and grabbed my arm.

This was harassment! Hadn't anyone told him that body contact is a political minefield? We'd just received a memo from the Law Society in chambers about it last week.

'So that's it?' he demanded as one whose determination knows no safe limits. 'No let's be friends? No it was great while it lasted? Just fuck off? Is that what you're telling me, Evvy? Is it? Because I wish you'd just tell me to my face? I mean I can't see why you can't at least be civilised about it.'

It was that word *civilised* that pushed the eject button on my self-control.

'Civilised?' I screamed.

We had stopped outside a stand specialising in gay pornography and the customers trying to get through to the smut were shuffling past us nervously. None of them looked on for limb tearing – in fact if push came to shove this crowd would probably side with Giles.

But I was beyond gender bias now. I was a one-woman mob of righteousness. 'What do you mean by civilised? Was Goldilocks in your bed civilised? Under my duvet? Was that civilised, Giles – was it – was it? Because if that was civilised so's this!' And with that I walloped him with my pilot-case. Fair and square in the groin.

As Gran said – the only place to love a man or fight a man is below the belt!

I stormed off down the Embankment. I felt I'd made my point. I'd been erudite and crystal clear. I'd pressed my case home with conviction.

I didn't look back to gloat at his writhing form. I was bigger than that. Cathartic therapy is as good as Prozac. It put a spring in my step and left me light-headed. My mood had lifted insurmountably.

The peak-hour mob were pressing and knocking into me, but I felt like I was strolling through Elysian fields. There were no cabs, but hey, I thought, I love my fellow man! I had a smile for all those sweaty joggers that passed me, a penny for all the huddled forms along the waterfront. I bought a dozen copies of the *Big Issue* from one of the homeless patrolling the station.

I was therefore pretty taken aback when Giles caught up with me – still nursing his manhood. 'I'm sorry, Evelyn. But I can explain. I didn't mean for you to find out . . .'

This man was priceless. This man took the cake and ate it then vomited it up and ate it again. We had a puppy that used to do that – but at least the puppy died in the end! For a legal counsel he lacked a sense of justice. I mean, I bet Genghis Khan thought he could explain. The Moor's murderers could explain. Fred and Rosemary West could explain. Nixon could explain. Explanation does not a reprieve make. Couldn't he see his appeal had no future? His case was hopeless. The best he could hope for was life out of my sight.

'Please, Evvy, can't we go somewhere to talk? It wasn't what you think. It wasn't.'

Then I saw it. In the distance, a black cab painted shocking pink advertising pizza was coming toward me – with its light on! I dived out into the traffic to take what was rightfully mine from the scores of pinstriped-suited jerks and two-piece-suited jerkesses as we ran at the cab like untouchables mobbing Gandhi.

Chapter 11

I was still kind of hopeful he thought of me as a sentient life form

Three minutes later I was coming to on the pavement with footprints across my Dolca Gabanna pinstripe, wondering if I could claim the cleaning bill on legal aid?

Julian must have seen the whole thing because he was crouching over me with Giles. I was propped against the wall of Temple station observed by an ever-increasing mob.

The gay porn stand had been moved to take full advantage of the crowds and a few beggars were milling around with their hands out, seemingly doing very well out of my tragedy.

Add to this scenario the bloke I'd bought all the *Big Issues* off who was in the street gathering up my strewn copies – probably to resell them I thought bitterly – and a dog wearing a red neck-scarf who was sniffing at my laddered stockings sadly and you can see what I was up against. This was worse than a ring of steel – this was a ring of uranium. What a relief I'd worn my sexiest Calvin Klein knickers.

While I took in the post-accident sideshow, I could feel my head growing another frontal lobe. Julian was on one side of me (squatting off the ground to preserve his Armani). He had his arm around me – which was heaven. Giles the super-bastard was on the other side of me in his Gieves and Hawke suit – which was hell.

I didn't know whether to be ashamed, furious or grateful. So I did what any modern woman would do in my situation. I burst into tears.

Not those tearless tears that accompany Gabby's whine when I catch her eating cream buns in reception. Not the tears of Warren our head clerk when there was talk of ending his ten per cent commission – heavy tears that streamed soundlessly down his Pink's shirt.

No, my tears fell with full stereophonic sound and waterworks – my lamentations were amplified and unabating. Everyone within a mile radius clustered around me asking what had happened . . . if I was all right. The dog howled with me. There were quite a few people itching to take the drama just a little bit further by calling an ambulance.

One of them was my *Big Issue* vendor. 'Are you sure she's all right?' he asked, eyeing up my support team suspiciously. He was one of those short men that me feel guilty for being so tall. I noticed that his scarf matched the dog's.

I nodded.

'Well if yer sure then?' he mumbled doubtfully. 'Just looks a bit strange like, don't it?'

'We'll look after her,' Giles assured him.

My champion didn't look convinced, but he hoisted his plastic satchel over his shoulder and slumped off anyway – his small black mongrel licking at his feet sadly.

'Can I take you home?' asked Giles as they helped me up.

'It's OK, I've got my car,' said Julian. 'I may as well drive her.'

Her? What was with the *her* thing? 'Hey, guys, thanks a lot but I can speak for myself!' was what I felt like saying, but I was almost fainting with the excitement at the idea of being in a confined space with Julian. So I just whimpered my assent.

He put one of his strong arms around me and led me to his car. 'Let's get one thing clear,' my hormones were saying. 'This bloke can speak for you any day!'

Hell he could have my vote if he asked for it!

Somewhere along the line I must have said yes to an ambulance too because as I was being tucked into Julian's BMW (what else) it arrived, all sirens blazing.

'I'll call you,' Giles shouted above the cacophony of the whirring noise and the interested crowd.

On the way home with my double-fronted frontal lobe

pressed against the window, I thought about how this desire Julian had aroused in me could be just what the girls had ordered. Maybe being a sperm bank wasn't the worst thing that could befall a modern girl after all?

I think it was a combination of the smell of his long lean muscular body so close and my concussion that made me think I was in with a chance. I thanked him for the hundredth time in a row and he looked at me and smiled – a knowing smile. I was on the point of persuading myself that this remarkable turn of events practically constituted a date, when he replied, 'God, I'd do the same for anyone.'

'Gee thanks,' I thought, feeling stupid. But I still couldn't help imagining what his body looked like under the drapery of his designer clothes.

'That's quite a lump you've got there,' he remarked.

I looked at my clitoris, ashamed. But then my heart leapt – he was showing his concern. 'Yeah not very flattering huh?' I joked.

'I guess it will pass in time,' he reassured me. His legs were stretched out on the accelerator and clutch pedals – and all I could think of was what it would feel like to have those legs wrapped around my torso. The pulse of my libido was careering out of control.

'Are you OK? I mean . . . are you fine to direct me?' he asked.

I couldn't concentrate – I was mesmerised by his hands and their light tan and I couldn't remember a time when I hadn't wanted to kiss them. Eventually I made a strangled sound he took to mean no.

'Well give me your address and I'll try and work it out. You *can* remember your address can't you.'

Christ what did he think I was – brain dead? I knew I wasn't doing a lot to impress him, but I was still kind of hopeful he thought of me as a sentient life form at least.

I retreated back into silence.

'It's been quite a day – I mean with one thing and another,' he mused as we waited for the lights to turn green. The car beside us – a red Mercedes with the hood down – was blaring out reggae music. The black guy looked at us under his shades. I was wondering to myself if Julian would try and race him when the lights changed. It was a test of phallic = car sorts I guess – only I hadn't decided what I'd do if he failed it.

'I don't think I've had one quite as mad before,' he went on as the lights changed and the red Merc tore off in the distance. 'I think there was one point there when I didn't think it could possibly get any worse – and then he pulled out that fucking foreskin. I've never seen anything like it!'

We looked into one another's eyes as we laughed. Seeing my reflection laughing back at me from those cool green eyes got my clitoris heavy breathing. I laughed louder so he wouldn't hear it. We continued to discuss the case as we crept past the Albert Hall and the crowd of paparazzi outside Kensington Palace and finally up Kensington Church Street. The traffic was deadly but the air was heady with the smell of freshly mown grass. I felt like I was waking up from a two-year sleep.

I even managed a few right and left instructions as we approached Ladbroke Square. I was just relaxing into my desires as the white stucco of Georgian terraces flowed past when he mentioned Giles.

'And how *bizarre*' – he put it quaintly – 'that we should all run into each other like that. Well, I know it was awful for you under the circumstances – but how incredibly bizarre.'

'Bizarre!' That was Giles' word. 'Darling,' he would whisper as he stroked my head lying on his chest as we recovered from marathon sex. 'Making love to you isn't incredible – it's *bizarre*.'

And suddenly I was back in Oxford. It seemed as if we had lived and loved in a perpetual drizzle for those four years we were together – and now I realised I must have been drugged to have fooled myself it was real. It was a dream – a soft, grey, felty haze of dreaming spires. The romance of the century we called it.

Giles had me at a disadvantage from the start. He was in his last year at Oxford – a wide circle of friends, a social life, a family two hours away by train. I was in my first year, my only friend was Wally the stuffed wombat, I had no social life to speak of and my family were twenty-four hours away by plane. He looked like a god. My friends said I looked like a Belsen victim – with the exception of my breasts which could feed a nation.

When I was fourteen my mother had announced, 'Evelyn's got Aunt Kit's breasts.'

'Well who the hell got mine?' I pleaded.

Aunt Kit had died before I was born so it wasn't her, but I was convinced that out there, walking the streets, was some bitch with a pair of A-cups that should have been mine!

That was another thing Giles told me – he liked his mammary big! Why didn't I run then from this flame-thrower of compliments. Mammary? Get over it, girl.

There were high points I admit. In the beginning, before I got my brain back, I was fighting for breath with love for him. Would he ring? Would he call? Would he like my new shoes? To me, you have to understand, these questions were as lofty as any asked by the great philosophers.

I guess I go for quality pain men. You know the type – intelligent, witty, sensitive, generous, sweet, built like poets, genetically programmed to cheat. Men that remind me of the big black Labrador we had at home – he was always straining at the leash to get away. That's my sort of man. Educated women call this ideal man *super-bastard* but we didn't have *bastards* on the curriculum at the Loreto School for Gentlewomen.

Chapter 12

The good dyke/bad dyke routine

We pulled up outside the flat around eight o'clock. The garden was full of residents canoodling, reading, chatting and children playing. The smells of picnics and barbecues wafted onto my taste buds. I didn't need to invite him in. The girls sitting on the balcony saw *man* and went berserk.

'Hello! Hello!' they screamed like parodies of convent-school girls spotting their first man out of a cassock. 'You're coming up aren't you?'

'Um? Well . . . I . . . I mean, I . . .' Julian prevaricated. Nothing had prepared him for a couple of lesbians on a semen mission. Persistence isn't the word.

'Of course you are!' they yelled. I was surprised they didn't throw a rope down.

'Evvy, what have you done to your head?' Charles asked as we came up the stairs. Whitney Houston was crooning, 'Ooooh I wanna feel the heat with somebody – ooooooh I want somebody to love me . . .!' Subtle or what?

She was still in her wing collar having just come back from court in Brighton. The V&Ts were already poured. Sam passed them to us before introductions were even under way. She winked at me. I didn't have to ask how much vodka was in Julian's drink.

Sam insisted we all crushed up on the Mae West lips sofa facing the velvet vulvas. *Cool it girls*, I thought, but I enjoyed the

75

body contact none the less. People were playing tennis in the rose-covered court below and the popping sounds of balls against rackets provided a languid rhythm to our group.

It was clear the girls were going to stick to us like Tarzan-Grip. I willed them to leave us alone. I prayed. Finally, in desperation, I pinched Sam in the ribs.

'Ow! Evvy, why did you do that?' she squealed. 'Are you trying to get rid of us so you can be alone with this nice gentleman?'

Julian and I both blushed.

The conversation didn't exactly flow. Stifled I think was the word. 'What a nice flat!' Julian declared like a Home Counties matron during one particularly long silence.

(It was such a cliché even I who looked on him as a god almost threw up.)

The girls cooed as if it was the most original thing they'd ever heard.

'I love the table and high-backed dining chairs!' he added.

(He didn't mention the red velvet vulvas gaping at his face.)

'What a great sense of space! Who did the vanilla treatment on the walls – very quattrocento,' he trilled.

Again, I'd heard it a hundred times before – as had Sam and Charles who threw themselves into the discussion as if they'd been longing for such incisive conversation all their lives.

'I don't think I remember a hotter summer. Are you going away?' he enquired.

I half expected the girls to say, 'No, we're hanging around for a sperm donor,' but they prattled on about tropical destinations as if they kept them awake at night.

'Do you play tennis?' he asked after we'd been listening to the pop-pop-pop of the ball on rackets for an interminable length of time.

No one even bothered to answer that. Sam and Charles were making gog eyes at his muscles.

'I go to the gym to keep fit,' he announced eventually.

(Oh gee as if we didn't guess.)

The evening yawned on. Why wouldn't they leave us alone?

Everything was so polite and measured I was falling asleep. I was reminded of tea with the Monsignor at the convent. But after a few teacups of brandy even the Monsignor cut the crap and brought out the strip-poker cards.

After all, we were all young and, I prayed, single. We were all educated and, I flattered myself, liberated. So why were we discussing wall treatments and tennis?

Listening to him making facile small talk with the girls, I felt like screaming, 'Say something! This is the nineteen nineties – we don't have to talk about sport and the weather – be controversial. According to Candida scandals and dark mysteries surround you! These girls aren't my chaperones for Christ's sake – do something. Try kissing me for instance!'

I was just about to inject myself with a lethal dose of vodka when Sam said, 'So tell me, Julian, do you believe that sperm is an inalienable right?'

He spat his drink back into his glass like a kid spitting its dummy.

Charles slapped him on the back. I jumped up and stared at them. What was it with these two? Why didn't she just stick a pipette into his testicles and suck the stuff out?

It wasn't as if I brought a man home every day of the week. I mean this was it – the first break in a manless existence spanning twenty-four months!

'Ignore her, Julian, she's a filthy sperm-hungry dyke,' I snapped as I went off to the kitchen to get some more ice for my head.

'Yes, don't be so prurient, Sam. Ignore her,' insisted Charles, smoothing down his tie.

'Com'on, Jules,' bullied Sam, nudging him in the ribs, 'tell us what your sperm count is!'

'Sam! That is outrageous!' squawked Charles.

In the kitchen I stuck my head in the freezer and wondered how long it would take for me to die of hypothermia.

'Julian doesn't mind. Come on you must have some idea. How often do you spill your seed?'

There was an ominous silence.

'Sam!' Charles yelled as if horrified.

'No, seriously, the more times you ejaculate the lower your sperm count.'

'I hardly think Julian wants to discuss that, do you, Julian?' Charles asked as if hoping he did.

Oh God, I thought, *here we go – they're doing the good dyke/bad dyke routine again.*

Chapter 13

Taking the testosterone host
into my own hands

Needless to say, Julian made a rapid retreat. He knew danger
when he saw it coming towards him with all the subtlety of a
lipstick lesbo on a sperm hunt.

I waited for the door to close before I performed the apocalyptic
tantrum I'd choreographed in my head earlier – in the cool light of
the freezer. I don't lose my sense of decorum often, but when I do
I throw everything – including my manicure – at it.

We were talking ballistic. 'Batten down the hatches and
prepare to die girls' was written all over my face by the time I
said goodbye to a man I now realised was the only man I could
ever love. 'How dare you,' was my predictable opening gambit,
but once I was in my stride, twelve years' education at the
hands of the female equivalent of the Jesuits shone through. Six
vodkas helped too.

I blasphemed till the heavenly hosts appeared in our sitting
room. I attacked them on everything from their selfishness to
their sexuality. I ranted, I raved and I pulled no punches.

Ladbroke Square gathered below our window, believing
themselves the privileged recipients of an impromptu equivalent of Glyndebourne. Old and young, dachshunds and children
huddled in the moonlight on rugs, impressed by what they
thought were wafts of Carmen arias rather than a crapulent,
concussed man-hater who's just seen the light in the end of the
celibate tunnel bricked up.

I had Sam and Charles cowering on the cushions, scraping and bowing at my feet and eating their now sizeable teddy collection. I made it clear that I was no mere heterosexual pawn to be sacrificed for the greater good of reproduction. I was meant to be their friend for Christ's sake!

'How dare you,' I wailed. 'He was my friend! A human being! Who the hell do you think you are to treat him like a fucking sperm bank?'

My oratory knew no bounds. I knew as I held forth on the sanctity of friendship that this speech should have been taped. Visions of my grandchildren listening in awe to the genius of my manifesto flashed in and out of my blurred vision. Today I had looked down the nozzle of Keith of Shepherd's Bush's foreskin and I was not to be trifled with.

I think they knew when they were beaten. Their arguments were as legless and impotent as their capacity for zygotes. They knew I was holding the cards to their future happiness. Like the intelligent life forms they are, they started sucking up like mad.

CHARLES: 'Oh, Evvy, you poor thing, what a day you've had!'

SAM: 'We didn't realise . . . Oh God, we're so selfish.'

CHARLES: 'We're so sorry – how can we make it up?'

SAM: 'Sit down, I'll make you hot chocolate.'

CHARLES: 'You look exhausted and what with your bump . . .'

SAM: 'Tell us how your case went . . . Did you win? Did you slay them in the aisles?'

CHARLES: 'Julian seemed nice – I'm sure he likes you, Evvy!'

And that was what did it – that one little phrase, 'I'm sure he likes you, Evvy'. A throwaway line of dubious validity, but – as any girl who's ever had a crush knows – it was all the encouragement I needed. I was a kitten in their deceptive lap.

'Do you think so?' I purred wide-eyed.

'Of course,' they cooed. They knew they were on to something.

'Bleeding obvious – I mean he couldn't . . .'

'. . . couldn't take his eyes off you,' stroked Charles.

'He did seem quite attentive, didn't he?' I asked, like a child pleading for sweets.

'Definitely.' They agreed in unison. I turned over so they could stroke my belly.

'I think he was really sweet,' Charles sighed. In lipstick-lesbo speak, he was a man worth *not* kicking in the balls.

Sam went in and stroked under my chin. 'He's gone on you, Evvy. Don't say you didn't cotton on?'

The only thing I wasn't cottoning on to was that I was being stitched up.

'It's just that ... he's really shy,' Charles explained.

Sam expatiated. 'Yeah, I think you'll have to, you know ... ask ...'

Charles jumped in. 'You know ... make the first move!'

Oh, WOW. 'Tell me something new, girls,' I meowed sarcastically, suddenly aware of where I was. I mean ever since I can remember, I've made the first move.

Gran used to say there comes a time in every girl's life when she has to take the testosterone host into her own hands.

And it was always that time with me. I'd always done the asking out. Later on in some post-coital moment, I'd ask my chosen one, 'Why did you wait for me to make the first move?' I had this huge hang-up that if I hadn't pushed Joseph Mendez et al into dating me, I'd still be a virgin.

But I had my pride. I sat up as if appalled. '*Me*, make the first move?'

My eyes were falling out of my head like bungee jumpers. As if they'd asked me to give a total stranger head ... not that that wasn't off the cards in their latest endeavours. 'I couldn't,' I spluttered prudishly.

Sam reassured me. 'Of course you can. It doesn't have to be a big deal – just like ...'

'Yeah!' Charles added. 'Just casually like ...'

'Well, we were thinking ... that well ... why don't we have an, um ...'

'We discussed it briefly before you came in,' Sam jumped in.

'We thought of having a party!' Charles called out from the balcony where I presume she felt safe.

But she needn't have worried. Maybe the girls were talking sense, I reasoned like a suicidal chump who tells herself that ten Valiums should do it.

Charles came in from the balcony uttering reassurance.

'Nothing huge, just some friends, just some . . . you know close . . . um . . .'

'Men?' Sam whispered hopefully while looking me in the eye.

There was a silence. Out in the square the audience had decided the show was over and were packing up their picnic hampers for the night. Sam and Charles looked at each other. I knew what they were thinking – they'd said the 'M' word and I hadn't gone into a snit.

'Yeah, men . . .' Sam tried out the word again.

'. . . And stuff,' Charles added quickly.

What a fool. The lust thing must have had me blinkered. There I was, like a little kitten lapping up its cream while the collar was being placed around my soft little neck. A party with men . . . and stuff. Well, we all knew what the stuff was!

Just discussed it briefly – my foot! They had already had the invitations printed. Gold embossed on heavy card.

> The fountain of life springs eternal.
> Celebration of life party
> 70 Ladbroke Sq. W11
> Dress – minimal.
> Champagne – on us.

The date was set for next Friday. It would be so simple, so natural to ask Julian to a party. I was sold. Sam made hot chocolate and we drew up a guest list. As I lay in my room going over the day, I realised that I hadn't told the girls who my persecuting counsel was.

Chapter 14

These things are sent to trial us

When I arrived at the Old Bailey the next morning – on time – Julian was nowhere to be seen. I wandered disconsolately about the marble-clad hall as stranger after stranger appeared out of the metal-detection booth, frightened that he'd asked someone else to take over. When he did finally appear – like a god stepping for the first time into the twentieth century – he looked right through me, before shaking his head and declaring.

'Sorry, Evette, I didn't recognise you there?'

Evette? What the hell was this? Five hours in court together, followed by my accident, followed by a lift home, followed by drinks. My friends were already planning how to spend his sperm for Christ's sake. I would have thought that justified remembering my name?

'The name's Evelyn,' I corrected, all school ma'am authority.

He was wearing the same suit with a tie that looked like it had been bought in an art gallery. How does anyone get this perfect? He had no idea of mortal suffering – what it meant to pluck eyebrow hairs or suck in your stomach. His was instant beauty – he came out of a machine like that.

We made our way down to the Cells where Keith was as happy as a lamb on Valium. He'd been diagnosed as depressed and had been sedated – to the relief of the guards. I was feeling better too – even the smell of prison food and urine, wafting down the corridors like a steam inhalation, did no more than reassure me of my growing competence.

I was getting used to the smell, just as Julian had prophesied. My lipstick line was straight and professionally applied today – a subtle burnt umber. My gown was on the right way out, as were my wig and my collar bands. The guard paid me the compliment of remembering me and enquired as to my well-being. Keith told me I looked *nice* and I beamed at his slumped and unassertive form hunched in the chair.

Satisfying ourselves that all was well with our client, we made our way up to court. Giles was already there, as was the seedy clerk from the CPS who was lazily picking wax out of his ears while reading the *Mirror*.

Giles was distractedly shuffling notes and bending his head to listen to his solicitor. Periodically he stroked his collar bands. I had a flashback to one of my weekends in London with him when we had wandered arm in arm down Chancery Lane. He had declared that when I was called to the Bar, he would buy me my collar bands and have them blessed by the Pope.

'All persons draw near and give their attendance, oh yea, oh yea, oh yea!' cried the usher.

I should have sued him for breach of promise, I thought bitterly. The learned counsel for the prosecution had lampooned my love for him! This was a man who had got away scot-free, while I suffered two years of celibacy. I needed no trial by jury to convict this jerk!

But I was forced to watch him now with a modicum of respect as he presented his textbook case of GBH with a flair of delivery that I could tell the jury were not blind to. Every eye in the courtroom was on him and mine were no exception. His voice rose and fell in a mellifluous, intoxicating soliloquy that put Keith to sleep.

Giles was made for the stage. He led the jury through the night of the attack as if he were describing the martyrdom of Francis of Assisi.

I remembered him reading the dedications on memorial stones pressed against me in the Catholic chapel at Oxford in that same style. 'Stop it – my body belongs to Our Lady,' I'd teased. The old women laying the altar, tut-tutted their disapproval. That was when he first proposed.

The first witness was sworn in. Keith smiled down on him

kindly from the dock. Father Malone of Bermondsey was as soused as a newt.

'A good day to you,' he called out to the judge and jury, waving gaily as he made his way to the stand.

Giles looked distressed. He pulled the constraints of his wing collar and tried to limit his questions to the time and place of the attack. But that was bad enough really – the priest gave the date of the attack as several years in the future and became agitated when Giles pushed him on the point.

I saw an opportunity to increase Giles' misery. 'I hesitate to interrupt, my lord, but my learned friend is leading the witness.'

'Just ask your question, Mr Billington-Frith. You know not to put words in the good priest's mouth.'

I looked at Giles and smiled smugly.

I declined to question the cleric myself, he'd said enough already to serve my purpose. Giles was red-faced. His next witness was most precise on the date and the place. The interesting nugget hidden in this chap's evidence was that he made continual reference to 'Keithy'.

I shot a glance to Keith, but he was on one of his nod-offs. Julian turned to me and grinned. We were basking in the light of our rising star.

The last witness should have been remunerated by the defence – he was priceless. He wasn't prepared to be limited even to the offence in question. As far as he was concerned the accused was responsible for just about everything from World War II to the delays on British Rail.

Before Giles could shut him up, he'd turned Keith's act of violence into a farce. The crime became more varied, more frenzied with every minute he stood in the witness box. At one point a shotgun was mentioned. The police officer who'd made the arrest wept into his notebook. There's such a thing as gilding the evidence but this bloke was encasing it in lead.

He declared, 'As sure as God's my witness that Keithy's bad news. You mark my words, you wanna 'ave 'im locked up and frow away the key. If I see 'im on the street again I'll kill 'im myself I will!'

'Confine yourself to answering the questions, Mr Timms,' ordered Judge Camp.

By the end, when Giles declined to question the witness

further, Mr Timms shook his fist and threatened, 'You'll regret this, yer fucking wanker.'

I was getting a feel for this case. And it felt good. It was obviously we were dealing with a vast web of intrigue that spanned beyond the head-butting of an innocent man while innocent passers-by watched on in astonishment. Maybe I was defending an innocent man after all? Giles sat down and cradled his head in his hands.

I rose to question the witness – he was as putty in my hands. I lured him like a whore into the brothel of his lies. I seduced him into great feasts of diatribe against Keithy. What's more, he didn't dress his hatred up for the consumption of the confused members of the jury who were now beginning to get alarmed.

He spoke in a crude and menacing language that made more use of sexual obscenities than the Censorship Board's cutting-room floor. At one point he spat at Keith. The jury recoiled and sank into their seats. He was threatened with contempt – but contempt was a lifestyle to Mr Timms.

Finally he was led out, threatening to put Keith down himself if the jury didn't do it for him. All the while my client was smiling like a kindly village idiot from his perch.

By the time Giles finished his closing speech I think he could see the Grim Reaper hacking at his case. I was almost tempted to smirk, I was so confident. I rose to make my closing speech with the certainty that both The Honourable Mr Justice Camp and jury were in agreement – that given a dark night in an unlit station they'd take the bovine Keith rather than any of the three witnesses.

As I rose, Judge Camp winked at me. 'I think the accused might require a prod – unless he'd rather be tried in his absence?'

The Securicor guard prodded Keith.

'My lord, I'm sure he's paying attention – he's just relaxing,' I offered. Laughter rippled through the courtroom like an electric massage. Keith opened one eye and smiled. I wanted some of that Valium stuff.

I drank my audience in with my eyes – twelve good and true persons about as representative of society as any dole queue. This was my day. Julian was beside me, waiting to be impressed. If I was ever going to astound and allure him – now was the time. I straightened my wig and faced the jury and waited for my dramatic pause to centre their attention. It was just like the nativity play at school – only then I had played the donkey. This was my chance to be the star – if not the saviour.

'Members of the jury, we have all heard the evidence as outlined by my learned friend and the varying reports of all three witnesses. One who claims the attack is yet to take place. (Laughter.) And two who would appear to know my client Mr Keith Conan – or should I say Keithy – rather better than we were led to believe.' I took a drink of water to allow this to sink in.

'As you have heard, these witnesses are clearly not impartial. Perhaps you will feel that given their determination to see Keithy "put away", their version of events cannot be relied on. They knew Mr Conan – well enough to refer to him as Keithy. You've heard my client protesting his innocence. He insists that he was set upon and only fought off his assailants using reasonable force. You might feel having heard the evidence that this rings true. He hit back under attack. Just as you or I would.'

Giles coughed.

The judge curdled him with a stare.

I smiled up at the bench the way I'd smiled up at my father over the lipstick on the encyclopaedia episode. 'Daddy,' I had said, 'do you really think I'd be so silly as to write my own name on the books?'

'Look then, ladies and gentlemen, what we have here is no simple unaggravated assault but plain and simple self-defence.' I announced this point with a meaningful pull on my gown. 'Any way you look at it, Keith Conan has been *stitched up* by those he looked upon as friends.' I could see my use of the vernacular had struck a chord. Oh yes! This was brilliant.

'Members of the jury, we have all fallen foul of those we would trust.' I gave Giles a metaphorical kick in the balls with my eyes and continued to stare at him as I said, 'We have all known the humiliation of allowing those we were closest to, to do us harm!'

The jury were nodding knowingly. 'I ask you to look at the accused, members of the jury.' The jury dutifully looked at Keith smiling kindly at them from the dock. 'Mr Conan states his innocence emphatically. He went out for a night of drinking with his mates.' The jury were visibly moved. 'And on that night he was set upon by those very people he counted on as friends!' I dropped my voice. The jury craned forward to listen.

'Standing in the dock is not a man who has *done* wrong but a wronged man! While considering your verdict, I would ask you to think of this. Has Keith been guilty of grievous bodily harm as accused? Or is it more likely that he has been a victim himself – a victim of betrayal by those he loved?'

It took ten minutes for them to get back with a not-guilty verdict.

I breathed out. With Keith's exoneration came my own. I was worthy after all. I had earned my two hundred quid on legal aid. I could handle my briefs as well as the next man. And more than that Julian would start thinking of me as competent.

After the jury were released, the guards woke up Keith. Watching him walk out to freedom, I was stung with a needle of unease. How long would the Valium last? *But ours is not to question why*, I told myself, *defend, prosecute, litigate and die.*

I allowed myself to sneak a glance at Giles but he had already left. Well, that was a relief. Now came the big moment – I turned to bask in Julian's praise, but to my horror he was also standing to leave.

'Look, I've got a lot on,' he explained gathering his stuff together. 'So I'm going to have to rush off – no doubt we'll meet again. Oh and watch yourself on the roads.' He slapped me playfully on the upper arm.

I felt as one who's just bought a pair of shoes on sale, only to find they don't really fit. This was not my chosen post-triumph scenario. At this point Julian should have been carrying me aloft while laurels flopped engagingly from my brow. We were at least meant to nip off to Benjamin Stillingfleet's to toss around a few of the more glorious bits of my summing up over a barrel of wine.

It felt like he'd slapped me across the face.

'But, but, but . . . You can't go,' I stammered, all traces of my oratorical prowess swept away.

He laughed. 'Sorry, but listen that was great. No doubt about it, I'll be using you again.'

Gee thanks, I thought, *I can't wait. Your generosity defies comprehension.* Was that really what I was looking for in life? To be used again?

He began to walk away.

'Hey wait a minute.' I stalled, searching for the invitation that had been burning a hole in my jacket pocket all morning.

'We're having a party.' I passed the card to him.

He read it with a wry smile playing about his mouth.

'Thanks.' He looked at me with renewed interest. 'Yeah, I'm free that night. I'll see you then.'

'Look forward to it,' I said as tersely as I could. But listening to myself, it sounded like an 'I Do'.

'Are Sam and Charles going to be there?' he enquired.

Brilliant! I thought. I'm Evette while they get to keep their real names. Is this screw-Evelyn's-ego week or what?

'Of course they'll be there,' I snapped.

He laughed. 'They're brilliant!'

'They're lesbians,' I stated pointedly.

'Oh I worked that out,' he laughed. Then he smiled a smile that made me cross my legs to stop my womb falling through. I was gone on this man and there was no going back. So what if he intended to *use me again?* my hormones cried. Use away!

A warning voice inside told me this was not what Camilla Paglia meant when she spoke about a woman being *empowered by her sexuality*. I could hear the suffragettes groaning in their graves. I knew I should be running in the other direction – out of the danger zone of my feelings for this man.

I mean, he apparently found me about as enticing as a *gelato* in winter – whereas he thought Sam and Charles were brilliant. Which roughly translated means – even a couple of dykes are more attractive than you, person whose name I can't even remember.

But it was useless. 'I want to fuck you!' was coming up in Braille all over my forehead.

Chapter 15

Mad, mad extravagant men!

I walked into the chambers' meeting a few minutes late, to be greeted by a stony silence as if I was walking into my own funeral. Everyone looked very embarrassed – except Candida. She was sitting at the back, wrapped up in her new baby seal skin coat.

'Sorry, Evelyn, we'd presumed you'd forgotten,' she meowed like a cat with the cream still sparkling on its whiskers.

'I see,' I muttered lamely.

'We were wondering if you've had any thoughts on the summer party?' explained Graham, one of the European law specialists.

Thoughts? Good God, I'd arranged a gala occasion that would forever change the way our drab little chambers' get-togethers were viewed. I was going to make an impression. I'd sweated for weeks to make sure that this summer party was the best bash 17 Pump Court had seen. I was going to make my mark with this *do*.

'I hope I've done a bit more than thought, Graham,' I started. 'I think I can comfortably say arrangements are—'

'Of course, if I had time on my hands I'd have done it,' Candida interrupted. 'But with all the work I'm bringing into chambers I don't have time for my own life.' She puffed her bouffant wearily. 'But that's me,' she laughed philosophically. 'A career woman to the end.'

So excuse me, what am I? I thought. *Your eunuch?*

'And besides which,' she went on. 'I think it's best to leave these gatherings to the younger members of chambers with time on their hands to arrange. I hope you're not neglecting the arson I gave you while you make these forays into the entertainment industry, Evelyn.'

I felt my self-assurance collapse from under me like a pair of Vivienne Westwood platform shoes. I wanted to say something bitingly clever. I wanted to scratch out her eyes with my wit. But I just sat there like I had when Mandy Maddocks told Sister Conchilio that I had tried to coerce her into having an abortion.

'Well, if that's all sorted out,' interrupted Vincent Felton. 'I'd like to take up the matter of clerks' commissions again if I may?' Vincent – referred to disrespectfully around chambers as Vinny – was on an economy drive.

Vinny should have taken silk ten years ago, but his personal hygiene standards weren't up to it. So he had taken to making his mark by trying to revolutionise chambers. Bringing it into the twentieth century, as he put it.

He put forward ideas such as employing office administrators and replacing our expensively decked-out and well-stocked kitchen with a coffee machine. But his big drive was getting rid of our head clerk, Warren, who wielded about as much power as anyone with a licence to write cheques in someone else's name.

Warren had been a clerk at 17 Pump Court since before my mother was born. He was seventy-four and indefatigable. Particularly when it came to spending chambers' money. He prided himself that 17 Pump Court was his responsibility. Basically, Vinny and Warren were at war with each other. But Warren had his fight-back planned. He'd discovered that Vinny was the man who had been regularly running down the batteries of his transistor radio every weekend when he came in to play computer games. He saw his chance to lay down the evidence.

'Oh please. We're talking a few batteries every weekend. I don't see how that signifies,' Vinny sneered haughtily.

'Don't you,' sniffed Warren, raising himself to his full six foot reed thin two. He knew the mood of the meeting was firmly against the arrogance of this man who didn't see why he should bathe daily. 'Well perhaps you had better get your own house in order before you start attacking my allowance, Mr Giblin. People in glass houses and all that.'

'That's right, Vinny,' added Duncan. Where there was trouble there was Duncan's spoon stirring it.

'Oh for heaven's sake, I'll pay for the bally batteries then. Really!' Vinny snuffled.

Warren put out his hand. 'Come on then! Four batteries a weekend, over eighteen years at two quid a time. Come on then,' he insisted. He had that resolute look he had had at last year's Christmas party – two hours before he was found paralytic in the loo with his pants around his ankles.

Vinny looked at the hand like it was an absurd joke. He laughed lightly. He looked to the rest of us to join in. But we knew which side our bread was buttered.

We stared expectantly at Warren's hand.

'Well, you don't really expect I'm going to pay for a few wretched batteries do you?' He laughed uneasily, searching for possible eye contact. There was none.

'Come on, man. You just said you would not two minutes ago,' goaded Alistair Robbins-Brown as he winked at Duncan. It was common knowledge, the carnal relationship between these two.

'That's right. In front of witnesses,' pressured Duncan.

'Oh really, what have we come to? That two intelligent grown men should act like this over such a pettiness,' Candida interrupted in her imperious way. 'I think there are more important things than transistor batteries that need to be discussed at this meeting.'

Vinny slumped into his chair in relief.

'Such as the dreadful Gabby girl? I mean to say, no woman can feel safe with that little miss trotting about dressed like a Kings Cross tart all over the Temple. I can't imagine the ideas it gives the men. I'm sure Evelyn would agree with me?'

She shot me a warning glare – realising that I was about to point out that men had been getting the wrong idea millennia before Gabby and her exposed midriff came onto the scene – but I was saved by Warren who jumped to Gabby's aid. Warren was not immune to the mysteries of Gabby's pierced navel.

'I think that's a bit rich, Miss Raphael. She's a competent little receptionist is our Gabby.'

There were general grunts of assent from the meeting at large.

Mark Sidcup QC, normally silent in these things, joined the rescue party. 'And what's more she speaks German,' he added mysteriously. 'Her mother was an Austrian. Broke code in the war she tells me.' Our head of chambers was big on German.

'For which side?' muttered Candida acidly – with a toss of her bouffant. Our head of chambers smiled back deferentially – he was used to being spoken to by someone like Barbara Woodhouse correcting the gait of a dachshund.

The pointless and petty discussions went on for another half-hour. I tried vainly to gee up the room with my promise of a sparkling night of chambers revelry but the truth was, no one cared. For them, the chambers' party was nothing other than a bonding exercise of dubious worth – a noblesse oblige they could do without.

But this party mattered to me. Sometimes it was as if I didn't exist in their minds at all – as if there was a conspiracy to render me invisible. The only work I seemed to get came courtesy of Candida strangely enough – and came with a price tag I was still trying to interpret. For a woman who hated me so much why was she so keen to take me in her confidence and to pass me the scraps from her brief pile? Because without her I'd be ruined.

Warren offered the odd flasher or shoplifter but for the most part I was invisible in their eyes. I saw this party as a way of making them notice me. I was very naive then.

I'd planned the party in every detail. No dry biscuits with cheese and Californian bubbly for me. I'd hired gorgeous waiters to serve Moët and canapés and my *pièce de résistance* was to be the background music provided by The Hothouse Jazz Quartet.

OK, I know it's not spine-rattlingly hip but you can't go at a chambers like 17 Pump Court like a bull at a gate. I was going to approach the matter like the wily Odysseus and sneak my way into their affections inside a disguise they were comfortable with – class. I wasn't after much – just the odd returned brief.

Warren was right behind me. He took his sense of pride from our cases and, besides, the matter of spending chambers' money was close to his heart. He encouraged me to hire the very best that chambers' money could provide – to take the heat off his own office extravagance, I imagine.

★ ★ ★

It was two hours later when we finally filed out to reception exhausted by our own pettifogging to find Gabby barricaded into her desk by a floral creation so various, so large, I fell down and worshipped. Julian had come through at last!

I smiled coyly and blushed.

'Check it out,' said Lee as he came through from the clerk's room. 'Ooze it for then?'

'Well I . . .' I mumbled shyly.

Gabby's muffled voice called out from behind the blooms. 'They're for Miss Raphael. They're from some bloke in Monaco.'

Candida then showed us skills that any Home Counties amateur dramatics member would recognise. 'Oh that wretched, wretched, silly man. Wildly extravagant as always.'

She thrust her eyes heavenward and her arms towards the flowers. 'Lee, take them into my room will you. I'm sure Gabby doesn't want to be swallowed by exotic orchids while she's trying to work.'

What she meant was that exotic orchids had no place in the life of that dreadful Gabby girl. That was Candida all over – even her concern sounded like a fatwah.

'It's all right. I don't mind,' called Gabby. 'I quite like them. It's like being on holidays.'

'Dear, dear girl,' Candida twittered as would a charity dame to an Aids patient. 'I can't imagine where you go on *your* holidays?' If Candida had her way, the Gabbys of this world wouldn't get holidays.

I decided the time had come to save the dreadful Gabby.

'Candida, could I have a word please?' I asked.

'Of course you may, Evelyn. I just have to make one teeny weenie phone call to the Duke to thank him. Mad, mad extravagant man that he is. But I'll join you in your room as soon as I can.'

Five minutes later she burst in – as usual without knocking – just as I was dropping into yet another daydream about Julian.

'So, darling, how can I help you?' she asked, dripping gold baubles like tennis stars drip sweat.

'Nothing really, it's just that well . . . to be honest, Candida, my curiosity was aroused by what you were about to say about Julian yesterday.'

'Julian?' she asked. I watched, as she mentally flicked through her heavy file of suitors.

'Julian Summers – you know, the solicitor? I prompted. 'Your friend Max saw me with him at the Old Bailey yesterday? You said there was something I should know?'

'Oh him? You're not interested in a *solicitor* are you?' she asked, spitting the word solicitor out like a loose tooth.

'Well, no, of course not in *that* way,' I lied. That's the thing about lust – it gets you sinning like none of the other venials can.

'No, of course you're not,' she said and then she gave me a saucy leer as if we were sailors sharing a dirty joke. I must say her look struck me as strange at the time, but I let it pass – eager to get to the heart of the Julian matter.

'Well, Evelyn, no doubt your affairs are your own concern,' she said, yawning. 'You know as well as anyone how I hate to spread idle gossip, but as it's common currency, I really can't see what harm it can do . . .'

And then they came. My bouquet. Not as large or as various or exotic as Candida's, but, as Gabby brought them in, I decided that Candida's loud blooms looked vulgar compared to the quiet sophistication of my dozen white roses in their ivory parchment box. Julian had come through after all. How had I doubted him?

Candida ushered Gabby out as no doubt she was used to doing with room service at George V in Paris. To my annoyance she also took the card out proprietorially and read:

CONGRATULATIONS
on your win.
It was a privilege to be against you.
Giles.

Chapter 16

Something was stirring within me –
my brain maybe?

It was a case of the right flowers, wrong man. Why can't men get their flowers right? White roses were Giles' calling card. He distributed them to friends and family like alms to the poor – which says a lot about the bankrupt state of his imagination. They could come in dozens or singles – as long as they were white. The last time he'd given me a white rose was the last time I'd slept with him.

Sending me a dozen was like his way of saying – let's be friends. But as Gran always said – don't hang on to a sock that's lost its mate.

It was time to look to the future. The past was dead. OK, he'd seemed like a good bet at first, but that was just a disguise. All that stuff about putting the toilet seat down and enjoying shopping was just an elaborate ruse.

The way he never complained when I dragged him around Bond Street and tried on clothes I couldn't afford was all part of a sneaky plan to put me off my guard. Once he bought me a Versace frock for my birthday and it was *my* size, *my* colour, *my* everything! OK so maybe he wasn't all bad!

But he was a bastard nonetheless. A coiled bastard waiting to strike. The evidence started coming in when we were making plans to share a place together in London. I was sitting my final exams. He had just been accepted into a set on the edge of Lincoln's Inn. Our future was mapping itself out as a river of togetherness but, even then, hidden along the bank were levees about to break.

The notice to quit the Garden of Eden began on a Friday night after I got back from my tutorials. There was a message saying would I mind not coming down to London this weekend as he was preparing notes on a big case.

Sex to die for – cancelled for notes? I mean Christ! I was sitting *the* most important exams of my life – I was about to do something that would go down on my permanent record in ink and yet I was prepared to undergo British Rail hell to be with *him*! It felt like unfair dismissal.

Devastated, I took it like a stoic and spent the weekend dying my hair colours that didn't suit my complexion and drinking wine in quantities that didn't suit my liver.

The next weekend I went to London, but Giles was acting strangely. He picked me up at the station as normal – but for some reason he didn't want to take me back to his place. Making up this mad story about how the landlord had just had the place painted and he didn't want me to inhale the fumes. Maybe I was holding one of those plaques that read 'innocent abroad' or something?

We went to the cinema, the theatre and all-night dance clubs – when all I wanted to do was to get back and fall asleep on the wet patch.

After two more weekends of these 'we can't go back to my place because . . .' excuses, I did what any woman in my situation would. I blamed myself. Maybe I was losing my appeal? Maybe my vagina smelt? Could it be thrush?

So I went to the Well Women's clinic and demanded a thorough going-over with the biggest breakthrough in misogynous instruments of torture – the expanding stainless-steel phallus. I got the all-clear the next Friday, at the same time I got his last message telling me he was working on a case and couldn't see me that weekend.

I didn't know it then, but I was sitting in darkness while a firing squad took aim. There were neon signs all around me flashing READY AIM FIRE! But I was keeping my blindfold firmly in place.

Why couldn't he come up to Oxford? I asked.

'I'm snowed under with work,' he said.

Fuck you, I decided and I took the train anyway. I convinced myself he'd be pleased to see me. Denial was a river in Egypt as far as I was concerned.

It was a hot sultry night – erotic. I was drugged up to the eyeballs with adrenaline and the journey seemed to take forever. The train was full of lovers consuming one another's faces. As we rattled through the darkness I had experienced a strange sense that I was about to be derailed from my innocence. Something was stirring inside me – my brain maybe?

It was midnight by the time I arrived at his house. I had been turning over this idea that I was going to silently undress, creep into his bed and blow job his brains out.

His house was in darkness, but they kept a key under a cement cat in the back garden. Maybe Giles had fallen asleep studying his notes, I kidded myself. There is none so blind as a girl sitting in darkness with a blindfold on.

All the way down the corridor I visualised his reaction. But by then even I could hear the sounds of the bullets being loaded.

My body was wedged tightly against those of my fellow commuters on the train to Notting Hill – the bloke opposite was grinning at me as if I was a bowl of water and he was a dog with rabies. First rule of train travel in this city is to pretend that it's not really happening to you. This is somebody else's problem and if you keep your head down long enough it will go away. Treat it as an out-of-body experience – because if this was really happening to your body, you could take every bastard on this train to court. Keep your eyes to yourself and your legs tightly together.

I clutched the flowers, thorns and all into my chest – God why not? I was on pain overload. It was so hot my underpants were slipping off me. And this was not the place I wanted to be knickerless. I prayed that today the IRA would leave the Circle line alone. I prayed the tracks wouldn't melt, and there wouldn't be a train derailed on the line for urgent repairs and, last of all, I prayed that this train wouldn't explode with shell fatigue.

I said all these novenas while I stared outside at the blankness of the tunnel. Sam and Charles were right. It was time to leave the past behind. Giles was a bastard but that didn't mean I had to live my life as if I had venereal herpes.

But I was still no closer to hearing Candida's gossip on Julian. Then again she was hardly known for the validity of her evidence, and, ipso facto, I was better off without it.

Once she had used a handwriting expert in a fraud trial who turned out to be the accused's brother. She was a use-and-do-and-say-what-suits-you sort of girl. But her hinted warning was there nonetheless, like a chip in my nail varnish that I couldn't paint over.

'Hey, you with the flowers!' some bloke called out.

Oh my God it was the bloke with rabies – now I recognised him. It was my *Big Issue* vendor and his trusty dog in neck-scarf.

'Fort I recognised you like. So owz it goin'? I figured that was quite a knock y'got yesterday. I saw it all y'see. That geezer wiff the blond 'air an' the glasses was 'assling ya. I would a' 'it 'im if you'da said.'

Everyone in the carriage suddenly found the point to their life in our conversation.

'That's very kind of you, Mr . . .'

'Jock. Call me Jock. I don't believe in surnames and stuff.' His crusty features grinned. He didn't believe in courtesy either, I thought, as he roughly shoved the old man beside him along the seat and motioned for me to sit down.

I shook my head vigorously. The old boy pointed reassuringly at the spot. My wedgies moved apart so I could get through. I reminded myself that this wasn't happening. It was all just an out-of-body experience.

'That's OK, I prefer standing,' I insisted.

He shrugged. The old boy beside him stretched out, pulled out his teeth and studied them.

'I could tell you was different from the others straid away like,' Jock explained, looking at me with those gimlet eyes you get when reality is just a distant memory.

'The others?' I asked confused. Everyone in our carriage looked around them.

'You know . . . everyone else. You just came up and bought a whole pile of the *Issue* offa me. Wild or what?' he laughed madly. Everyone averted their eyes. 'Made me day like. I mean, I dun normally notice most of 'em.'

What was happening here? I wondered who I could pay to

stop this – whatever it was – from going on. Did he want me to buy more of his magazine? Was that what he was after. I asked him if he had another copy I could buy.

He looked at me as if I were to be pitied. 'The next issue izzen out for a week. 'Ere let me give ya anover one.' He fumbled in his plastic satchel and produced a magazine. 'Go on, it's on the 'ouse.'

'No please, you must let me pay,' I insisted, flapping uselessly about for my bag. The last thing I was about to do was accept charity from a man such as Jock who probably slept in an old polyester blanket in a doorway. Legal aid may be meagre, but I had my pride!

But he was resolute. He passed the magazine to the old bloke who still had his dentures in his hand. I could see the saliva trailing over the front page as he passed it on to the bloke, nearest the woman, closest in the wedge to me.

My worst fears were recognised – I grabbed it on the wet bit.

'You're one of us now!' he declared, thumping his chest.

Brilliant, brothers and sisters in saliva. I wiped my hand on my Dolca Gabanna.

'One of us?' I enquired stupidly. By now everyone else in the carriage was tuning into their own out-of-body Zen experience like mad. If this bloke went AWOL with a knife or even his bare hands, they wanted to be on another plane.

'Yeah, you're not like all them others.'

I had a loony. Two stops to go and I had a loony. A lot can happen to a girl with D-cups between Gloucester Road and Notting Hill Gate I thought to myself. I started ticking them off on my mental check list. Everything from ABH to murder. The best thing to do was to say nothing. But Jock wasn't so easily put off.

'It was a look you had in ya eyes.'

I can explain that, I thought. It was the look of a woman who's just spent a day at the Bailey on ecstasy – defending a man who keeps snapshots of his pit bull under his foreskin.

I thought about screaming for a guard. I couldn't have got my leg free enough to kick him if I tried. But I felt even worse when the train pulled into High Street Kensington. Everybody evacuated the carriage except for Jock, his dog, the old bloke and me.

I sat down close to the door and put my back to him. *Why hadn't I taken a taxi?* I cried out inside. *Because you are broke with an overdraft the size of most people's mortgages and you're trying to appease your guilt before you splash out on the Agnes B sunglasses.*

I felt a hand on my shoulder. 'I can tell stuff like that ya see. I've got the sight. I can see right froo people.'

I felt suddenly exposed. This was a conversation I wanted out of and now. What was he doing on the train anyway? Wasn't he homeless? Wasn't the whole point of homelessness that he had nowhere to go?

I have this propensity for attracting the Jocks of this world. When other kids were followed home by stray dogs, I was followed home by tramps and hobos.

I put up a tent in our front garden in Mosman once so an old tramp I'd discovered sleeping rough near the Harbour Bridge could stay dry. It was down where my father moored his yachts. 'A view people pay millions for,' my father shouted aghast as he dialled the police and had the old boy moved on. And now I had Jock. That was the trouble with me – I attracted the wrong sort of men.

'I can tell you're special,' he was murmuring. I could feel his breath on my ear. I looked down at my feet where the dog had fallen asleep on my shoes. The old boy put his teeth back in.

There was no way, I argued with myself, that Jock was going to be pitching his blanket in Ladbroke Square tonight. As the train pulled into the station, I thrust the flowers into his hands and ran. I was over white roses, but more than anything else I wanted to be over the wrong sort of bloke.

I kept running all the way up Kensington Park Road like a prairie oyster after a hangover. Past the Pakistani shop and the temple where a hundred or so West Indian women milled outside in their finery – as if waiting for a second coming.

When I got to the taxi rank I was about a hundred yards from home but I was desperate and the temptation was too much. I had just put my hand on the hot handle of the door when I saw him. I almost didn't believe my eyes, but it was definitely Julian driving past – that navy BMW was unmistakable.

'Follow that car!' I shouted. If Julian had business on my turf, I bloody well wanted to know about it!

My cab driver took my instructions about as enthusiastically as a hike in mortgage interest rates. By the time he found himself in the mood to pull out from the kerb, Julian was already parking between Leith's and L'Artiste Assoiffe.

'OK that'll do,' I told my driver who ignored me and sailed straight on.

'Stop here!' I demanded as we drove beyond Westbourne Grove.

'What?' he enquired, opening the window.

'Stop here!'

'But you said follow that car.'

'Exactly and it just pulled up over there,' I cried out. I turned around and caught a glimpse of Julian – he was already walking down Westbourne Grove. The driver slowed to a halt. I threw in five pounds and charged.

I ran straight for the turnstile near the smart loo designed by Piers Gough – in W11 even the public loos are designed. But there was no sign of him. I was at a crossroads in my life – I was being offered my dignity. I could abandon this mad quest now and go home or even take a stroll up Westbourne Grove to Agnes B and spoil myself with those glasses – and a bit more debt. After all, it's not every day a girl humiliates herself over a man quite so thoroughly.

But an inner voice told me that now wasn't the time for dignity – dignity is something to comfort yourself with in your old age, Gran always said. At twenty-four I was too young for dignity.

Then I saw him in the florist. More flowers? I wondered hopefully. I strolled nonchalantly over towards Tom Conran's Deli. After all it was my area, I had every right to buy prosciutto if I so desired. I ordered a modest amount while keeping my eye on the street. The meat was already on the scales when Julian came out.

'Actually I'll take it all,' I told the snooty salesgirl who looked as if she's been waiting all her life to serve me – not!

'You said one hundred grams,' she sniffed.

'Yeah and now I'm saying I'll have it all,' I explained. God, move with the times, girl.

'Do you want low fat?' she suggested. Obviously this bitch wasn't schooled in the art of sound-bite marketing. Anorexic women do not offer heavier women 'low fat'.

103

'Do I look like I do?' I challenged her. 'Just ring it up will you!'

'But that's three kilos,' she bayed.

'And three thousand women just contracted breast cancer in the time we've been arguing over this. So just tell me how much it costs and let me get out of here. I didn't come here to buy bloody salami anyway,' I huffed.

'No?' she sneered.

'No! Oh, fuck it.'

I abandoned my purchase and ran from the shop just as Julian ducked up Colville Road. He was lugging the biggest bunch of blood-red roses I've ever seen. And, no, they weren't the sort of flowers you buy for a sick granny. They were get-your-knickers-down flowers that usually come hot on the tail of champagne – the sort of flowers you give to an object of desire. And with a sinking heart I knew I wasn't that object.

That was all I needed when I was still on my seduction trainer wheels – competition. And in my own area for God's sake. Hadn't he heard of discretion? He turned down Lonsdale Road and disappeared into Boom Boom – a cafe bar with wall-to-wall twentieth centuriness. How obvious. That was when the first wave of shame swept over me.

What was I thinking of – stalking my solicitor? What had happened to me? People live their lives in fear of people like me. I toyed with the idea of going home. I honestly did, but not for long – if he had a paramour in my area, I bloody wanted to know who. Like I said, two years in the celibacy closet and I was rampant. I mean I was that close to storming into that bar and demanding on-the-spot cunnilingus.

The bar was big and loud and U-shaped with wall to wall TV screens. People stood in the shadows and looked cool and vague and not the slightest bit like people in the sixties probably imagined people in the nineties *would* look. It was as if time had stood still – only the technology had changed. This was intravenous, in-your-face, up-your-nose, down-your-eardrums cool. They were all very young and I felt suddenly old. Adrift from my generation.

I had the choice of going right or left, but in the end I did a complete lap three or four times – each time more frantically than the last. All of them under the critical gaze of the not-so-now generation.

I felt like I had when I lost my mum in Counterpoint shopping centre in Sydney and ended up amongst the polyester kitsch of the racks in Katies. My mother was *so* embarrassed, she practically disowned me. I mean if I was going to get lost, she didn't see why I couldn't do it in the marble aisles of David Jones at least.

There was absolutely no trace of Julian. And that was when the full force of my situation hit me. I was a stalker about to be sprung by her prey. He must have gone upstairs which meant he was on the balcony bar which meant when I walked out – he was going to look down and see me.

I tucked my face into my chest and ran. The last thing I heard was my name being yelled from the balcony and a barman rushing down the street after me.

'Madam, madam. You've left your shoe behind.'

Chapter 17

She made the face I'd seen her making only last month – after she'd taken a speed and champagne rollerball

I was so glad when I got home to find I was alone. When you're two-hundred-pounds worth of Gucci shoe lighter the last thing you want is an audience. I had also shaved off the leg of one stocking on the journey home but even that didn't upset me as much as the flowers. So Julian had another woman?

We weren't even dating and he was already cheating on me! And with a local girl! I mixed myself a V&T and sat outside on the balcony overlooking the square. We spent most of our summer evenings on this narrow space luxuriating in the riot of colour in our key-garden. It was somehow humanising to come home from work and watch the old women walking lapdogs and the children playing hide-and-seek along the overgrown footpaths and hedged passageways.

I was about to go inside to attack the vagaries of my wardrobe – you know, follow the three-point plan to getting a together look. 1: Throw out anything you haven't worn in the last two years – does that include the snake print Morrisey Edmondson mini I bought in the Strand Arcade in Sydney last year? Eeek! Surely not! 2: Throw out anything that's not in my size – oh right like ninety per cent of it. Come on, seriously, one day I will be a size eight I promised myself. 3: Throw out anything you have more than two of – sure like all eighty-six little black dresses. Very likely!

Sam burst into my musings with a rustling of Mothercare bags.

'Evvy, look. Look! Look what I've got!'

I laid down my drink and looked – as only a true friend can look at the instruments and the contraptions that are meant for the hanging and dangling and swinging above babies' cots.

'Oh bloody Jesus what happened to your foot?'

I stuck it under my bum. 'Nothing.'

'Shit! It looks like you stuck it in the waste-disposal unit.'

'Can we drop it?' I pleaded. 'They look like fun,' I offered, to change the subject.

'Fun?' she said crestfallen. 'They're meant to be stimulating,' she groaned as she slumped into the sofa, wearing one of those shapeless maternity frocks with the absurd bows on the front.

'Stimulation is fun,' I argued.

'S'pose,' she said, like a tired jury member falling to the force of the majority. 'What I was thinking of was hanging them above our bed and kind of road-testing them. You know, get in on the baby's angle.'

Do babies want us grown-ups muscling in on their angle? I wondered. 'How do you think Charles will feel about that?'

She looked at me like I'd called her a hairy dyke. 'Charles is cool. She wants what's best for the baby,' she pointed out – singling me out as the one who didn't.

'So do I, Sam – I'm the woman who's got to come up with the raw materials, remember.'

'I know, Evvy. I'm sorry, it's just that . . . well, you know . . . my hormones have knocked me for six.'

I found that a mite troubling. I mean if this was the pre-pregnant Sam, what were the hormones of a pregnant Sam going to do? This motherhood business was beginning to sound increasingly dangerous. I offered her a drink which made her recoil with a sharp intake of breath.

'Evvy! You don't seem to realise what effect alcohol can have on a foetus. Haven't you heard of Foetal Alcohol Syndrome? Do you want our baby to look like this for the rest of its life?'

She made the face I'd seen her making only last month – after she'd taken a speed and champagne roller ball.

'But you haven't got a foetus yet, Sam!' I explained. Someone had to set this girl straight. Her reality principle needed sobering up with a few little home truths.

'Not yet, but I'm doing the groundwork now. A healthy body nurtures a healthy foetus.'

I poured myself a triple and downed it in one. The prospect of this kid was starting to inhibit me – and it wasn't even a zygote yet. It's not that I hate kids or anything – I love them. I love tossing them around, crawling about with them, blowing bubbles and making hideous faces for their delight. But talk foetus and this girl runs for cover behind the pages of *Vogue*.

I hear the word foetus and I think labour, stretchmarks and post-natal depression. I think about shitty nappies, sick on the shoulder and pretty soon I'm in birth-control mode. I know that as a woman my DNA should cry out for children, and it does – other people's. Preferably with nannies.

It's the sick-making lifestyle changes of motherhood I find so hard to bear. Once my sister actually asked me to change my adorable nephew's nappy.

'Change a nappy?' I cried as incredulous as the begum asked to do up her own clip-on ruby and diamond necklace. 'With this manicure? Get real.'

Charles came in. She kissed Sam on the cheek, dangled a few zoo thingies in the air and turned to me.

'Well?'

'Well what?' I thought she was talking about the mobiles. 'Yeah, gee, aren't they great,' I chortled.

'Your case, idiot! How'd it go?'

'I won it!' I said without enthusiasm.

'No? Evvy, that's great. That calls for champagne. I bought some yesterday just in case, but given the circumstances I didn't think you'd well . . . Sam, can you get it, sweetie, I've got to collapse? I've just had *the* most trying day in court,' she groaned while flinging her black-stockinged legs over the side of the vulva. Sam slumped out to get the champagne.

'A tough one, hey?' I sympathised.

'Thank God it's Friday's all I can say. Oh, Evvy, these millionaire twins – you wouldn't believe it. I told you about them, remember?'

'Are these the ones who were sued for damages after having that couple evicted by mistake?'

'Yeah that's them. The Bigg brothers! Unreal! They had no court order remember? They just had their *muscle* dump this couple's gear on the street while they were at work. Thieves stole the lot naturally. That's the old news. They were ordered to pay damages and now they're appealing.

'I told the solicitor that the appeal's hopeless from the start. But, anyway, I met with them today to discuss the case which is warned for next week and they fired me! Can you believe it? Just because I told them what I was professionally bound to tell them? Sorry, anyway, I'm going on. Tell me what happened to your case?'

So I told all. All about Keith being sedated, the priest being drunk and how the other two were obviously peppering their evidence. 'Basically the verdict was handed to me on a platter by the prosecution. Anyway you won't believe this – Giles sent flowers to chambers. Oh, I forgot to tell you that part. He was counsel for the *persecution*.'

Sam returned with the bottle of Veuve Clicquot and handed it to Charles, then she rummaged around in the Mothercare bags and held up a contraption that looked like a Looney Tunes gym.

Charles ignored her. 'You're kidding? Oh, Evvy, how hateful. Good thing you won then. Why didn't you mention it? But hang on – he sent you flowers? Saying what?'

'Just congratulations.'

'What a turnaround. Oh, Evvy, that's so sweet. He can't be that bad if he sends you flowers,' she exclaimed.

This wasn't what I wanted to hear – my ex-super-bastard described as sweet. 'For Christ's sake, even paedophiles shell out for sweets!' I reminded her.

'I thought we might hang these above our bed,' Sam interrupted, standing there looking like *The Blob* in her capacious frock. Was this really the dark dynamo of the disco floor I've lived with for two years? The svelte punk I'd rarely seen out of plastic, leather or sequins on the weekend?

Charles must have been thinking the same thing. She looked at her like she'd just suggested an orgy with the gardener.

'What ever for?' she asked crossly.

'To see what it feels like – you know for the baby.'

Charles finally prised the cork off the champagne and put her mouth over the bottle to catch the ejaculation of bubbles.

'Get real, Sam. I'm not having a kid to study child psychology. And I'm not going to have that falling on my head in the middle of the night,' she exploded through spurting bubbles. 'Just cool it a bit will you. Let's wait till we *get* pregnant. Could you get some glasses please, honey? We've got something else to celebrate.'

After another gulp of the champagne she said, 'So Giles the super-bastard sent you flowers? What sort?'

'White roses.'

'Oooh, Evvy – watch out. He's going for the kill again.'

'Well he can bloody well find another victim this time,' I snapped. 'There's no way in the world I'd even give that bastard the time of day.'

Sam returned with the glasses. The girls looked at one another. I could see they were afraid that the 'how to string men out on mountainside' diagrams, were going to make a come-back.

Sam ran to stem the haemorrhage. 'Absolutely, Evvy . . . the man's a bastard. That Julian's so much sweeter anyway.'

But I knew what she was really thinking. Julian was a big possibility as far as donor material went.

'So where are these flowers then?' Charles enquired, looking around the flat while she poured the bubbly.

'I gave them to some bloke on the train. He usually sells the *Big Issue* outside Temple tube station. And guess who I saw?'

'Julian?' The girls squealed, pausing suspended like expectant fathers on their seats.

'He had a big bunch of roses with him.'

They raised their eyebrows.

'Big red roses,' I pouted. 'And I don't think they were for me.'

But we were interrupted by the door buzzer. Sam and Charles both went to answer it. While they were away I watched over lovers on the commemorative chairs in the garden – smooching. I felt suddenly lonely and hopeless.

I would never forget the sticky sweetness of Chanel No 5 in the air. I still couldn't believe he'd done it. The memory of her lying under the duvet we'd bought together at Habitat. It still hurt. I had stood and stared at her. I had to strain my eyes to see in the half-light cast by a streetlamp outside. But finally, out of the shadows, I made out the form of a Goldilocks in my bed. Her long blond strands trailed possessively across the pillow. The bitch incarnate.

Her face bleached white against the darkness was beautiful. Giles had revealed that honour when we first slept together – that he had only ever slept with beautiful women. Conversely I had the good grace to keep from him the fact that I had only ever slept with bastards and nerds.

Besides I didn't need the proof of her face. Her A-cups in all their mocking compact glory were an epic poem to my indignity.

A moment later the door slammed and I heard the furtive whisperings of Sam and Charles. I got up to see what was going on and sprung them both in the corridor, reading a card.

The card read, 'To Sam, Charles and Eleanor (*sic*). Thank you for last night. I'd love to come to the party – see you Friday!'

There was no getting away from it – we were a threesome in Julian's mind – and I was the last in his order of preference. He couldn't even get my name right. What was it going to be next? Egor?

'He said he couldn't come in,' explained Charles, looking as guilty as hell.

'Yeah he really wanted to . . . like,' insisted Sam. 'Look he bought you this – Cinderella,' she said, producing my Gucci from behind her back. 'So now you'll have to tell us what happened?'

Could life get any worse? I pushed my way through to my room. I was going to test the mettle of my non-run Lancôme mascara.

Chapter 18

I felt like a cab driver clicking on the meter for a fare to Heathrow

Monday's are all bad-lipstick days. Drinking champagne the night before can only make it worse. I woke up with a boiling stew in my head. Putting on my stockings was a major test of dexterity. I broke five nails trying to do up my suspender belt. It took a packet of Panadol and a litre of Lavazza coffee just to get me moving.

How many times have I said I am never drinking champagne again?

Alighting from Temple tube, I was overtaken by an irrational loathing for life and all those inhabiting this overcrowded planet – a condition known to London's psychiatric community as London Underground Syndrome. I strode head-down through the rays of tentative summer sunshine spreading across the cobbles of the Temple.

Charles had done the rational thing and stayed in bed. Sam was still surfing the loo in preparation for the first trimester of her pregnancy.

Warren greeted me in the clerk's room like I was the prodigal daughter. 'Congratulations on your first win at the Bailey, Miss Hornton,' he said.

Lee was stirring his coffee with a broken digestive biscuit. He looked up and grinned while the biscuit dissolved in his fingers. 'Wait till you see what Warren's got waiting for you in your room, Miss Hornton.'

'Get away with you,' laughed Warren, playfully clipping Lee's ear with the *Sun*. 'I've put you on an appeal. The Biggs brothers are quite distinguished in the property world.'

'East End gangsters 'e means,' Lee explained.

'Now, now, don't go getting too big for your boots, lad. This could be quite lucrative for you, Miss Hornton – if you take my meaning.'

I did. We were talking folding money – not the pitiful pennies of legal aid. I flirted with the idea of kissing Warren's Churches but I decided my hangover wasn't up for it. Now I could afford that gorgeous little Ozbek number tantalising the shop window of Bond Street.

'They're in your room now, waiting for you. They sacked their counsel yesterday and so they're looking to you to carry this appeal for them,' he explained.

'Villains the both of them,' Lee added. 'They're in there with Ken Trumpington from Judge, Rape and Scythes. It's your lucky day, innit? They're making an appeal on a damages award. A bit of civil for you.'

So Charles' twins were now employing me to make their doomed appeal? And paying folding money? As I calculated the consequences of this case that could pay for itself, my hangover disintegrated like one of Lee's digestives.

I felt like a cab driver clicking on the meter for a fare to Heathrow. My luck was looking up.

After the brothers Bigg and their solicitor left I gathered up my wig and collar bands. My client was entering a guilty plea on a charge of ABH at the Inner London Crown Court. I didn't imagine it would take more than an hour. A small dissertation on the mitigating circumstances was all that my client required. A guilty plea's like sliced white bread – and it went down easily with a hangover. There was no jury to perform to and the prosecution was unlikely to harp on.

Giles was guilty. All it took was a change of postal address and he was out of my life. After discovering Goldilocks I had moved into a bed and breakfast. I had the Post Office redirect my mail and gave no forwarding address at my old rooms. I only had two weeks to go at college so I had put my head down and studied. I dyed my hair black, wore Doc Martens, drank red wine, read a lot of feminist literature, saw films we would never have seen together and tore up his letters without opening them.

After the exams I went to Australia to visit my family. On the surface I looked normal, but I felt like my head was rotating round on my neck and six priests were exorcising a host of demons from me. I asked British Airways to refrain from sitting me next to any male passenger they didn't want badly injured. I moped and I cried and I read Simone de Beauvoir. My parents asked me about Giles. I said who? They knew enough to drop it.

He was never mentioned by them again.

When I returned to London I moved in with Charles and Sam and started Bar school. Twelve months later I passed with flying colours and started a pupillage in the Chambers I'm still at – 17 Pump Court.

I had reinvented myself as a full-time, post-feminist professional with no time for men. And now the work looked like it might finally start coming in. The phone rang as I was planning the details of my new wardrobe.

'Hi! It's Julian. Listen, I'm just calling to tell you I'm sorry I missed you on Friday.'

'Oh yes, never mind,' I replied, trying to keep the embarrassed quiver out of my voice.

'I saw your shoe though,' he laughed.

'Yes, well, thank you for returning it,' I said curtly. What was he doing, trying to strip me of any residual vestiges of human pride? All right so I lost my shoe – I had stalked and lost. I have been tried and humiliated accordingly.

'Like Cinderella running from the ball,' he carried on, confident that he had the safety of all the technology at British Telecom's disposal between me and him.

'Was there anything in particular you wanted,' I asked, attempting to freeze him from his embarrassment drive.

'I actually wanted to apologise for running off on Friday. Look you were brilliant. It's just that I had a personal matter to attend to.'

'Not too personal I hope?' I probed, suddenly keen to chat away.

'No,' he laughed as if he sensed it. *'Finished* personal business, you could call it.'

I was trembling with excitement. Either he'd just had genital

115

warts removed or he was what's known as *between relationships*. And those flowers sure as hell didn't look like a 'goodbye to genital warts' bouquet.

'But anyway,' he continued, in a voice that was made for telephone sex, 'I just wanted to apologise about running off after court. We should have gone out for a drink. I mean that was superb – your speech.'

My vanity was rushing up my body like a red Versace dress coming down the catwalk. 'That's OK, I had to get back for a chambers' meeting anyway. By the way the *girls* received your note,' I added, fishing for clues. I mean, maybe he had a thing about lesbians. Maybe he was one of those kinky blokes that get off on two girls making out?

He didn't miss a beat. 'Did they? Excellent. They're brilliant,' he replied without a trace of irony in his voice.

'I'll tell them you think so. But, listen, what about a drink tonight?' I suggested going for broke.

There was a hesitating silence before his answer. 'Well look, really . . . I'd love to, I'm just not certain *yet* if I'll be free. Could I get back to you this afternoon?'

As I put down the receiver I was determined to get the dirt on him from Candida. There was more to this man than met the eye. I was sure of it.

As I was leaving for court, Lee burst in on me to give me warning that I was about to be ousted from my room as of Thursday – while it was *spruced up*.

'But don't worry, Miss Raphael's agreed to let you bunk down with her. Sorry about that. It was meant to be discussed at the chambers' meeting, but you know how these things are?' he added sympathetically.

'So how long is this sprucing up going to take?' I asked, reeling from the concept of sharing a room with Candida.

'Oh, you know.'

'What? A week, a year, an eternity?'

'Don't panic, it won't be that bad – it's not as if you'll be out in the cold. You'll be sharing with Miss Raphael. You know, girls together.'

He'd slammed the door before I had a chance to get the point of my stiletto in his eye.

Chapter 19

The anti-girlfriend

Candida was to my ego what Rasputin was to morality. She whittled away at my self-image until I started to think that maybe at twenty-four I was too old for short skirts and stilettos.

After ten minutes in her room, which was decked out like The Lanesborough Hotel, it was clear that sharing with Candida was everything I'd *never* planned for myself and more. It was like sharing a room with a boa constrictor in a steam room of Diorissimo. But what really, really, really grated was the way she constantly referred to me as *your sort*. As if there was a caste of people just like me out there.

I mean, that is not what you want to hear when you spend three times more than you make trying to strike just the right eclectic note. I'm a millennium woman! A post-baby boomer – carnivorously individual. A wild child. Unpredictable. One month I might wear nothing but *black* Sonia Rykiel and then the next month OK so I'll wear nothing but *black* Gucci.

'What do you mean *my sort*?' I demanded once and for all.

Candida rolled her eyes as if in one of those dervish trances. 'You're not going to ask me to spell it out are you?'

'Well, you're going to have to. I haven't got a clue what you're talking about.'

'Oh, Evelyn, you don't fool me. You're not as innocent as you look.'

'Innocent? Me?' I squealed, incredulous as a nun accused of

having a clitoris. I'd always resigned myself to the fact that innocence does not sit well with Aunt Kit's breasts bursting forth from my chest. But Candida refused to go into it. After a few more bouts of tongue clicking she went on her next offensive. My hair!

She visibly shivered as she meowed, 'If I'm going to put up with you sitting opposite me all week you're going to have to do something about your hair.' She puffed up her own incredible hairdo for added emphasis. She then went on to decry my hair as one of the seven horrors of my generation. The way she said *brown bob* made it sound like forensic evidence.

'It's not that bad!' I argued weakly.

'My dear girl, how bad does it have to be? I mean you're off down to Hove on one of *my* cases tomorrow. And it matters to me that you look your best. Not that the verdict won't be an absolute walkover, but appearance is all, as they say. Now, as it happens, I can arrange an appointment for you with one of *the* hair artistes of London. Stefan of Mayfair. I wouldn't let anyone else touch *my* hair.'

'Stefan?' Was this woman on a maintenance dose of LSD or something? Did she really think I was going to entrust something so close to my brain to a man that created *that* bouffant? *What's the matter with my brown bob anyway?* I wondered. *There's a lot of it going about the Temple these days.*

That was how I had the inspired idea to invite her for a drink at Benjamin Stillingfleet's. A bar on the edge of the Temple where the young and brave knock back verdicts and sentences over gallons of wine. And – more constructively – where a hundred brown bobs could give testament to my view that you don't need a bouffant to be a barrister.

Later that afternoon – after the Biggs had lost their appeal (surprise surprise) and paid me in cash (no surprises there either) – Candida agreed to accompany me to BS. As predicted the bar was full of brown bobs just like mine. Brown bobs, spine-rattling music, smoke, wig & gown bags and pilot-cases strewn all over the floor. The Temple goes Boom Boom – minus the TVs.

Candida turned up her sizeable nose and held the *Telegraph* over her head as if she was walking through a food fight. I took control and sat her at a table near the bar while I ordered.

'Quite a lot of brown bobs about the place,' I pointed out.

She wiped her glass with her napkin before agreeing to sip at the V&T I brought over.

'Quite,' she exclaimed, rebouffing her hair.

I tried another angle. 'I suppose under the wig no one even notices my hair.'

She looked at me sadly. 'Your client will notice, Evelyn. However much they're paying – and granted in your case that's woefully little – clients have expectations of their counsel. You have an image to uphold.'

But we were forced to drop the topic of my crown of thorns when Julian walked in with four gods from the mountains of Olympus.

'Eleanor! Candida! How's it going?' he muttered vaguely as if passing the neighbour's dogs on the street.

I wanted to call out something witty and cutting to him as he perched on the other side of the bar with his mates. But my brown bob let me down.

The bitch from hell was smirking as a blotched red and greenness spread up my neck and face till I looked like one of those face-painted protesters that tie themselves to trees and railings.

'So are you going to tell me what it is with that guy now? What's his big secret?' I snapped as nonchalantly as I could with my ever-spreading facial tattoo.

She puffed her hair. 'Well, Evelyn, I'm really not one to spread a rumour,' she purred, practically climaxing in the juices of my discomfort.

By now I think Candida could tell that I was prepared to cavort with the Prince of Darkness if it meant discovering Julian's secret. She was smiling at me like a Cheshire cat on Prozac. 'I didn't realise how keen you were, Evelyn.' Which meant that now she did know she wasn't going to tell me.

The music punched its base beat into my embarrassment as I watched Julian and his friends laughing animatedly in the shadow world on the other side of the bar – as bob after brown bob burst into the room like a squadron of Daleks. We were a bloody army. After all this time thinking of myself as an

119

individual there was now no getting away from it – I was a clone!

The truth hit me like a chain saw. No wonder Julian had never noticed me. No wonder he'd never even remember my name. Girls like me came off a production line. Black two-pieces, brown bobs and pilot-cases. We were like bewigged members of some loony sect.

It was too dark to lip-read but I convinced myself that Julian et al were lampooning brown bobness. Maybe the unthinkable had finally happened. Maybe Candida was right.

'What were you saying about Stefan, Candida?'

So that was how I allowed myself to be dragged off to Mayfair where Stefan, I was assured, would do to me as women all over the world had prayed he'd do to them. I reasoned that it wasn't such a bad idea. Looking at my track record, I wasn't having a lot of luck seducing Julian so far. In fact the only man this haircut had attracted was Jock – the *Big Issue* seller!

'I can't tell you how lucky you are to get an immediate appointment!' she cooed after she'd got off her mobile. 'Why, Stefan doesn't just *do* anyone. He's an artiste in the true sense of the word, darling! And, believe me, hair artistes are rarer than two-way streets in Mayfair. Why, women come from New York and Paris just to be *done* by Stefan . . .' she oozed.

She might have won the hair point, but it would take more than that to bring us closer together. As she babbled on like a *grande dame* to a pug dog as we started to leave, I prayed that she'd trip over the treacherous arrangement of pilot-cases strewn all over the bar and land sprawling and humiliated at my feet. But of course she didn't.

She asked one of Julian's juicy friends for a hand 'to escape', as she put it. Then she tiptoed like Ginger Rogers clasping Fred Astaire and squealed and 'darlinged' her way to popularity. By the time we got to the door, the whole bar was cheering her. God, I hated this woman.

Chapter 20

Where was this woman when the suffragettes needed her?

What was I doing trusting a woman like Candida with my hair? After all, in the manifesto of sisterhood, girls boost other girls. Girls tell one another that they have great legs, winning smiles, A-grade personalities and the charity of an angel. Girlfriends pick you up when your own ego slacks off. When you know you look like a Westminster Portabin, they tell you you're going to stun him with your wit.

Not Candida – she was what's known around the sisterhood tracks as an anti-girlfriend!

I must have been mad. Candida was right when she spoke of Stefan's reputation. He was the only serious competition for the Nicky Clarke throne. His signature cut was the 'done' look which when it was trendy looked like something out of the sixties and when it wasn't it looked like Candida. As a consequence, Stefan was the darling of the Chelsea Knightsbridge set – women who lived for The Season, who lived for Stefan to *do* them!

We circumnavigated Mayfair for about eight quid. That's how I measure distance in London, in cab fares – just like a junky measuring smack. It was here in Mayfair, where adjectives such as gracious, elegant, sophisticated and sublime trip off the tongue like coins into a parking meter, that I first hatched my new vocabulary to describe Candida. I sensed that I had the support of the cabby. As we entered Grosvenor Square for the ninth time, Candida threatened to report the driver to the Taxi

Confederation for not knowing where Stefan's was.

'I can't see that it's my business to give you directions to *the* greatest living hair artiste in the civilised world,' she hissed.

'So, you've no idea of the address then, madam?' the driver probed.

'Address? Address? I said Stefan's didn't I? Do I need to say any more? You're meant to be the one with *the knowledge*!'

The driver closed the adjoining window with a thud.

'That's the trouble with society now,' she went on, loudly so the driver could hear. 'Everyone requires spoon feeding. It's the thin edge of the wedge when a London cab driver finds himself lost in Mayfair.' Then she re-fluffed her unbelievable hair and settled in amongst the Lacroix jacket that had arrived in chambers the day before – yet another gift from her 'mad, mad, extravagant duke'.

We glided on down Green Street, Park Street and the lanes and yards of Shepherd Market as the cab explored every nook and cranny of Mayfair's Georgiana. I watched the meter as it clicked into figures that resembled my fee for representing Keith the head-butter.

'So you've *absolutely no* idea of the address?' I insisted.

Candida threw her shoulders into the air and pouted ever so slightly like a child about to admit to killing the cat. Then she glared at me like she might bite. 'Of course *I* know the address. I just don't see how this man can lay claim to *the knowledge* when he hasn't heard of *the* salon in London.'

I refrained from taking her gilded neck in my hands and satisfied my thirst for blood by biting my lip. 'Well, tell *me* the address, Candida. After all, we don't want to keep the maestro waiting do we?'

This seemed to bring the colour back to those heavily rouged cheeks. 'Oh all right then. Ormond Yard . . . of course!'

I patted her on the knee. 'Great, Candida – we've just spent half of what I make in a day driving through the one-way-street system of Mayfair, searching for something that was in St James's all the time?'

I saw her lip twitch. For a second I thought she was about to apologise. But no, I was still just on my trainer wheels where this *femme fatale* was concerned.

She rubbed her temples with two delicately sun-lamped,

manicured hands. The driver at this point, having had the good sense to listen in, had made a beeline for St James's.

'I take it, it is Ormond Yard you want, ladies?' he called out just to double check.

'Of course it's Ormond Yard, you wretched man. I wish you'd just do what you're paid to do and drive us where we want to go. These irritating road checks of yours are giving me a migraine. I hardly think it's my job to memorise the London A-Z!'

This woman took some beating. The Women's Movement could have used her as a secret weapon. Where was she when the suffragettes needed her? But Candida was a cause of her own. Her battle was a lonely one. She had her hands full just looking after number one.

There have always been women like Candida – women who cried 'Feminism? Who needs it – I don't need liberating!' And now I could see their point – it wasn't Candida that needed liberation. It was the rest of us – the cabby, Gabby and myself. The little people. We needed armed protection from this woman.

My knuckles were white by the time we arrived at Stefan's. I paid the driver and asked for a receipt. He must have felt sorry for me because he handed me a book of them. Candida had already abandoned me on the pavement and by the time I struggled through the rotating door, the air kisses were all but over and champagne was being poured.

'Darlings, I'm giving up cabs!' she declared in a toast to the gaggle of trendoid geeks surrounding her.

'Oooh . . .' cried a creature I took to be Stefan (there were pictures of him kissing an array of stars all over the salon) and his fussing lackeys with concern. He was about thirty-five with a nose that looked like it was going on ninety. He had a mane of auburn hair – 'aubergine' as it was written up in the press. He was holding a small Jack Russell, with a runny nose and a diamante collar famous at the catwalk shows, which started snarling at me.

'No!' Candida insisted. 'They've had their last fare from me, darling! The wretched man hadn't even heard of *you*!'

'Nooooooo . . .' cried Stefan and his boys, bug-eyed with the shock of it all. Stefan of the tumbling aubergine locks fanned himself with his photograph. They looked at one another as if it was a matter to be taken to a higher authority.

'Did you hear that, Mr Pog? Did you hear that, my baby?' crooned Stefan to the dog.

'Yes!' shrieked Candida. 'And you won't believe this,' she said in a lowered voice.

Stefan and the lads gathered around.

'He thought Ormond Yard was in Mayfair!'

This delighted them. They threw their heads back and squealed like skewered pigs above the din of Pulp singing an ode to the common people.

I was gripping the periphery of this geekoid group with grim resolve. At least I was close to the exit here, I reasoned. Whereas looking down the marble sweep of steps I saw a world I was innately afraid of. The interior designer who put this fearsome look together probably sold it as classical. My stomach was lurching with a dread Odysseus and friends must have known as they fought their losing battle to steer their ship clear of Aeaea where Circe lay waiting to turn them all into swine.

I hate having my hair cut and when I do I prefer to have a friend do it – you know, someone I can get revenge on later if I have to. If forced to seek outside help, my idea of a salon is a few girls on the high street who can turn out a respectable feather cut or bob for twenty quid. At least if it goes wrong there is the satisfaction that it didn't cost much. I mean why spend money on hair when you can buy yourself some Agnes B sunnies?

Below me was a world of men in bondage trousers with nasty dyed-black hair reflected in sinister multiples all around the mirrored atrium. These creatures of Pope Innocent IV were standing over their paying victims with instruments of torment. Hairdryers that looked like they'd been ripped from the wings of Boeing 747 jets and tongs and crimpers.

One thing was clear – these men were not beautifying women's hair, they were at war with it. They made pampering look like torture. They snarled and bitched and squealed with nasty laughter above the bludgeoning sounds of Retro Pop as they stuck pins and combs in their prisoners that they'd pulled from their own mouths. I was looking at *Childsplay III*.

There was a woman in the corner whom I vaguely recognised from a serial about lawyers – with what looked like an electric-shock apparatus over her brain. She looked about four hundred years old, no doubt a survivor of the Counter Reformation. If Candida thought I was going to pay to be on the receiving end of this, she had met her match.

Watch my lips, Candida, I thought, *they're saying, 'Not on your clitoris, girl.'*

'Darling, this is the colleague of mine you've generously agreed to *do*.' She pushed me forward. Mr Pog's nose dripped lavishly on my hand.

Stefan's acolytes dilated as he gripped me like a lost child. I smiled weakly while he stalked me – walking around me the way polar bears at the zoo do before they tear into your flesh.

'Yes, yes, mmm, mmm, I can see what you mean. Mmm, mmm, take a little off the sides. Mmm. Mmm. And then go in like this . . .' He flayed my hair back across my skull. 'Mmm. Mmm, yes it can be done, darlink. What do you think, Mr Pog?' he asked the dog.

Mr Pog snarled nastily at me.

'No? Mr Pog thinks *non*?' Stefan and his aides screamed with laughter.

I felt like a bull in the ring with a battalion of loony matadors armed to the hilt with clippers.

'I don't think it needs much. I like the natural look,' I explained hopefully.

Candida and Stefan led the troops in the screams of laughter.

'The natural look?' they howled.

Candida, struggling not to spill her Moët, turned to me and patted my shoulders. 'From the mouths of babes. Didn't I tell you she was priceless?' she asked, drawing me to her gold bosom. I drifted into a state of semi-consciousness, choking on the vapours of Diorissimo.

'Priceless!' Stefan echoed, but I knew my price tag was showing – and it read, 'charge like a wounded bull'. Stefan and his boys joined in the patting of me. This was worse than the polar bear enclosure. At least polar bears do you in with one mighty club from their claws. I was being pawed to death by these Rottweiler puppies.

'Paul Smith, very nice,' exclaimed one of the puppies, pawing at the label down my back as he strapped me into a kind of black plastic straightjacket.

'We'll make you anything but natural, won't we, girls?' asked Stefan suggestively of his boys as he steered me into the dungeon of marble and glass.

I couldn't quite place his accent, it was sort of W1, meets Russian, meets French, meets Cockney in LA. I guess it's what the smart set call an international accent.

'The only thing that's natural here are the products, darlink,' Stefan explained proudly as he put Mr Pog down to snap at my ankles. 'No animal testing, no toxic chemicals. So just relax and enjoy. Tea, coffee, wine; red or white, Evian, Perrier, Moët?'

He fired off the choices like an automatic round of rubber bullets as he fastened me to a chair and pushed me towards the sink and a pimply boy of about fifteen – who looked about as pleased to see me as I was to see him.

'Wash and dry,' he instructed and left.

I don't think the boy heard him though. He had his own agenda. There was a type of woman that he lived to hate and it was me. He smashed the back of my head down into the igneous rock of the basin and sprayed me with a hot shower that excoriated my scalp. Then he scrubbed and scratched at my skull till it was raw and bloodied with this abrasive substance they hadn't even bothered to try out on a lab rat!

Was this really meant to make me feel relaxed? I hate rats. I want to know that they suffered at least as much as me. Not only did the shampoo burn, but it stunk like bottled rat. Maybe that was the key. They hadn't tested it on the lab rats because they'd liquidised them to make the stuff.

When the boy tired of hurting me, he twisted what was left of my hair into a white towel and dragged me by it over to Stefan who was smoking a cigar over a woman whose head was shoved up a kind of lobotomy dome. Mr Pog went berserk as I approached his master – previously he was snarling and yapping happily at cigar ash as it fell onto the dome.

'So, nice and relaxed, darlink?' he asked, clapping his hands loudly.

I get it, I thought, *this is like one of those establishments where women in pinstriped suits pay money to be whipped and urinated on.* Mr Pog sunk his teeth into my shoe.

It was time to back-paddle. 'Look, that was great, Stefan, but I think I'm going to have to get going unfortunately. There's a bit of a party back at chambers. Obligation calls and all that . . . But I'll come back another time . . . Seriously, I can see you're an artiste.'

Stefan seemed to find my explanation a glorious joke. He put his knees together and giggled. I could see my communication skills had met their match. Head-butters and bastard landlords from Stratford all fell to my charms – but not Stefan. Mr Pog looked up at his master solemnly.

'Candida has just gone to do a little shopping. She'll be back in half of one hour. You have plenty of time, darlink,' he reassured me in his West Coast/French/Russian brogue. Mr Pog snarled.

Stephen babbled on. 'Believe me, darlink, it is change you are afraid of! Today you become a new woman. No more saggy old brown bob! [He said the word bob as if it referred to something that belonged in the rest room.] Today you become the super-you! *Non*? The old you is dead meat, darlink. A shell you will cast aside. The new you I will release – personally.'

He said this with some pride, pumping and poking his chest out like a Cossack dancer might before he falls to his knees and tears about working off the vodka. The question was, did I want this man of the steppes of Russia rebirthing me?

There were many questions going around in my head, but only one answer. No! Categorically and definitively . . . No! No! No!

I shook my head.

While I pleaded for my release, the bondage boys had been releasing their own prisoners, plying them with products to carry on their own torture at home and ringing up their bills at the till. Now they began to draw in around me like a jury about to deliver a verdict that would end with my head on the block.

I was going down.

Chapter 21

I felt like a new religion was sprouting up around me – and I was its first sacrifice

I lapsed in and out of consciousness over the next half-hour. I would come to – to the sound of Candida's excited chatter and the growling of Mr Pog – cast an eye over the mirror, realise the horror of my predicament and fall back into a faint again.

I was the only customer left in the salon now – which meant they had focused all their diabolic arts on me. I was pinned to the chair like a specimen on a museum wall.

They kept reassuring me that I was having the old me hacked away. That was one way of putting it. Let's be honest, though, I was being stitched up here. Stefan the Cossack owed some ancestral debt to Candida or something, but the upshot was, I was paying out. I had trusted a woman not made for trusting any more than Margaret Thatcher was made for turning.

What Stefan was doing to me defied medical explanation. Tomás de Torquemada, the king of all Inquisitors, had been reincarnated in the guise of Stefan. This bloke could hire himself out to the Bosnian Serbs.

If it was national secrets he wanted, I would have given them gladly. My virginity, if it was mine to give, was his for the asking. A ransom? I'm sure my father would oblige. But no, Stefan wanted something more vile than money, or state secrets, or sex.

He wanted the *new me*.

★ ★ ★

When the new me finally emerged from underneath the canopy of curlers, tongs, pins, gels and sprays and indescribable metallic paraphernalia, I think even Stefan knew he'd gone too far. There was another sharp intake of breath apart from mine when the unveiling of the homunculus was complete.

I flapped about in my straightjacket to get my fist out, but it was useless. Even Mr Pog was ominously silent.

'Darlink, I luf it, I luf it, I luf it,' Stefan exclaimed finally in a newer thicker accent.

It was the operative word here.

'Darling, you are a genius. What can I say?' Candida gushed.

I'll tell you what you can say, I thought. *I'll tell you in a language that is clear to everyone from Newcastle to Siberia*. But my concise and clear opinion was drowned out by the effusive warblings of Candida and Stefan – not to mention the lackeys now sweeping the old me off the floor.

'My lord, why have you abandoned me?' I cried out. But my anguished cry was blown away by the engine of the Boeing 747 which Stefan attacked me with.

How could I describe the indescribable fury sweating in my fist? Five words summed it up – I'll see you in court. My days of milk and honey were over. Where hours before I had walked with a head as high as any Dalek into this den of Excommunicamus, now justice failed me.

Something told me my head clerk wasn't going to like the *new me*. Something told me that this haircut confirmed all my enemies' opinions of me. This definitely wasn't the haircut to seduce a man with lashes that curled up like Siamese fingernails.

It was lank, it was hacked, it was of varying shape, it clung to my head like clingfilm and yet stuck out at odd angles – like the ears I had on my snow-cap as a child. 'It's so, it's . . . it's . . .' I struggled.

'*Très* grungy!' someone murmured.

I looked around for the literary genius who had put in a nutshell what I couldn't have managed with a thesaurus in seventy languages.

Stefan clapped. Candida clapped. The sweepers of the old me

clapped. Mr Pog barked appreciatively. The Pet Shop Boys'
platitudes were muffled by the applause.

'Très grungy,' Stefan repeated. 'Très grungy.'

He had his mantra and he was sticking to it.

Candida joined in. 'So grunge, so grunge. You are a grunge
genius, darling!'

I felt like a new religion was sprouting up around me and I
was its first sacrifice.

'And *they* say grunge is dead,' Candida sneered after a while.

I didn't like the way this was going. Why did they say grunge
is dead? Who said it? This grunge was the new me? What did
she mean, *they* say grunge is dead? Were *they* telling me they
had killed off the old perfectly happy, natural me and rebirthed
me as something dead?

'What do *they* know, darlink?' Stefan pooh-poohed.

I don't know, but *they* could be on to something. This hairstyle
didn't look very lively to me.

'Well, Evelyn, what do you say?' Candida asked.

Finally it was my chance to express myself.

Under my breath I said something like 'you'll keep'. 'Words
cannot express Candida, what I feel at this moment,' I said
truthfully.

'Très grunge,' muttered Stefan.

This bloke was in nirvana. I knew the look of a mystic when I
saw it. Sister Bethlehem was wearing that look just before she
admitted to being the Virgin Mary and men in white coats came
to lead her away. I knew nothing I said would reach him now.

I looked at my watch. The best and finest of 17 Pump Court
would be steeling themselves for their annual crimes against
their dignity by now. My chambers' party would be underway.
The party where I was to make my mark. The party where I was
to stand out amongst the pinstripe suits and the old boy
network of my peers.

I gave Candida a look I hoped would wither her, but she was
a woman that fed on such looks. You don't get sent Lacroix by
mad, mad, extravagant dukes for being a witherer. I was the
witherer and now I had the haircut to prove it.

When the time came to face the auto-da-fé for the reading of
my sentence, Stefan's accent slipped back to the Geordie/LA.
'Well, my dear, that will be one hundred and forty-three pounds

for the cut and blow dry and ninety-two pounds for the products to keep you looking grungy!' Mr Pog snuffled in his arms.

'I think I'll forego the products today thanks, Stefan,' I explained firmly. I wasn't completely lacking in backbone, you know.

'No, no, no, I insist!' he purred. 'Even I cannot manage without my salon products.' He pushed the pile of salon products across the marble counter. Mr Pog bared his teeth.

'Just the same, I think I will have to forego them,' I pushed them back.

I hadn't shared a cell with Keith of Shepherds Bush for half an hour for nothing. If push was coming to shove, I was prepared to use my black-belt. As far as I was concerned, this guy had just written off my chances of ever seducing a man whatsoever – let alone an image-conscious bloke like Julian. I had suffered most of the indignities ever suffered by my sex in the pursuit of a *new look* this afternoon, but I knew when enough was enough. Those ninety pounds worth of products were staying on the shelf.

As a junior member of chambers reliant on the goodwill of my colleagues, I could hardly tell Candida where to go – but this guy with his trumped-up accent, his snotty-nosed dog and bondage trousers was another matter.

Candida was displaying signs of irritation – tapping her nails on the counter. 'Evelyn, don't be difficult. Just pay the poor man and let's go. The party will be under way by now. I for one don't want to miss Judge Hawkesbury when he comes down. Besides, Stefan is the expert.'

'Fine and I'm not arguing about paying for what he's done to me – but I'm not going to buy a lot of gunk I don't need.'

Stefan was fanning himself with his photograph again. This was hard on him I could see. His boys were huddled around, no doubt expecting their tips. Mr Pog snapped lazily at a fly. It was dawning on me that there was no easy way out of this. Did I really want to stand around and argue my rights with this band of experts in coercion? Rights are what you can get away with, I seem to remember reading on a toilet wall somewhere – and tonight I had that sinking feeling that I wasn't going to get away with much change.

I fished the bundle of cash out of my cleavage and passed it over.

★ ★ ★

We arrived at chambers at seven o'clock. Just in time to see Giles
rushing down a side street with Goldilocks. I'd recognise those
A-cups anywhere. Small beads of sweat burst from my brow.
Had I died and gone to hell or what? I clung to the Zimmer
frame of my faith to support me out of the cab. Was this some
kind of divine retribution being meted out here? I got the feeling
that if I had an only son he'd be lying on a makeshift sacrificial
altar down at the Temple church. I looked up expecting to see
the hammer of JHVH bursting through the clouds.

Was this what my Gran referred to as comeuppance? Maybe
this was my payback for that childish prank I pulled in third
year. 'OK, I know she was a nun but this is a bit over the top
even for you, God!' I argued. 'A bit Old Testament, don't you
think?' I chided, hoping to hit a note of reason with His
Divineship. First the hair and now Giles flitting through my
misery like some kind of profane streaker? I'd offer this up to
the souls in purgatory if I wasn't convinced I was already there
myself.

Chapter 22

The seventh chamber of 17 Pump Court!

It wasn't as if I'd looked forward to this party, but, let's be frank, I hadn't bargained on facing it with a haircut that challenged the view that humans are superior to the apes. I looked like a chimpanzee that Darwin might have worked with. I looked like a joke person – like someone who lets Japanese tourists take photographs of them for a pound.

The revelry was well under way by the time Candida and I arrived at 17 Pump Court. But instead of the strains of the jazz band I'd hired wafting down the street, I heard the Four Seasons played on a combination of brass and snare drum. It sounded like an American shopping mall nightmare.

What the hell was going on? This wasn't the sound of the sophisticated soiree I'd planned. I scaled the steps two at a time, all thoughts of purgatory and Giles and vengeful gods shelved for the mo. Most of chambers were in their cups already, but they sobered up at the sight of me. The snare drum fell crashing to the floor.

'Miss Hornton! Your hair?' My junior clerk was not a man to mince his words.

'Never mind my hair, what's this cacophony?' I demanded.

'Darling, no one wanted jazz,' Candida sighed loudly. 'We wanted something a little more restrained. I took the liberty . . .'

'You took liberties all right!' I screamed.

'Had an argument with a client was it?' Alistair joked.

'Representing Edward Scissorhands by any chance?'

'Such an improvement, don't you think?' Candida prompted, fluffing her own hair proudly.

Gabby giggled. I stopped her with a ferocious stare.

'Well, now that you mention it, no, I don't,' answered Alistair, moving forward to get a better look.

'Good God, girl, what's happened?' asked Mark Sidcup QC.

Candida drew herself up to her full five feet five inches (in Walter Steigers). 'Well I think it's a big improvement – much more suitable for a girl *her* age!'

'Yes. What is your age exactly, Evelyn?' asked Duncan.

'Twenty-four,' I said, feeling like an errant schoolgirl before the board of governors.

'Well, you look like a complete turd if you don't mind me saying,' Alistair slurred politely.

Mark Sidcup QC and Judge Hawkesbury both coloured and took a deep draught of what they were drinking. That was when it dawned on me that I wasn't drinking anything. So I left them holding forth on my hair and went in search of a drink.

There were lots of attractive-looking young men swishing past with inedible-looking battered Thai canapés, but as far as I could tell the drink was off. For one chilling second I feared it had all been drunk. Or maybe Candida had sabotaged the Bolly too. Brilliant! My party would forever be remembered as the one without booze.

I eventually discovered him – the drinks' waiter, guzzling Bolly from the bottle in the clerk's kitchen. As he saw me his face threw several emotions at me at once – shock, fear, embarrassment, guilt, resentment and horror. Then he broke into hysterical laughter.

'Oh God, I'm so sorry,' he yelped. 'It's just that, that, that, that . . .' he babbled incoherently, pointing and floundering for the word to describe the monstrosity of lank locks wrapped about my skull.

'All right, so I look like shit. Just pour me a drink,' I ordered.

He knew when he was facing the Evolution of Man gone wrong. He drained the bottle he'd been drinking from into a glass and did his best to stifle his guffaws. I downed the glass in one and stood eagerly waiting for him to open another bottle.

The cork came out slowly and silently. Like a virgin sighing – that's what Giles would have said if he were here. Or had he just been here? What did he mean by running past my chambers with that bitch?

'Yeah, sorry about that just then,' the drinks' waiter explained. 'It's just that they were all so boring in there. I had to get away and get a drink to keep myself going like and then you came in with your . . .'

He started smirking. I tried to tell myself that he was just a sad drunk who'd lost control of his reason, but then he pointed rudely at my hair and started giggling.

This was too much. I was bred for better things than the taunting of a twenty-year-old sink-waiter, whom I was no doubt paying more than I earned in a day. I snatched the bottle from his lips and pressed the neck of it into his chest.

'That's enough of the champagne and enough of the attitude,' I sobbed. 'We're paying you to do a job – do it!'

His training at the Brentford Hospitality Centre came flooding back into his cheeks.

'Yes, madam. Sorry, madam. I'll just go and refresh the other guests' drinks, madam.'

After downing a few more Bollys I tried to sneak into a toilet to see what could be done to my hair, but they were all in use.

The jazz quartet was playing 'Greensleeves' now. The scene I entered reminded me of the really bad art films we used to go to see at college. Like la Dolca Vita goes Da Da in Romania. Duncan, who is only about five foot in insteps, was chasing Lee around with a fly-swish he'd brought back from a recent holiday in Egypt.

Alistair – his closet lover – was sulking over by the photocopier, listlessly taking copies of his hand. Vinny was telling our new pupil, Jennifer, how pretty she was as she swayed to the music like a drugged Thai prostitute. Gabby was showing her pierced navel to Mark Sidcup QC. The two European law experts from upstairs were challenging one another to an origami competition.

What had happened to my careful months of planning – my elaborate and not inexpensive efforts to make my mark by organising the finest most memorable chambers' party 17 Pump

Court had seen? This was one of those memories I was prepared to pay good money to forget. I could already tell I was going to need heavy duty rebirthing to get over this.

Judge Hawkesbury came out of the toilets and approached Alistair who showed him some of his handprints. Judge Hawkesbury didn't appear to find anything at all odd about this – in fact he offered his own hand for copying. And they say the old boy network is dead. This was a male bonding thing that a woman can never understand or be part of. I was so busy watching their cute little tête-à-tête, I didn't notice Vinny approaching. Vinny is tedium with his flies unbuttoned. Think of every man you've ever wanted to run from and you've got Vinny.

'So, Evelyn!' he hailed.

'So, Vinny?' I replied.

'Not a bad evening, eh?' he cried out too loudly, slapping me harder than necessary on the back. 'Old Judge Hawkesbury seems to be enjoying himself over there, what?' He prodded me in the chest.

'Photocopying his hand you mean?' I asked, taking as hard a swipe as I could at him.

Vinny belted me back heartily. 'Well, he doesn't get a chance to get out much nowadays, I suppose, since the um . . .'

'The IRA attack?' I asked brutally, like a priest sticking the word sodomy into a sermon.

Vinny looked at me like I'd just broken the Secrets' Act. Chambers had been staked out by Special Branch since Judge Hawkesbury had sent the Bradford Three down for life. He looked about to make sure no one was listening and then he did this thing with his face that entirely changed my opinion of him.

First he got his eyebrows to join in the middle in a kind of Masonic handshake and then he pursed his lips out like a cherry about to fall off the branch. I think these contortions were meant to remind me of the numerous threats and ultimate attack on Judge Hawkesbury's life which had resulted in his pit bull terrier Margaret being blown up by a car bomb.

'But surely that's all over, Vinny. Now that the IRA have laid down their arms?' I said comfortingly.

'No! No! No!' he shouted, as if his spaniel had just shat on his foot. 'Laying down is not the same as handing over. They could pick them up at any . . .'

But by then the fight had already started over by the photocopier. In the last thirty seconds Duncan had laid down his fly-whisk and strode over to the happy association of Judge Hawkesbury and Alistair still mindlessly chortling at the sight of their handprints pouring forth. He looked distinctly maleapausal. Something told me the old boy network wasn't working for him.

Lee sidled up to me and jabbed me in the ribs. 'Brill party, Miss Hornton! Love the band – class act, girl.' Then he slapped me hard on the back so I fell forward into Vinny's belt. Both men laughed politely, as if it was a little trick I'd prepared earlier for their amusement.

I could have taken them through my black-belt moves, but I was distracted by Duncan poking Judge Hawkesbury in the chest and flicking his tie into the judge's face. He hissed something I didn't catch.

Now, even those of you with no legal background must realise that judges are not there for the poking any more than their ties are there for the flicking. This was a scandal – one of 17 Pump Court's finest. That years of dodging car bombs should see Judge Hawkesbury so vilely attacked by one of England's own sons – at my party! I rushed over to the gathering.

'Go on then, go on. You've got a problem, let's sort it out,' Duncan goaded, giving Judge Hawkesbury a vicious poke in the arm.

'I have no idea what you're talking about, old boy. I have no problem. Alistair and I were just having a little harmless fun with this machine thingamy here,' he explained, laughing lightly. He gave the machine an innocent pat.

'That's right, all sorted out now. Let's move along shall we?' urged Graham, one of the European law specialists. Up until that moment, I'd always thought he looked like he'd just walked out of a tomb. But he came to life for us now as he bravely grabbed Duncan's arm and attempted to pull him away.

Duncan shook Graham's guiding hand off as if it had leprosy. 'Stay out of this, Boffins,' he snapped cruelly.

Boffins! Oh my God this party was going straight to the High Court of disaster. Boffins was our private name for Graham. We had never called him that to his face! But it was that kind of night – when things that should never be said or done were going to be. This was just the beginning.

Boffins slumped off to his companion, now putting the last touches to a Japanese water crane. He was chatting with my sink-waiter who was now openly drinking the champagne. I didn't like the way they were laughing in my direction.

Alistair had disappeared in the heat of the moment, leaving Judge Hawkesbury alone and undefended. Duncan looked menacingly deranged. There was no one to stop the carnage now, unless you count Vinny or Gabby or the new pupil – a wet girl just out of Bar school who wore her hair in a side part with hairgrips and called all the men 'sir'.

I could tell, bad hairdo day or not, it was time for all good women to come to the aid of the party.

'So, Gabby, I don't think we've ever seen that tattoo of yours have we?' I enquired.

This was Gabby's chance to secure her job for life.

The mood of the group changed immediately. We all knew where this tattoo was rumoured to be situated. Even Duncan was distracted. He dropped Judge Hawkesbury's tie and wandered over for a closer look as Gabby lifted up her skirt.

Lee nudged me in the ribs again. 'Great party, Miss Hornton.'

Under the thin film of nylon pantyhose, Gabby was wearing no knickers. On close inspection, a small rose was just visible. Mark Sidcup QC, returning from his annual party hiding place – the loo – stooped over to join us as we bent over Gabby's bottom.

It was about the time that Vinny was knocking my teeth through my gums in his excitement that I realised that Candida was nowhere to be seen – nor was Warren. The two people most likely to have prevented this fetching display.

I could tell that Duncan had calmed down by the way he was stroking Judge Hawkesbury's tie. I detected in the judge's eyes, a look of one who wants to be back upstairs safely surfing Judgenet. I asked Jennifer to assist him up to his room while I grabbed an opened bottle from the table and wandered off for a little quiet drink.

My room was still flooded with paint tarpaulins and other spruce-up gadgetry so I crept off down the corridor to Candida's where I reminded myself my sandwiches lay untouched in a drawer. It had been a long day and I was starting to feel peckish.

At first when I turned on the light, I didn't comprehend what it was I was witnessing. It was like an anatomical puzzle I had to put back together before it meant anything. All I could make out at first was a pile of luminous flesh pulsing on the desk.

But then I heard a muffled sound like someone crying out in pain.

'Oh, Miss Raphael. Oh, Miss! Oh, Miss!'

I started to put the figures together. Warren's legs were sticking out one side of the desk wedged between Candida's thighs. I worked that out more or less straight away. At first it looked like his bum was on Candida's face and his head between her legs. But surely that wasn't medically possible?

Then I think Candida realised I was there and she gripped Warren's groin to a standstill with her milky thighs – giving me the second I needed to put two and two together. Warren was fucking Candida while wearing his toupee on his bum!

I made a small involuntary yelping sound. Candida took the hair-patch in her hand and threw it in my face.

Looking back this must have been an undignifying experience for Warren. He cowered into Candida's bosom emitting muffled sounds I can only imagine were sobs.

'Get out! Get out, you fucking bitch. Go on get out,' she screamed.

I'll never know what it was that made me hang on, but I just stood there frozen to the spot, staring at this beast with two backs and fiddling with the hair-swatch in my hands until Candida hurled another torrent of abuse at me. I eventually uprooted myself and slammed the door behind me. But where does a girl go clutching a clump of her clerk's hair?

I stood hapless and confused, shuffling in the corridor. I had an urge to put Warren's toupee somewhere. On my head maybe? No, it smelled all greasy and sweaty. I tried to hang it on the outside door handle, but I deduced it would fall off when they opened the door. I tried to push it under the door, but the new carpet with the corporate stripe was of a sufficiently high pile to seal the gap.

By now I could hear howls and panicked discussions taking

place inside. My face was burning red. What was I to do? I couldn't just run off and leave Warren's dignity in a pile outside the door. And yet I didn't want to stand here in the corridor like an embarrassed footman waiting for them to come out.

Then I observed the drinks' waiter coming out of the kitchen so I hissed and gestured for him to come down to me.

'Look, there's someone in that room that's lost this,' I explained, showing him the damp swatch of hair.

He laughed immoderately. 'You're having quite a night of it on the hair front aren't you?'

I gave him my most cutting stare. What kind of impertinent drinks' waiters were they breeding in Brentford nowadays?

'Very funny,' I snarled through gritted teeth. 'Look, it's just that it would embarrass the person who's lost it to find I have it. So what I'm proposing is you wait here with it, or tap on the door when I've gone and give it back to him.'

I placed the mat of hair on the tray and removed the bottle hopefully.

But my sink-waiter was not so slow.

'You're joking?' he chuckled, putting the toupee on my head and snatching the bottle back.

'I most certainly am not,' I insisted, with my best Loreto head-girl voice. I replaced the wiglet on his tray and reclaimed the bottle.

'Fuck off, luv, I've been trained to serve drinks not toupees,' he maintained with some truth. A sound argument, I had to give him that, but I hung onto the bottle anyway and glided off like a phantasm. Leaving him to tap on the door.

I entrenched myself in energetic back-slapping discussion with Vinny until Warren discovered me and said with a great deal of composure, 'Miss Raphael would like a word please, Miss Hornton.'

Chapter 23

The fly was in the ointment the day I was born a girl!

'Torch Me!' They were Gran's last words. Two words that were for ever to sum up her existence. I'll never forget that vigil. We'd been gathered around her bed for days waiting for her to die. She wasn't any happier about it than us. She looked as bored by her existence as we were. Finally it looked as if she was even tired of receiving the last rites she'd insisted on daily for the last week.

Father Guy looked bored too – holding those ivory hands of hers as they clutched at those ebony rosary beads. He had leaned towards her ear and said, 'Tell me, Evelyn [I was named after her], do you have any last words?'

I think he was just trying to break the boredom. I don't think he really meant anything by it. But we all craned forwards, waiting expectantly for those last words to be delivered like players of a monopoly game waiting for the *Get Out Of Jail* pass.

I was personally hoping she'd say something like, 'You were my favourite granddaughter, Evelyn, and consider my fortune yours.' I guess Father Guy was hoping for, 'I'm off to sit at the right hand of the father, Father, and I'll be sure to give you a mention.' But we were both light years off the mark.

'Torch Me!' she yelled like a banshee with her last breath. And all hell broke loose. The priest grabbed his heart and collapsed. My mother fell on top of him. The rosary beads scattered all over the floor. My father grabbed the bedhead for support and blasphemed rigorously. My siblings ran from the room babbling in tongues.

Gran was dead before the last rosary bead fell, but the scandal outlived her. So did the debate. Was she referring darkly to an afterlife in Hades? Or merely suggesting how we should dispose of her earthly remains?

'Life is an eternal mystery,' the priest had extemporised at her funeral.

The next half-hour was to prove him right. Standing outside Candida's door I was reminded of another door I had stood outside some ten years before. My progress up the ladder at the Loreto College for Gentlewomen was halted rather suddenly after I caught Sister Catherine playing poker with Father Young from St Ignatius Loyola Jesuit school for young men.

'*Ad magorem Dei gloriam.* That's forty quid you owe me, you old tart!' was what I walked in on. The repercussions were revolutionary.

Let's get this much straight. Before I even turned the handle on Candida's door I was prepared to say or do or admit to anything just to get out of that room with my womb still in place. And before you accuse me of being spineless, may I remind you I've read *The Crucible*. I knew my script and I knew that after a few minutes of full-frontal abuse by Candida, I was going to admit to fiendish deeds of evil if it meant an early release.

'You slut. I'll destroy you. If you think you're going to get away with this, you tart, I'll kill you,' she explained before even turning around to face me.

It crossed my mind that I was in a confined space with a psychopath. I toyed with the possibility that she had one of those sadistic analysts who suggest fully expressing your emotions. Maybe she was lynching me – as a means of purging herself of menopausal tension? A kind of cathartic Evening Primrose equivalent.

As she tore into me like a frenzied evangelical preacher in languages Berlitz will never translate, one thing was certain. These emotions hadn't been cooked up over a toupee and a sexual indiscretion. This was deep stuff. This was the sort of hatred that had been fermenting for a very long time – this was like . . . ancestral stuff. It was like I'd always said – as far as Candida was concerned, the fly was in the ointment the day I was born a girl!

'Don't fool yourself – they all know what you're about,' she spat. 'Always slinking around, you little bitch. You, you . . . slut. Acting the little Miss Innocent. Oh, you've wanted to get something on me for a long time I've no doubt. You stupid little cow. I've seen it in your eyes. So jealous and grasping, aren't you?'

She paused long enough for me to answer. I opened my mouth but decided against words. Throughout her philippic I felt as futile and as victimised as Eve after she'd been caught nibbling apples – overreaction didn't even come close.

After she'd collapsed in a sort of spent heap I attempted a defence. 'I'm very sorry I walked in on you, Candida, I truly am. But, come on, I was literally just in the wrong place at the wrong time.'

She put her head back and laughed hysterically as she had with Stefan only hours ago about how ingenuous I was. Priceless was how I think she described me then. That terminology was all water under the bridge now though I sensed. She looked at me with the eyes of a Nuremberg jury facing Goebbels.

'You expect me to believe that it was an accident?' she asked, as if even I, in my guise as the vessel of all evil, couldn't expect her to believe that.

I nodded in a dreamy, Valley of the Dolls fashion.

'You must think I'm stupid!' she hissed.

I denied the charge energetically with my eyes.

That was the point at which things took an unexpected turn. She fluffed up her hair, snuggled into her chair and turned around to face me. 'Well, maybe you're right. Perhaps I am being overly harsh,' she agreed briskly.

I gulped.

'Maybe I should just let bygones by bygones.'

My eyes retreated into the back of my head. Had someone spiked the champagne with hallucinogens? I mean, she was crusading down the path of forgiveness like Christ himself. Had I been at the ecstasy bottle again? I wondered briefly. In hindsight, of course, I should have stopped her then. I should have insisted she flay my flesh – is that the word? Whatever, I should have said, 'Treat me like one of those Singaporean prison guards treat drug dealers. Take to me with your fists. Whip me, thrash me.' I should have pleaded, realising that the deeper she drank from the cup of forgiveness, the bigger would be my hangover.

Candida swivelled her chair around to face the wall again where a rather bad expressionist painting of her own profile smiled menacingly out at me.

'You think you're pretty smart don't you?' she enquired without facing me.

'Not at all, Candida. I look up to you.' I kept my eyes on the painting.

She laughed lightly – seemingly flattered. As she turned around to face me, she smiled and said, 'You know, I know you're one of *those*!'

I was stumped. Was she referring to the painting?

Confound your enemy, Gran always advised.

I was confounded. 'Ah? One of those what?'

She dropped her voice to a whisper. 'Oh, little Miss Innocent. Did you think I couldn't tell you were from Lesbos?'

I was floored – speechless as they say in intellectual novels. 'What?' I squeaked.

'Oh, I've never said anything before. I can be very discreet when I *choose* to be,' she hissed.

'But you're wrong, where did you get *that* idea?'

'It's pointless denying it. I've known since you first came to us. I know all about Charlotte Macer. I know she's one of those . . . one of those . . . she makes no bones about it. She'll probably take silk because of it. I know how the Bar Women's Group is all for that left-wing sex stuff.'

Left-wing sex stuff? I felt like a kitten who's lost the end of its ball of yarn. 'Hang on a minute, are you saying I'm a lesbian here?'

'Oh grow up, Evelyn. I'm no stranger to the world of perverts. What do you take me for?'

I rocked mindlessly in my chair. As the Count of Monte Cristo said, 'Wait and hope.' So this was what she had meant by all those dark references to *my situation*. I began to see a long stint in chains ahead of me. Not that I was appalled at being labelled a lesbian. At times I might even be flattered, but, as I'd seen before, in the hands of Candida even a hairstyle could become a weapon.

'Living with Charles doesn't make me a lesbian, Candida,' I reasoned uselessly. 'And so what if it did?'

'Is that what she calls herself? Charles? How typical. It sounds like something out of *Goodbye Berlin*. You can say what you want, darling, it's of no moment to me and quite honestly *I* don't care . . . not personally. As long as you don't try any of your filthy ways on me.'

I bridled at the very thought of anyone, let alone myself, trying anything on this gold-encrusted crab apart from a noose.

'Charlotte may enjoy the safety of a liberal chambers,' she purred on, 'but I don't think I need remind you that Warren takes a very grim view indeed of *your sort*.'

I was right. This wasn't about me catching her and Warren in flagrante. There was a much broader agenda here. As head clerk, Warren held my earning capability in the palm of his hand. If he was to find out that I was the sort he took a grim view of – my earning capability would plummet.

Up until now Warren and I had a pretty cosy relationship. He saw me as a nice young Catholic girl of high moral calibre. You've got to realise that as a devout Presbyterian, Warren wore morality like a jockstrap. Forget *his* moral duplicity. One's own sins are always easier to forgive. But homosexuality was another kettle of fish entirely. We're talking about a crime against decency – a crime against nature. We're talking about a man with major league anal blockage.

'So now, little Miss Busy-Body,' Candida started up again like a crazed doll rewound. 'I think it would be wise for you to keep your head down in future. Knowing what I know, I'm sure you'll do your best to keep me happy.'

'Keep you happy?' I dribbled. Keeping Candida happy was surely a Herculean remit – a bit like keeping the leaning tower straight.

'Well, shall we start with winning the cases I have the kindness to pass to you? I believe you have an arson of mine down in Hove tomorrow?'

I wanted to say something rational like, 'Isn't that up to the jury?' But my mouth got stuck. I dribbled some more.

'Let me make this quite clear. When I talk verdicts, I'm not talking options, darling.'

It was a bit like sexual harassment. I felt abused and violated and angry and impotent. In fact, forgive me, sisters, but I felt like wrapping her fallopian tubes around her neck.

Torch Me!

Chapter 24

I had the feeling I was in one of those dyke plays where the hetero bimbo doesn't get a speaking part

Life wasn't meant to be easy. So said a great Australian politician once. He was routed at the next election for it. And now I knew why – all I wanted was an easy life. I sure as hell didn't want these merciless realities that had been raining down on me lately. If this was life, I wanted something else. Something more benign. Anything! An out-of-body experience in somewhere like Jamaica would go down well.

Sitting in the auditorium of the Underground, looking down my tunnel of wrecked dreams I tried to remember halcyon days when the only thing that kept me awake at night was fear of a visible panty line.

Now here I was being harassed about my sexuality by a rabid bouffant. What happened to sisterhood? What would Gloria and Germaine say about this? I mused. I doubt that even Camilla Paglia would have a one-liner for me now. One thing I learned at convent school was that fighting a woman is so much deadlier than fighting a man.

At least men have testicles to kick. Candida's Achilles heel wasn't so easy to find. She was a fortress and a dragon all rolled into one. I kept going over the facts in my mind. I walked in on her fucking the head clerk and I'm the one with the tail between my legs? Excuse me? This lesbian threat was just a front. True or not true, Candida thought she had a hold of Damocles' sword. And by the look of my hair she'd already had a go at me with it.

'What happened?' I asked the universe out loud – like all the other loonies on the platform mumbling away to themselves. One minute I had the world at my feet – I had my tenancy, a big case at the Old Bailey, and a brown bob. And now I've got a rabid bouffant after my cervix. I had an urge to read Sylvia Plath.

And I haven't even told you about the latest blow. Just as I was descending the staircase of chambers, Candida had come running after me and thrust what I presumed was a letter bomb into my hands. 'Oh by the way, darling, this arrived for you while we were out – it looks rather personal.'

It was a large envelope addressed to me. The sweeping curves of the handwriting were familiar enough not to open it straight away, so I plunged it into the nether regions of my pilot-case – and my consciousness.

I meant to read it on the train, but you know how it is with public transport. I was too busy shelling out to Bosnian buskers and defending my derrière and avoiding eye-contact with the man with a snail trail of silver studs running along his eyebrow. He was picking at a scab on his dog's head. As Gran was always moaning – the general public is a brute.

As I walked up Kensington Park Road I was praying that the girls would still be up. I felt like some of that nurturing girlfriend stuff I'd read about in magazines. One article I'd been particularly impressed by was in *Tatler*. It had scoffed at the American dependence on analysts while lauding the British girls for their reliance on the good old-fashioned girlfriend network.

'Evelyn, your hair!' screamed Sam from the balcony. 'Charles, quick, come and see Evvy's hair,' she yelled. Just in case anyone on the square hadn't heard her the first time.

'Oh my God . . . your hair,' squealed Charles. Gran called it stating the obvious for the sake of a good laugh.

I looked up, noticing the flashing of lights going on all along the square.

'Can we wait till I get inside to have this conversation?' I pleaded.

Despite the all too frequent attacks on my dignity, there's a lot to be said for living with girlfriends, I reassured myself as I ascended the stairs. OK, so they can be embarrassing at times, but at least you don't have to face the malaise of the twentieth century alone. Girlfriends provide a soothing backdrop to the slings and arrows of life. You get to share clothes, magazines, electrical appliances and gossip.

Sam and Charles were waiting at the top of the stairs for me in their shorty pyjamas. Sam was holding a turkey baster loaded with some sort of alcohol which she fired all over my face.

'Look at you, Evvy. Oh poor baby!' Charles exclaimed, wrapping her long arms about my now moist person. Sam ran off – I suspected for more ammunition – but came back bearing Pimms and cucumber – in a glass. I ducked.

'Have some refreshment – that will make you feel better,' she chortled. 'But my God your hair! What have you done to it? Don't tell me before you've had a drink! You had your party tonight didn't you? What a bore! God that haircut, Evvy. This is what we've decided on for the party tomorrow night.'

She went on babbling excitedly at a thousand miles a minute while I drank the drink – straight Pimms through a sieve of cucumber.

Tomorrow night seemed light years away. I sat on one of the black cast-iron high-backed chairs. The glass-topped table was littered with hundreds of condoms, pipettes and paper cups. It was like some sort of bizarre 'Barbie goes berserk in the chemist' scenario. It was time to flush that girlfriend nurturing dream down the toilet.

I needed intravenous counselling.

'What do you think, Evvy? Pipette or baster?' Sam asked, holding up the various appliances.

'Aren't they great? Lia and Adrienne gave them to us!' She handed me a bundle of condoms.

I recoiled from them as if they were used.

She wasn't fazed, plopping the whole mass in my lap. 'They used the turkey baster method too. Oh, Evvy, I can't wait to see how much sperm *you* manage to collect,' she squealed excitedly like a child waiting to see what its Christmas present is. She started gathering up the cucumber from her drink. 'Anyway, all you have to do is collect it in the condoms like this,' she announced, depositing some cucumber from her drink into a condom.

I started to feel woozy.

'And then tie a knot in it like this!' She tied a knot in the top of the condom. 'And then run it into us and we'll suck it up into the turkey baster and up the cervix and *voilà*! Babykins.' She explained all this with actions I could have done without. Charles was beaming supportively at her like father watching his wife give birth. My jaw was scraping about the floor like a hoover.

This was just what I needed. Not! I'd just seen my party turn into the fall of Sodom & Gomorrah. Candida's inner being probed by a toupee. I'd been threatened with exposure as a dweller of Lesbos. For the last twenty minutes I'd been watching some urban barbarian picking scabs off his scrofulous pet. And now this. I felt a bit faint. Apart from the onslaught from fate, I was bloody hungry.

'Can you just give me some time out for a bit here?' I begged. 'For two years I haven't so much as kissed a man and now you're laying out a banquet of condoms – enough to end this third world population explosion thing I worry about at night. And correct me if I'm wrong, but I get the impression you're counting on me using at least a few dozen of them?'

They blinked madly – like this was exactly what they were thinking.

'Well, darling, you have been experiencing a rather long drought. We hoped you were praying for rain – a flood even.' Charles pouted.

I felt the saints in heaven fall with me when I fainted.

I came to being sprayed with Pimms from the turkey baster. This was one of those movies you close your eyes in and when you open them it's gone from bad to worse. They were my girlfriends for Christ's sake! They should be tuning into my pain – nursing me through it.

After all, I went to convent school! I know better than anyone what this girlfriend thing's all about. I could write *the* girlfriend guidebook and this scene would sure as hell end up on the editing floor.

The girlfriend rule book states clearly that girlfriends do face masks together. Girlfriends do calorie charts. Girlfriends tell one another when they've got lipstick on their teeth. Girlfriends reassure one another that all men are bastards. They share self-defence tips while watching *Fatal Attraction* cuddled up on the sofa together. And as I came to from my faint, the thing I most wanted to get through to these girlfriends from hell was that they were breaking every girlfriend rule known to woman.

I had very real problems I needed to talk about. Apart from this haircut, I was being blackmailed over a specious assumption that I was a lesbian. I needed my girlfriends like I'd never needed them before.

But this script had been written for me, not by me. I could tell I was in one of those dyke plays where the hetero bimbo doesn't get a speaking part.

'Did you know the Gnostics ate cucumber all the time because they thought the seeds made them more jism?' Sam prattled on as my brain cells decided to stop making even the most basic connections. Was there no stopping her? OK, so she wanted a kid but this girl was seriously possessed by her theme.

'Isn't that sweet?' she cooed like some crack-fucked grown-up on *Sesame Street*. 'I bet it would have been easy getting hold of men's spunk in those days. Apparently it was like a meditation to them – every orgasm brought them one step closer to an enlightenment kind of thing. I s'pose they fantasised about the passion of Christ and stuff like that. What do you think, Evv, you're the Catholic? Do you think your nuns masturbated their way to enlightenment?'

Now she had gone too far. Even for an end-of-the-Millennium girl who had a few gripes with the Pope and his infallibility, this was too much. I could feel my tongue lolling down the back of my throat. I'd seen a girl in the throws of an epileptic fit once. Helen Maddocks. She was doing badly in Maths' and Sister Catherine had started tapping the blackboard with a big yard ruler. Usually when Sister did that, it led to the girl in question having to come up to the front of the class – for like a total baptism of humiliation. But then Helen had this fit and threw all Sister Catherine's sadistic plans into confusion.

I wondered if an epileptic fit would help me now?

Chapter 25

As straight as a dildo!

Charles came to my rescue in the end. 'OK, Sam, I think Evvy's had enough for one day. 'Why don't you run her a bath and we'll hear what the hell happened to her hair?'

I had been freed. I felt like a prisoner of Hezbolah kissing the hand of the good guard. I ran to my room and waited until the smell of lavender essence alerted me that it was safe to come out.

Sam had put on some Chopin on her way to the bathroom. It's strange the way music can trigger things. We'd played that CD to distraction over the last two years – in fact it jumped on the fourth track. We loved it to death. When we were on a Stolly binge we'd sing corny romantic lyrics to it, country and western style. The sort of things Chopin might have sung to George Sand if he'd been born in the Wild West. But tonight a shiver crawled up my spine as memories I'd done my best to forget fought to be reclaimed.

The first time Giles had undressed me in his room, 'Preludes' had been playing in the background. That part where the keys go all tinkly gave me a sense of vertigo – like I was on the precipice of an emotional cliff. As we made love in front of his fireplace in New College, amongst his neat piles of paper and shambolic arrangements of antiquarian books, I thought I'd found true love. Erk! That was when I remembered the big envelope Candida had thrust into my hand as I left chambers. Giles! I went all weird and wobblyish like something was about to happen.

I fully intended to look at it after my bath.

I was gloriously immersed in the bubbles by the time Charles came in with her bag of hairgear and Sam came in with the iced chocolates and carrot cake. This was more like it. This was what girlfriends were all about. *Tatler* was right. Pah to analysts. Pah to intravenous therapy.

'So tell us about your hair?' Charles urged.

So I told them. A snip-by-snip account of Stefan and his fellow inquisitors.

'Stefan? Who's Stefan?' they asked in unison as I explained the antecedents of my ordeal.

'For Christ's sake, don't let Candida hear you say that! As far as she's concerned Stefan is to hair what vodka is to Bollinger.'

Sam and Charles fell about giggling.

'You mean you let a man going by the name of Stefan touch your hair?'

As the crumbs of carrot cake flew about their faces I loathed them as no other. Sam pumped the plunger of the turkey baster and ejaculated a spray of bubbles into the air above us.

I gave them my most injured look. 'Can you two try and take this seriously for a minute? What am I going to do? I've got an arson in Hove first thing tomorrow and if I lose it I'll be sweeping the streets. Plus I've got Julian coming over tomorrow night and now Candida thinks—'

The Julian reference made them snap to attention (for Julian just read sperm). 'God yeah! What are *we* going to do? It's the party tomorrow night. I mean, no one's going to want to make love to that!' Sam stated pointedly, squirting a crown of bubbles onto my head.

I felt like a lamb at a sacrificial altar trying to discuss its heartburn with the high priest. 'I get the feeling I'm nothing more than walking sperm bait to you two,' I whined.

But I was ignored – or rather mown down by Sam's Panzer division logic. 'What on earth made you subscribe to Candida's hairdresser anyway? Christ, she's hardly a woman anyone in their right mind would seek advice from in aspects of grooming by the sounds of it.'

'Oh, so it's my fault now?' I snapped. 'Look this is serious. Forget the hair for a minute and the condoms and that bloody baster. I've got bigger things on my mind than your zygote, believe it or not. I'm being threatened with exposure as a lesbian!'

'A what?' they answered in tandem.

'A lesbian.'

They looked lost. Like Sister Bethlehem did when we asked her if she'd ever had an orgasm.

'Hello! Earth to Jupiter. You know the clit-club? You're fully-paid-up members, remember?'

'All right, all right – go back a bit. Who's a lesbian?' Sam asked.

I enunciated slowly. 'Well, Candida thinks I'*m* a lesbian.'

'The bouffanted bitch that made you get this thing done to your hair?'

'Yeah. I walked in on her fucking the head clerk and now she's saying if I tell anyone what I saw, she'll tell Warren I'm a lesbian.'

'So don't tell anyone,' Sam said as if it was decided. Then she shot a cold stream of bubbles under the water with the pipette. 'See – sorted!'

'Oh sure and it's that simple? Can't you see she's convinced she's got something on me? Not that she cares. She hates me – she wants me out of chambers. This haircut was just the start. A warning shot. Candida's not the sort of woman to let the truth stand in her way. She can use this lesbian thing as a lever against me anytime she wants and there's nothing to stop her dropping hints in the meantime. For instance this arson in Hove. It was one of her cases she passed on to me and she's basically saying WIN IT OR ELSE!'

'Or else what?' Charles asked.

'She'll tell everyone I'm a lesbian.' Something told me I wasn't representing myself very well.

'But you're not a lesbian!' Sam piped in with all the logical ability of Timothy Leery on acid. Boy, were the Lesbian Rights lobbies lucky not to have this sister at the helm of negotiations.

'Can't you see, she could ruin my life at Seventeen Pump Court?' I explained desperately.

'Would anyone care if you *were* in the clit-club though?'

Charles enquired. 'I mean it's no secret in my set which way my preferences lie,' she laughed.

I could see they weren't taking my problems seriously, but I persisted. 'Well that's just the thing, see. She mentioned you when she told me I was a lesbian. In fact she's done her homework on you, girl. She made a reference to your liberal chambers and how being a lesbian could be enough to get you silk. But that's not how it is at Seventeen Pump Court. If she tells Warren – I'm up shit creek without a paddle as we say in Sydney.'

'Sure, sure, I've taken all that on board, Evv, but it brings us right back to the main point. You, my dear, are as straight as a dildo. A vanilla bean. A hetero bimbo, if you'll pardon the expression.'

'Stupid me. Why didn't I think of that? I'll just take a blood test shall I?' I snapped sarcastically. 'If you think that's got anything to do with the price of Poppers in Soho, you don't know Candida. She's not bothered by the formalities. As far as she's concerned I live with you and that's that.'

'So what's Sam then – my spare dildo?'

'Ooooh yes please,' Sam cooed wrapping herself around Charles.

I picked up a razor – only used once or twice before – and thought about slicing their throats and mine in a lunatic murder/suicide. But that would only delight Candida all the more. I settled on shaving under my arms. 'Oh don't even look at it that way. If Candida finds out about Sam she'll label us a *ménage à trois*. Which means Warren as senior clerk will starve me of work.

'Can't you see? It doesn't really matter to Candida what I am? The point is, I'm a woman who won't play court to her and she doesn't want me in chambers. The haircut's all part of it. She probably paid Stefan to do this to me – or rather told him to charge me. She knows that all it will take to get rid of me now is to convince Warren that I'm a lesbian – which in Warren's mind makes me about as wholesome as Myra Hindley.

'You know yourself, Charles, that at this stage in my career if Warren takes it into his head to stop my trickle of work he can. I've hardly got a client base to keep me going. Warren is the source of all work to me – the Nile, Thames Water. If he turns off the tap I'm . . . I'm . . .' I looked up at them with a look I hoped would convey my despair.

'Fucked?' suggested Sam. 'But anyway the first problem on the agenda is still your hair.'

I felt as misunderstood as a rape victim at a police station. I'd filled in all the forms, shown them all my bruises and torn clothes but they still weren't convinced I hadn't asked for it. Everything I had achieved in my life seemed to be as likely to go down the plughole as this bath water. I submerged myself under the bubbles, thinking that maybe the best thing to do would be to drown myself. That would make them take notice.

Sam was holding up the magnifying mirror as I emerged – the one we used to squeeze our blackheads with. The evidence of the last six hours folly was inescapable. If Julian had been cool towards me before, this was the haircut that was going to snap-freeze his juices. I was looking at the reflection of a ball-breaker.

'See what I mean, Evvy?' she pointed out with some truth.

'Yes, the case is cut and dried, my girl,' Charles agreed. 'A jury wouldn't even have to go out on this one. Looks like there's only one sentence!'

'Off with her head!' they cried.

Sam and Charles and I often did one another's hair. Charles' blond crop came from a bottle and a pair of Remington clippers. Sam's feather cut was put together by Nicky Clarke, but in a pinch I could keep it in trim. As for my brown bob, that was . . . well, let's let bygones be bygones.

As I climbed out of the lavender-scented bath it was already twenty to one in the morning. We decided after some dispute – again I wasn't granted a speaking role – that I should have a crop like Charles'.

We were ten minutes into the cut when Sam dropped her napalm. 'Oh by the way, Julian rang you up tonight,' she said casually, as she sheared off the *new me*. 'He was making sure you were straight.'

I gagged on a bundle of hair as I spun around in my chair. The clippers drove painfully over my left ear.

'What?' I screamed as my blood ran down my shoulder. I gazed in disbelief – searching for half an ear lying amongst the strands of the old me on the floor. I was struck by an urge to post it to Julian.

Chapter 26

The Hoves and the Hove nots

Julian cared. That was the first thing I thought of as Sam woke me with a cappuccino at six. After all, checking out someone's sexuality is the late twentieth-century equivalent to finding out someone's marital status.

Sitting on the end of the bed in her honeycomb white robe, new from the Conran shop, Sam reminded me of a Madonna. I knew then that she would make a great mother – her whole silhouette cried out fecundity.

She rubbed my near-bald head affectionately. 'Sorry about your ear, Evvy.'

I put a hand to my ear, bumping the large Elastoplast we'd patched it up with. It felt like a bee sting. In the end we'd decided against the peroxide. Looking at it in the cool light of day the iodine was an obvious mistake.

'Don't think about it,' I smiled. After the news about Julian's phone call I was feeling magnanimous.

'You look like a diesel-dyke that's been in a fight,' laughed Charles as she walked in and leant on the doorway.

I threw one of my pillows at her.

'That's not what she wants to hear, bitch,' Sam said, jumping to my defence. As her robe fell open I caught a glimpse of her Tom Gilbey waistcoat. The one that said 'weep arseholes' – to all the geeks on the trading floor, she'd explained once. Her brown breasts were just visible – well bulging obscenely basically. Charles had seen them too, I realised, watching her eyes pinned at Sam's chest. I settled into my remaining pillow, drank my cappuccino and watched the floorshow.

'You're the bitch that did it, bitch,' Charles snapped, throwing the pillow back at Sam, nearly impacting with my coffee.

'What would you know, you selfish bitch?'

I'd seen them like this before – they were on one of their *bitch* foreplay sessions. This could go on for quite a while before they got to the writhing bit on the floor. So I downed my coffee and went to the shower.

In the mirror I could see Charles was right. I looked exactly like a diesel-dyke that had just been in a fight. All I needed was a beard to be truly at home in Dyke's on Bykes, the bar down the road where dykes congregated in their button-up shirts and jeans. Obviously that had been Candida's plan all along – she had Stefan make me look like a lesbian before she spread the calumny. How could I have been so trusting?

I ruminated on Candida's ultimatum on the case while I showered and dressed. I opted for my sort of coffee-coloured Jil Sander suit – suitably understated for provincial court – and it matched the Elastoplast on my ear. I took a quick look at my horoscope, but there was no mention of triumph in it – just the usual inscrutable warnings about storing things up inside. And they call that a prediction? What the hell did storing things up inside mean anyway? What was I, a silo? And what things? Fluid? Cellulite?

I want good old solid predictions when I turn to my horoscope. Like – don't go out on the street today or you'll get run over. Don't get your haircut today or it will be a disaster, or you WILL fuck the guy you've been completely potty about since you laid eyes on him, or you will get the verdict you need.

Before I left I tried on my wig in the mirror – to see if the Elastoplast was still visible while I was wearing it. If I was going to win this case a lot depended on the jury not drawing the dyke on a byke analogy.

It was while I was scrambling around in my bag for my wig tin that I rediscovered the big envelope from Giles. Maybe that was what I was storing up? I looked at my watch. Help! It was seven-thirty! I thrust it back into the no man's land of my case as another one of those cold thingammies washed over me.

★ ★ ★

I arrived amongst the rag-and-bag tumble of Victoria station right at peak-hour flood. A few of the homeless were still lying on the seats outside the station, dazed and dislocated, half in and half out of their duvets. A small cell of them huddled companionably along the wall sipping at cans of beer. They looked at me knowingly. One of them held up a *Big Issue* which I felt compelled to buy. I thought it might be like the Irish flower women who put a curse on you if you don't buy some heather.

I passed him a pound coin and magnanimously declared that he could keep the change. But as I tried to take my paper, he pulled it away. 'Only if you don't mind, I'll keep this one. It's my last, like,' he explained.

Was I down on my luck or what? I couldn't even buy a *Big Issue* successfully?

'Hiya, Bruiser,' the ticket guard called companionably as I walked onto the platform.

Brilliant! My parents would be thrilled. Twelve years of the best Catholic education Aussie dollars can buy, a first from Oxford, a scholarship to Bar school, a tenancy in a reputable chambers. And a nickname that any member of the criminal world would be happy to share. Confidence is a fragile, sensitive thing and my ego was encouraging mine to file a suit against my haircut for malicious damage.

I changed trains at Brighton and shared a carriage with a barrister. He gave me an avuncular smile and sat down in the seat opposite. I probably should have said something networky but I was already getting pretty anxious. Not just about Candida's arson.

I was distracting myself with the bigger issues now – world starvation, Aids, the beef crisis, the rates of payment for junior barristers and what I was going to wear tonight. I was rigid with the excitement of a roller-blader about to hit a pedestrian in Hyde Park.

I was fairly set on the Versace dress Giles had bought me just before we broke up. Pigeon blood red and tight as a condom. But it was tainted by Giles. So big deal – wasn't it poetic justice that Giles should have bought me the dress I was destined to seduce Julian in?

Then I went through post-confidence jitters. What if Julian

163

didn't find me attractive? How could he with this hair? I could wear a wig – but the memory of Warren's toupee more or less quashed that bright one. I visualised my reflection in those green eyes of his. What if he turned up and declared that there was nothing he hated more than tight red dresses on tall thin girls with Aunt Kit's breasts and dyke-on-byke haircuts?

Then my doubt about my phenotype commingled with my doubts about winning this case. Let's be honest, doubts go with men like snags go with Donna Karan bodies. If you want security, girls, give up dating hunks. Marry a sad old impotent man who adores you just because you speak to him.

No matter how much I tried to keep Julian in perspective, I couldn't stop thinking of him as a god. That's how it is with men and me. If I fancy them at all – which is rare – I want to put them on a pedestal and worship their everythingness. And the more I abase myself, the more they want me to. Why was I obsessing about him when I hardly knew him? Maybe he was an utter pillock who left the seat up in the loo and called his girlfriends 'babe' in bed. I shivered at the idea.

There was something so fascinatingly synthetic about desiring a man I knew nothing about. Julian had a latex personality that I could twist and mould like a fantasy. There was a very real possibility that there wasn't even a real human being underneath all the bondage gear of my imagination!

The barrister opposite folded up his newspaper and stood up. As he towered over me as the train pulled into Hove station, I couldn't imagine doubts assailing anyone where he was concerned. Without knowing him I could read him like words from the headlines of his paper. Social Security.

He wore his unthreatening masculinity like a pair of cufflinks. The gene pool had stopped producing men like him five decades ago. He was a relic from an age when men were men and women married them and longed to have their children.

Julian and his pectorals were of a breed of man enjoying a genetic hiatus – the sort of man who offered little more than safe sex. And God how I longed to have his orgasms.

I almost jumped out of my clitoris when the barrister spoke to me. 'Would you like me to get anything down for you?' he asked.

Just my carnal appetites, if you wouldn't mind, I felt like replying.

Chapter 27

The case of the cable-knit criminal

I was doing my positive affirmations. *I must win this case, I must win this case*, I chanted to myself as I tore up the stairs of the court to glue my wig to my head. I had to win the case if my career was to be more than a brief history (full pun intended). But more than anything else, when I met Julian at the door of my flat tonight in a dress that screamed SEX, I was determined that it would be the cheek of a winner I proffered to his lips for kissing.

My client's crime was arson but his solicitor had insisted on referring to it politely as road rage – you know the crime of the tax-paying mortgaged classes? They say it's *the* crime symptomatic of the stress of the millennia. Ensconced safely in their bubbles, the psychologists tell us, the average driver is filled with an aggression they may not normally be endowed with.

Up to a point I agree. It's true, being in a taxi almost always pisses me off – watching my bank balance being clocked up to someone else's credit before my eyes. But it's nothing on the aggression I get when there are delays on the tube or I'm on hayfever pills. So what's the punchy little label for going berserk on antihistamines?

So here I was, a woman without a licence batting for a guy who suffered from millennia stress. That – I decided as I scanned the crowd for my client and his solicitor – would be the basis of my defence. Road rage – we've all done it. It had a pally ring to it.

Good jury sound-bite stuff. I could hear the plaudits in the judge's summing-up speech now. There'd be a write up in *Counsel* magazine and *Bar News* of course – I'd be the talk of the Temple. I would set the tone for all road-rage defences in the future. Sure! Like *not*! I was more likely to be Candida's bridesmaid when she married her mad, mad, extravagant duke.

As I looked over the heads and shoulders of Hove's criminals and witness support groups, I realised I was not looking for a head-butter type, nor was I looking for an East End gangster. I was after that least loveable of all crooks – the middle-class criminal. One thing you learn as a criminal barrister is that the middle-class felon is the worst sort of all.

He or she doesn't know the crime game you see – they don't play by the rules. When they're nicked they don't say, 'It's a fair cop'. They say, 'how dare you – this is an outrage!' Indignantly they tell themselves that, after all, they were only doing something any Saab driver cut off at the Worthing turn-off would do.

They think the criminal class has glass ceiling that prohibits people who drive Saabs or Volvos from ever making it. Hell, the opposite's true – crooks run an open door policy. No dress rules, no race, colour or sexual prejudice – break the law and you're in. It's that simple. Give me Keith of Shepherds Bush any day.

All the usual crown suspects were gathering around waiting for their slot: petty larcenists, joy riders, vandals and thugs talking to friends and family. The entrance was thick with smoke and the seedy smells of provincial crime, but as Mr Roberts waved to me in the crowd he looked like he'd just jumped off the set of a commercial for Imperial Leather. I could smell the smoke of his Aga on him. In his cable-knit sweater, with a smile that made me feel I'd never cleaned my teeth properly, he reminded me of Richard Branson.

'This is all very embarrassing,' he said as we shook hands. I couldn't imagine Keith of Shepherds Bush ever saying that.

'It's OK, Mr Roberts, we've all done it,' I soothed, trying out my lines. He looked kind of horrified. I guess you don't want to hear that your counsel is a road-raging maniac just like you. 'Well, no, I don't mean that actually. I've never actually been arrested for anything. But I want you to know that I've been pretty damn cross in cabs coming through Knightsbridge on a Friday night on antihistamines. And well, er . . .'

Lines from Sylvia Plath's poem Ariel ran through my head. I wanted to tell this man that I found him oppressive. That I wanted to free myself from both this case and him. I suggested to him that he should think about pleading guilty. That way, I reasoned, Candida couldn't blame me. But the way he looked at me I could tell my exoneration wasn't going to come that easily.

'So you honestly think I'm better off pleading guilty?' he puffed. Then he looked at me the way that American bloke had in the sixties when he'd vowed to bomb Indochina back to the stone age. 'Well that, my dear, is laughable,' he shouted mirthlessly. A few vandals closed in around us hoping for action.

What's with the 'my dear'? I thought, as in – if I wasn't acting in my professional capacity as a barrister, you'd be picking my stiletto out of your nostrils, shit-face. 'On a guilty plea you would be entitled to a lighter sentence,' I explained hopelessly.

'My dear, may I remind you that my record is spotless. I haven't hired you to lecture me on credit reduction. I'm paying you to get me off! Now, when Miss Raphael told me she was sending a junior, I didn't make a fuss. But that doesn't mean I'll put up with some law school flunky still wet behind the ears telling me to plead guilty because it makes her job easier.' He said this last bit through clenched teeth like gangsters do when they talk about hiding bodies. I felt sick.

To make me feel just that bit more like I was being inhabited by Sylvia Plath's spirit, his solicitor, Barbara Hocks, a flustered woman in a dark Laura Ashley print and sensible shoes butted in and demanded I call her Babs.

'Babs?'

'Yes, we like to do things the informal way down here. After all we're not criminals here.' She gave my shoulder a little pat and laughed lightly.

'Babs?' I repeated. 'As in Barbara?' I enquired, looking down on her. She was a good foot shorter than me, but not quite short enough to step on.

'Yes, as I said we're an informal bunch down here.' (Bunch of what? I hesitated to ask. Moonies?)

But she had already gone on to describe a scene from a surreal suburban nightmare. 'Edward is as law-abiding a man as you'll meet. A neighbour of mine. A Rotarian. He's not a common crook with his hand out for legal aid. He doesn't want a lot of technical talk about sentences and pleas. He wants our support.' Edward nodded earnestly at all this. Well at least he wasn't asking for a light yet, I comforted myself.

I looked from one to the other and gauged my chances of making a run for it. Maybe I could tell Candida that I couldn't find them – that I lost them. Maybe they'd forget that they'd ever met me. Like ships that passed in the night. Babs was still babbling.

'So call me Babs and Mr Roberts, Edward and we'll have a nice cup of coffee from the machine and discuss tactics informally.'

'Oh I get it,' I said, looking madly from one to the other like a crazed prisoner trying to work out which of her captors has the gun. 'I took a wrong turn and ended up in the Scientology tutorial?'

Babs and Eddie laughed heartily.

'I like that. A sense of humour,' Edward cheered.

'That's better,' said Babs. 'Much better than talk of sentences,' she oozed.

'Much,' Edward echoed.

It was the word *informal* that set the alarm bells ringing. Informal is when the formal social barriers that divide and rule us as individuals are relaxed. I like to think I'm as capable of informality as the next girl. Hell I'm Australian – we invented the concept. But informality's the last thing a girl wants when she's surrounded by hordes of violent, deranged criminals and a couple of members from a weird Scientology sect. I wanted barriers – barb wire, sniffer dogs and tear gas if necessary.

Our slot came up at eleven o'clock. By then Mr Roberts – sorry Edward – sounded reasonably clear about what had happened the day he saw fit to burn a complete stranger's fifty thousand pound phallic investment. It seemed to him a perfectly rational thing to do – given the way the Jaguar driver had inconsiderately cut him off at the turn-off.

If I had my doubts when I read the brief, my vocation for this case was on the rocks now I'd actually met my client – and Babs, who stroked the arm of his cable-knit reassuringly throughout the morning. But these doubts were not shared by Mr Roberts. His vocation as a man in a cable-knit who could do no wrong was unquestioned.

As I left to go to the robing room, he gave me a look that Richard Branson might give before opening a new airline. He even raised his arm in a kind of salute. Who was I kidding? This case was like my hair. A setup. Candida had landed me with a case that was clearly unwinnable then told me that if I didn't win it, she might be forced to ruin my career. This was what a bantamweight boxer calls a fight with a heavyweight – a no-win/no-win situation. I was out of my depth. Playing above my weight.

Offer it up to the martyrs, Gran would say. But I *was* the martyr here. Between Richard Branson, Babs and Candida, my future was about as certain as the pandas.

I started to feel sorry for myself. Can you blame me? Last night my best friends hadn't even bothered to pretend to take my predicament with Candida seriously. They'd treated the whole thing as a whopping great joke. I was tempted to write to *Tatler*.

That magazine needed to get a grip on reality before some neglected girlfriend took it into her head to Semtex it. I was being persecuted by a woman with the hair of Margaret Thatcher and they treated it like a jolly jape. But I knew I was in serious danger. Speaking from experience, when a woman in a bouffant gets it into her head to fight she always fights dirty. Babs and Edward proved that.

Amanda Maddocks had fought dirty in the first grade. She was possessed of the longest plaits in St John's Infant School history – until I came onto the scene with plaits that made hers look like pigtails. The thing was, Mandy wasn't a girl to say *die* to popularity that easily.

She told the nuns that I had tried to talk her into an abortion. Get a life! I should have said. I'm five years old. Where would I get the money for an abortion? She'd read the word in one of our Preparation For Confession Handbooks – *A Hundred And One Sins You May Have Committed In The Past Week*. It was on the number one reader list in the St Johns first grade.

Mandy had no more idea what it meant than I did, but that

didn't stop Sister Claire amplifying my crime at the parent-teacher meeting. 'There has been a worrying trend of abortions in the first-year infants' school,' she had announced to a sea of troubled parents who probably had no more understanding of abortions than we did. Our parents' sin-league was in the range of lewd thoughts and pride with a bit of light blasphemy on a Saturday night. People weren't exactly tripping over one another to get abortions in Kirribilli in the early seventies.

But by the end of that year I'd been accused of masturbation and sodomy as well – and I think by then everyone had done their sin research. Tongues wagged. When I finally made my first confession and rattled off my misdemeanours – selfishness, disobedience etc. – the priest said, 'Go on.'

Eventually I was hauled before the school governors. But not because of her defamation. By then I had decided to play dirty too.

Chapter 28

Various parts of my anatomy were already saying their goodbyes

The barrister on the train was counsel for the prosecution. His name was Mr Worston and he had tufts of grey hair wandering out of his ears, but despite this I liked him from the start. In the bonhomie of the robing room he tried to entice me to talk my client into a guilty plea to a lesser charge of criminal damage. I explained that nothing would give me keener pleasure, but that, regretful as it was, my client trusted in a middle-class jury to find him not guilty. It was all very polite – like sticking pins into an effigy.

'So you didn't have the heart to tell him that the average jury is just as likely to have come from the local branch of the Social Security queue as the ranks of the middle classes?' Mr Worston enquired.

'No, I told him that. He thinks they're likely to understand better than anyone why he was forced to torch a Jaguar. Not that he did torch it of course.'

'No?'

'No!' I responded firmly with a confidence I didn't feel.

We were up before Judge Neals QC, a middle-aged man of no outstanding feature apart from funky glasses with blue lenses and his controversial stance on Judges on Internet. He was known around the circuit as Judge Net. He got his kicks slapping barristers about the ego with his up-to-the-minute on-line legal reports.

After listening to a counsel's brilliantly argued point, Judge Neals would lift his head from his computer screen and declare that the same point had been overturned by the House of Lords just two minutes ago. (Na-na-na-na-na!)

I was slightly encouraged by the frog-green silk shirt the Jag driver was wearing which clashed gratifyingly with Judge Neals' blue lenses. But my confidence was not to last. When Judge Neals entered in his purple robes and grey wig, I felt a ladder of fear run up my body. Something told me he took a harsh view of Saab drivers who couldn't keep their petrol cans to themselves – even where the wearer of a frog-green silk shirt was concerned.

Mr Worston opened the case for the prosecution with the same old-world charm he'd shown on the train. The story, as told by the prosecution, veered from my client's version of events around the time that he was alleged to have set fire to the car. Which is a pretty major deviation I grant you.

My client claimed there was an altercation between the Jag driver and himself. The prosecution denied that any words were exchanged. According to Mr Eric-*check out my gold chain bracelet*-Tarr, the first thing he knew of the Saab driver's existence was when he heard his car go up in flames while he was watching *Home and Away*. Looking out the window, Mr Tarr claimed to have seen my client drive off.

The learned counsel for the prosecution was diplomatic throughout. He didn't lead his witnesses – the policeman and the one-time Jaguar owner. He didn't mount any objections of his own when I did. He didn't have to. Judge Neals did it for him. He had two objectives for this case: one – that it should be brought to a swift conclusion today and two – that it should be done with maximum damage to my ego.

Mostly he didn't even bother to raise his blue lenses from the screen. He just launched his rockets into my defence as if he were spitting grape pips. By the time it came to my summing up I was about as confident as Hitler was in his bunker in 1945.

'We've all done it,' I said, looking earnestly at my jurors. 'What one of us hasn't felt angered at someone cutting across us in a queue? After all, the defendant's life *had* been put at risk by this Jaguar's intolerance.' I pronounced the word Jag-uar like Hooray-Henry. I knew this went down well with the jury by the number of nodding heads I counted: one, two, three, four, five, six, seven.

My confidence was just about to rear its nervous head again when the judge moaned languidly, 'What a load of claptrap!'

The Jag driver, sitting morosely in his green silk shirt, lifted his big red solemn face spasming with the scarcely suppressed despair of a man who's just seen his Jag torched. He looked like a frog, I thought as I pulled my robe around me and waited for a wave of nausea to subside.

'My client admits to dousing the Jaguar in petrol,' I continued. 'He was angry. He admits that too. But what he doesn't admit to, men and women of the jury, is throwing a match knowingly onto the vehicle. And here is where you come in. I ask you to use your judgement.'

The jury looked gravely at me. I looked gravely back at them. The judge looked down on me over his blue-tinted glasses and clicked his tongue. 'Move along please, Miss Hornton, the jury know what they're here for!' I was momentarily thrown.

'Was there an altercation?' I continued, only for the judge to clear his throat and interject.

'Well, we've been told by the victim that there wasn't, Miss Hornton. Mmm?' He looked at me through those sky-blue lenses and gave me a look that might have withered even Candida.

'Yes, your honour, but with all respect you have heard the defendant's case and he insists that there was an altercation. And after all the Crown's case relies entirely on the evidence of Mr Tarr – given that there is no supporting eyewitness evidence to say the altercation did not take place. And if that argument *did* take place' – I spoke quickly to avoid more interruptions – 'is it not conceivable that the defendant, upset by the altercation, leaned on his car and lit a cigarette to relax himself?'

The judge cleared his throat again. 'This is supposition, Miss Hornton – claptrap and supposition. I am not going to allow you to waste taxpayers' money and court time on airy fairy supposition.' He stared at his computer screen as if hoping for pointers on how to further undermine me.

'Arson is a crime, members of the jury,' I continued bravely.

'Well of course it's a crime. We haven't brought them down to court for a tea party! Mmm?' He looked pointedly at his watch.

I smiled. 'Yes, your honour, a very serious crime.'

The judge growled and muttered something like, 'Well I'm glad we all agree on that.'

'My client admits to dousing the car in petrol. But petrol can be hosed off. Throwing petrol is not arson,' I explained.

'It's damn well not a handshake either,' the judge sneered.

'Yes, your honour. He was angry. But we all get angry, men and women of the jury!'

The judge looked angry now. He glared at me over his trippy glasses as if I were a hallucination he wanted to go away.

I soldiered on. 'After the argument, when Mr Tarr went inside, Mr Roberts has explained that he decided to have a cigarette. It had been a trying series of events. He'd forgotten about the petrol by the time he tossed the match carelessly away. I'm sure we've all been forgetful, members of the jury!'

'I hope I don't have to remind you what we're here for, Miss Hornton! This is a trial by jury not sixth class existentialism,' Judge Neals reminded us.

I ignored him. 'Think about it – it could have endangered his own life,' I insisted. 'It could have happened to anyone.'

'There must be a better way to earn my mascara money,' I sighed under my breath as I watched the jury walking out with my career sticking to their shoes like chewing gum. My mind flashed back to a conversation I'd overheard at the local video shop while I was hiring *Trainspotting* for the third time.

There was this private detective bloke over behind the horror section who was advising another bloke that he'd been hired to take *direct action* on him over an unpaid bill. By the tone of the conversation and the smell of nervous sweat in the air, I gathered that bloke number two was pretty scared of this direct action stuff.

Maybe Candida would pay someone to inflict a bit of direct action on me? Watching Mr Roberts smiling menacingly at the jury as they filed out, I wagered that he'd probably chip in. Turning to Babs who was fluttering about with some papers totally unrelated to the case, I decided I couldn't discount her fiscal support either.

Hell, maybe the whole Hove contingent of Scientology would chip in to have *direct action* taken on me. Various parts of my anatomy were already saying their goodbyes. Why had I ever agreed to come to Hove? What kind of a fool was I to defend a man who didn't even require legal aid? The whole thing was sinister from start to finish – everyone gets legal aid. From petty crimes to corporate giants. Why hadn't I hidden over by the coffee machine and refused to come out? Before I started crying out loud the jury decided that they were ready to deliver their verdict.

Chapter 29

My vital organs were beginning to feel nervous

Surprise, surprise, the verdict went against me.

My client looked as if he'd just been found guilty of supplying heroin to infants. He had the words 'direct action' written all over his face.

'This is an outrage!' he cried. OK, so he was angry. I understood that, but let's keep this in perspective Ed my good man. *You* aren't the one who has to face Candida. This verdict was a bad one for both of us. Only something told me he was going to get off with a lighter sentence. I had lost her case! And my vital organs were right to feel nervous.

Judge Neals looked at him sternly through those blue-tinted glasses with a gaze that would turn a Medusa to stone. He complimented my defence – pronouncing it admirable. When I bowed my head respectfully, Mr Roberts had to be restrained.

'Traitor, traitor,' he yelled. 'You won't get a penny from me . . . You set me up!' he continued foaming at the mouth. He didn't actually utter the words direct action, but the innuendo was there.

After Judge Neals threatened him with contempt his mouth lolled open like a cow with BSE and something told me I wasn't the first woman who'd wanted to shove his balls down it.

'Mr Roberts,' the judge explained, 'as admirable a defence as Miss Hornton conducted on your behalf, the jury was not taken in by it. They have reached a verdict and, I might add, it is a verdict with which I agree. You have wandered far and wide outside the parameters of the law in your quest for revenge against a fellow driver. You are a criminal, Mr Roberts. A hoodlum of suburbia and let all who follow your example be warned! I'm going to adjourn the case till the fourteenth of August for a pre-sentence report to be prepared by the probation service.'

Was this what's known as a black letter day or what? I felt like asking the judge to punch the dimensions of my coffin size into the Internet while he was at it!

In the robing room, Mr Worston was philosophical. 'Well you can't please all the criminals all the time,' he reasoned.

But what about Candida? I wanted to scream. I wondered if he'd be able to come up with such a pithy aphorism for her? There was something about his demeanour that made me want to confide in him.

We lunched together in the salubrious surroundings of the Grand in Brighton. While the string quartet tinkled lightly in the background and the succulent aroma of organic roast beef wafted seductively through the restaurant, I kept expecting a tory M.P. to come crashing through the ceiling.

Mr Worston was amusing in a dry way – at least he had the good grace to keep his dyke-after-a-fight comments to himself. I made a few incomprehensible remarks about Stefan and *très* grungy, but he pushed them aside as of no consequence.

'It'll grow out eventually I don't wonder,' he soothed.

Then we skirted around the gossip doing the rounds of the Temple at the moment and I realised I hadn't talked to a man like this since I'd sworn off them. Simon, as Mr Worston insisted I call him, had pale blue eyes which twinkled kindly when he was amused. He reminded me a lot of my father, which kind of made me nervous after a while.

My father's got this obsession with the way people hold their cutlery you see and he doesn't care where he is or who he's with when he feels the need to correct a wrong. He's what's known around the restaurants of Sydney as a *righteous diner*.

Gran used to warn us never to invite him to dinner at St Pete's – as she affectionately referred to the Papal Palace – if we had the good fortune to marry any of the Pope's illegitimate offspring.

It was pretty much taken for granted in our family that all Popes had illegitimate children and, furthermore, Gran had her heart set on one of us marrying one of them. Who knows, maybe one of them might even be a barrister? I guess it was like the Catholic equivalent of marrying royalty. My mother took up this baton when Gran died.

When I first moved to London she was on the phone constantly enquiring vaguely if I'd met any nice Italian men – now that I was so close to Pete's Palace and the like. But that's another story. The point was that if my father saw a fork being mishandled it didn't matter who was holding it – nuns, priests, judges – he'd just stride on in and correct the perpetrator loudly and forcefully. 'A stiff fork means a stiff stomach and the only winner will be your indigestion!' he'd boom.

But thankfully Simon made no such observations over lunch at the Grand that day. Just to be on the safe side though I ordered the sushi and struggled away with the chopsticks.

The wines were exemplary. My discretion, such as it is, was not fortified by two bottles of Hermitage La Chappelle. Like my father, Si knew how to order his wines. In bulk.

By the time the port came round I was unbuttoning myself like a drunken sailor. One minute Si was extolling the virtues of the surrealists and the next minute I was ranting on about my demented bouffanted colleague and her plans to take direct action.

Si took it in his stride. 'Bit of a Portia is she then?'

I waited for my eyesight to converge on him. Was he talking to me? 'Well she's got this weird sort of puffed-out hairdo,' I conceded, waving my hands wildly about my head as if warding off berserk pigeons.

'As in *The Merchant of Venice*,' he explained to me as if speaking to a foreign student trying to learn English on a day break. 'It sounds to me like you've got a Portia on your hands,' he announced.

'Oh. As in Shakespeare?'

'That's right,' he laughed. 'As in William.'

'Well she's certainly that,' I agreed. 'But she's more of a Lucrezia Borgia actually if we're being spesss – spess – whoops, accurate,' I slurred.

He put back his head and laughed.

179

Tiddle-de-pom, I thought to myself. So far so good. 'So what's your angle, Si?' I demanded loudly, now striding with assurance into my place at the helm of the old-boy network.

'Well, not being able to speak from experience you understand – the Borgias haven't broken into my chambers just yet,' he chuckled. 'In fact we've only just started taking women on in the last five years. But we already have four. No Borgias amongst them as far as I can tell.' He chuckled some more.

A little less of the chuckling, Si, I wanted to say. Somehow I didn't seem to be getting the seriousness of my problem across to people. But I could tell Si was on a roll so I held my counsel.

'Yes sometimes we chaps feel a bit outnumbered in fact. We accuse the women of closing ranks against us . . .'

'Closing ranks?' I bellowed, now desperately fighting my way out of the maze of the old-boy network. Men! You can't fault them for predictability can you? Just when you're about to pronounce one of them a human being they go all wobbly. You can set your watch by them, as Gran used to say.

I mean we had to throw ourselves under horses' hooves at the Derby and go bra-less and carry placards to get into the workplace and now that a few of us were winning the fight, men start moaning about positive discrimination. Closing ranks indeed!

'Poor lamb,' I scoffed in what I hoped was a very meaningfully and not too slurred a manner. 'All those nasty women trying to play with the boys and spoiling all their nice boysie games. Poor little boys . . .' I'm really quite good at sarcasm when I get going you see.

'I can see you're peeved, Evelyn, but if you'll just give me a chance here. What I was going to say was—'

'No, Si, let me help you. You were going to say that it would be all so much more civilised if we girls would just keep things in perspective. I mean the odd token woman in chambers is fine, but two's a crowd and three or more's a veritable riot . . .' I finished the last of my port and then realised I had nothing to throw in his face. So I called out imperiously to the waiter for some brandy.

Some of our fellow diners probably thought I was seriously pissed, but the truth was I hadn't even started. I mean, get real, what did I have to be sober about?

'Evelyn, I really think you've got hold of the wrong end of the stick. What I was about to say was that maybe that's what you should do. Next time your chamber takes on a new tenant. Push for a woman and close ranks against the Portias – or the Borgias for that matter.'

'Oh!'

'I'm sorry if I gave you the impression I'm sour about the number of women in my chambers. That couldn't be further from the truth. Truth is they're a damn diligent lot and as far as I'm concerned the Bar has been a ridiculous bastion of old boys for far too long.'

The wrong end of the stick? We were talking another stick altogether actually. A whopping great branch and it felt like it had just landed on my head. 'Ouch!'

'Sorry what was that?'

'Oh I just said, ouch. It's nothing really, just a bit of make-up falling off. I'll be back in a jiffy. And maybe we might shelve the brandy for another time, eh?'

On my way to the Grand's loos I overheard a couple of lasses from Liverpool talking. 'I'll tell yar wot – let's check out the bogs first!'

Sound advice, I thought. But it had come too late for me. Why hadn't I decided to check out the bogs before careering off like Naomi Wolfe with rabies? What a complete and utter cervix I had made of myself.

In the toilet, I wondered how I could ever make it up to poor old Si. He really was from another world – a world where men lift down heavy bags from luggage racks for women. Blissfully ignorant of Candida and her black arts. He probably thought direct action was a new Green lobby campaigning to ban French products!

How could I have been so senselessly aggressive? 'You're losing your grip, girl,' I said to my reflection. One of the Scousers now drying her armpits under the dryer looked at me and nodded.

OK, so it was one thing for me to wallow in self-pity, but the reality was if I didn't grab onto my destiny pretty damn smartly, I may as well flush myself down the bog here and now.

I knew what it was I had to do – just as I had known what had to be done with Mandy Maddocks. If anyone was going to take direct action it was me!

★ ★ ★

In the hot afternoons the nuns used to allow us a fifteen-minute reprieve from the Three R's in which to enjoy the gentle discipline of craft work. Scissor-craft as it was known.

It came back to me now as I rubbed a hand over my concentration camp cut *à la* Stefan. Mandy used to sit in the seat in front of me. I finished early one day and brooded on Mandy's latest accusation of bestiality. There was a fly buzzing lazily around my nose.

'Idle hands do the devil's work,' Sister Claire reminded me as Mandy flicked a plait tantalisingly over one shoulder. The red bow at the end of her braid flicked beguilingly onto the edge of my desk. It was as if the scissors acted independently. After the plait plopped sadly to the floor, I admitted to succumbing to the devil. But the damage was already done.

My direct action was evil and efficient. That was the last sin Mandy ever chalked up to my soul.

I rubbed a hand over my scalp and plotted.

Chapter 30

My Versace hung as forlorn as
a wallflower in my wardrobe

It was four-thirty when we left for the station. Mr Worston urged me to travel first class with him – not that I needed my arm twisted. I was well and truly over second class. I was shifting my focus on a lot of things – largely to do with the amount of booze I'd consumed at lunch.

Sadly though, British Rail wasn't over delays. Twenty minutes into our journey and our second whisky and soda, we came to a standstill.

'We apologise,' they told us through the crackling intercom. Hell! You're English, you'll put up with it! the tone seemed to imply.

They thought we'd all just take it on the stiff upper lip. Judging by the collective groan that went up in first class and the collective curse from the rest of the train, it sounded like BR had misjudged its audience. The EC was giving us ideas. These commuters had Inter-railed. There were sinister whisperings around our carriage that the sooner privatisation came the better. I could smell a new crime in the wind. It was called rail rage.

Si was philosophical about the delay – but then he didn't have a set of eyelashes that curled like Siamese fingernails waiting for him at home, I told myself. As minutes collapsed into hours, we lapsed into a humid silence. We shuffled about in our wigs and robes and pink ribbons for distractions. And that's when I came across Giles' letter which had laid dormant and cursed for twenty-four hours. I finally succumbed to the temptation and opened it.

Inside was a bundle of snaps and a note written on chambers' paper. The St George Chambers logo embossed on the corner must have caught Simon's eye because he leaned over.

'I say, who do you know there? That's my chambers,' he explained. I felt a sick knot coil around my lungs. God how had I been so stupid. Of course – he must know Giles!

'Giles Billington-Frith. He's um an old . . . sort of . . .' I only narrowly stopped the words, utter testicle, from slipping out.

'You know Giles?' he exclaimed as if I'd admitted to having met the children of Fatima. 'Sound fellow Giles. There are no angles to that lad, that's what I like.'

The man was clearly deranged. My affection and trust for Mr Worston was draining away as quickly as my enthusiasm for Network Southeast. I turned my attention to the drought-stricken fields simmering in the evening heat like some kind of metaphor for my love life.

Giles, no angles? I mused. God, we're talking five degrees here – the man was a knife plunging into the spine of humanity! He was an isosceles set square, slicing into the soft flesh of my love for him. The man was a viper, with teeth as sharp as any of Satan's equerries.

'Oh really?' I smiled sweetly. 'I'm afraid I don't know him well enough to recommend him quite so heartily.'

'No? Well take it from me. I usually like to keep a distance in my own set. It doesn't always follow that one wants to seek friendships with one's colleagues.'

Well at least we were as one on that point. This *one* had no intention of seeking any friendships at 17 Pump Court. Between Alistair and his photocopied hands, Duncan and his pugilistic tendencies towards judges, and Candida and her plan to destroy my career, I was better off chumming around with Jock the *Big Issue* salesman.

'But Giles is an absolute gentleman,' Mr Naive went on like a stuck platform announcement. 'Not that we see a lot of one another, mind you. But I have a lot of respect for Giles and his family. I knew his father up at Oxford – we were in the same college. No, they are a charming family. Oh they've had their problems like any family. Goodness, so have I. And girls can be the worst, mark my words.'

What was he boring on about? I wondered briefly. But I didn't ask, deciding silence was the best way to end the eulogy. Mr Worston could write Giles' obituary when I killed him.

I read the letter. It was just a note to say that he'd come across some photographs that we'd taken together. For some insane reason he thought I might like to have a copy? *Not as much as I'd like a phial of arsenic*, I thought darkly. I shuffled through the images disinterestedly. Snaps of days I'd burned from my mind. Days when we had thought one another's funny poses were funny.

There was one of Giles standing naked except for his bands. I had taken it in his Islington bedroom. I felt like sticking pins into his testicles. I looked around in my bag briefly for something suitably sharp. As I used a safety pin from my gown to lance his manhood, my face began to burn and that old feeling came back – like one of those faith healers had stuck his hand through my chest and was squeezing my heart. I shoved the photographs back in my case and went off in search of more whisky.

After three hours another message crackled with excuses about the heat melting the tracks. The whole carriage reverberated with fury. The sun was beginning to sink into the horizon. Casting long romantic shadows over the South Downs where I had gone walking with Giles three years ago.

We had set forth on an autumn day. Giles had borrowed a friend's orange Citroën to match the leaves of the chilly autumn morning. It was too cold to get out of the car when we arrived so Giles had made love to me, practically impaling himself on the gearstick during orgasm.

As we climbed out of the vehicle – stiff with the cramps of our carnal antics – we were approached by a group of children who'd found an arrowhead. They'd asked Giles in the earnest tones of twelve year olds what he thought it might be. He had given them a long-winded and wholly implausible story about a war between the Picts and the Britons.

I'd practically suffocated on my giggles. Watching the muddy-faced boys – their wide eyes dilating with wonder – I

185

had loved him as never before. Now I regretted not grabbing that arrowhead and stabbing him to death with it.

By the time the train finally clattered off into the darkness, I had despaired of racing Julian off. He would be there by now, I told myself miserably. In my flat, in all his Armani magnificence while my red Versace hung as forlorn as a wallflower in my cupboard.

It was ten o'clock before we arrived back at Victoria – no one but the sweepers and sleeping derelicts to welcome us back to civilisation. The dark threats muttered by my fellow commuters about how they were going to sue British Rail and vote the The Anti-Rail League at the next election had been deflated. Network Southeast had done their research after all. They knew the fight would be squeezed out of us by hours of tedium and vast quantities of free whisky. Our revolution had been squashed by boredom. Our dreams for commuter revenge were as lifeless as the last few sandwiches left on the food trolley – and so were my hopes for a union between Julian and me. *Get real, girl, he's probably found some other red dress to inseminate by now*, I told myself.

Chapter 31

I was the proverbial worm turning

Every step I took plunged me deeper into the realisation that I wasn't in the mood for a party. I didn't look remotely like the sexual predator Charles and Sam had cast me as. My suit was crushed, my stockings were laddered and my make-up was circumnavigating my face.

The square was reverberating with the competing sounds of our music, vying with the car alarms for airplay. Set off by the bass thump of the music, it was as if every car in the street was screaming for help.

As if in languid juxtaposition there was a poker game going on in the basement flat of our building. Fat men in vests and boxers looked up darkly from their game as I fumbled for keys on the steps. Two laughing girls, naked but for a few sequins and their tennis racquets, lunged through the door while I was crouching on the ground searching the tabernacle of my bag. The sight of my prostrate confusion delighted them – they shrieked with laughter all the way to the garden gate.

This was not the impact I'd planned to make tonight.

I climbed the stairs with a sense of dread, regretting that I hadn't touched up my lipstick in the toilet of the station. My Jil Sander, so highly commended by Si, now made me feel like a bag lady compared to the trendy scantiness of my guests' attire (mostly female it has to be said) as they spilled like sick from our landing.

Dressed in nothing much but the latest perfumes, a discreetly arranged sequin here or a leather thong there – and the ubiquitous Doc Martens, they were leaning over banisters and lounging on stairs, smoking cigarettes and joints, knocking back drinks, toying with nipples and kissing. A sort of hip, hedonistic parody of the men playing poker downstairs actually. I could already visualise complaints from the residents' committee coming in – under the resident rules we weren't allowed to have more than twenty guests at a time. Oops!

As I negotiated my way through the outstretched limbs and cigarettes, it was clear this line-up of extras from a Fellini film found me the height of nineties' entertainment. Clowns, put away those red noses.

'E-v-e-l-y-n!' Charles sang out to the tune of the latest pop anthem blaring from the quadraphonic acoustics of our flat. 'Sammy, it's Evvy!' she yelled through the multitudes.

The flat was thick with every half-dressed lipstick-lesbo this side of the Thames. As for men, well yes there were a few of those too – mostly cowering in small groups. In corners among their own kind – in suits not unlike my own.

Charles was dressed from head to foot in gold paint.

'Evvy, where have you been?' she pleaded, as if I'd been on the Missing Files for years.

I smiled weakly as if to say – yes, the beleaguered friend has returned.

She was smoking a cigarette, which, considering Sam's recent expostulations about purifying the world to prepare for the baby, was surprising – party or no party. She was drunk. I looked around for Sam, expecting her to swoop down on this nicotine wand like an avenging angel, but both Sam and her Mothercare accessories were significantly absent.

'So what happened, darling?' she continued. 'What can I say? You look like shit! Here give me that case. We almost called the police. Sam kept hassling me to, you know *ring them, ring them*! – but that's just because she thought they might . . . you know . . . come up with a bit of insemination material. She's not had much luck you see. Party's not been a huge success in the sperm department anyway. Seems like everyone's after the stuff these days – it's like *the* commodity of the decade. Last year ecstasy, this year sperm! Sam is irascible. So looks like it's down to you, big girl! Drink?'

And that was when I saw her.

Not Sam – although I spotted her too, also covered in gold paint, over on the balcony talking to Julian. They looked like they were really hitting it off. Bitch! No, on the other side, cackling with some half-dressed dyke-clones. Goldilocks – she of the A-cups. She who had turned the man of my dreams into a super-bastard.

A wave of nostalgic nausea crashed over me as I was transported to another time and place. Back to two years ago to that house in Islington.

When I'd first seen those features asleep in Giles' bed, I had turned and run. When I had first seen her hair, spraying out across the pillow like the snakes of Medusa, I was afraid I would never get my heart back into my chest. I was afraid I'd never cope with the pain.

But that was all ancient history now, I told myself as I grabbed Charles' drink from her hand and crossed the party floor, stepping over the odd sequinned leg, knocking the odd glass.

After I'd found her in Giles' bed – under my duvet – I'd gone to Australia to lick my wounds and had comforted myself with black female artists singing sock-it-to-'em lyrics. Seriously, I was in a bad way. There I was living in the western world, living the life people forged passports and took perilous journeys to live, yet I would gladly have swapped places with someone on Gaddafi's death list.

I'd just spent two years licking my wounds – getting over that bastard. Now after this shit of a day, after Candida and her fucking middle-class cable-knit clients and four hours waiting for Network Southeast to get their act together, I realised in a flash my time for direct action had finally come.

Crossing the room towards her I was the proverbial worm turning. In psycho-babble I was tapping into my anger – my bloody vengefulness actually. I was fucked off with being the victim. But, more to the point, I was fucking furious that she was standing in my party, drinking my champagne, looking gorgeous while I looked and felt like something out of *Les Miserables*.

A lot of things happened at once. After I'd done my Moses thing with the parting of the crowd, Charles shouted something at me. Sam became aware of my presence and Julian became aware of my existence. I was vaguely aware of someone moving aside to let me past, and of someone else knocking over the CD player as they ran from my approach. The music stopped.

My glass of Pimms and lemonade and floating bits of ice and cucumber made contact with Goldilock's face and almost simultaneously her fist made contact with my right eye. The gloves were off.

Goldilocks' friends, who only minutes before had laughed at her every joke, lost total interest in her. 'Fucking hell! Let's leave,' one yelled as Goldilocks and I fell into a torrid heap of fists, tits, teeth and legs on the floor.

At the time, rolling around, pulling out tufts of Goldilocks' hair by the roots while she sunk her teeth into my shoulder and bruised my left tit with the heel of her foot, I told myself I had the advantage. But I was wrong. Kick-boxing is a sport for the upright. Goldilocks had used her time wisely, learning the sport of scrag fighting on the playground. Whereas I had squandered mine, walking up and down stairs with books on my head under the watchful eye of Sister Conchilio.

The fact was feminism had failed us both. Here we were, sisters in genitalia – warriors of the same cause – tearing one another apart. Betty Friedan and Emmeline Pankhurst would weep in their graves if they could see us now. Think about it! The irony of it all was mega! That decades of fighting for breast scans should end in me getting a mastectomy at the teeth of a fellow bitch!

Charles and Sam dragged Goldilocks off me and Julian prised what was left of me off the floor. Once Goldilocks had spat out the remains of my breast reduction, she started screaming indiscriminate abuse at me.

You've got to comprehend how totally unexpected all this was from my point of view. Hitherto, Goldilocks had been something passive to me – a sleeper. This rampantly active side of her character kind of took me by surprise. But I caught my breath and started screaming obscenities in tongues any born again Christian would be proud of, getting that last bit of epiphanous catharsis in while I could.

I mean, let's get a few things clear – I was the victim right. She was the accused. In my decision to throw drink in her face, I'd kind of envisaged a scenario whereby she'd go red and run from the party like a moneylender driven from the temple by Christ.

This scenario of her hitting back and, indeed, getting on top of me and performing the breast reduction surgery I'd pencilled in for a qualified Californian surgeon once I'd taken silk, took me by surprise.

We were both being restrained from behind while our legs kicked and thrashed about furiously.

'You don't understand,' I babbled incoherently. 'She's the fucking bitch that I found in my boyfriend's bed. You bitch. You fucking bitch. You don't understand she was under my duvet!'

I knew I sounded like Mr Roberts outside Hove Crown Court. While Goldilocks on the other hand was limiting herself to straight expletives that, while basic and lacking in detail, hit the required note of outrage. Everyone knew what she meant – she'd been set upon by me . . . by a dyke with an Elastoplast still on her ear from her last fight. Everyone knew how she felt.

I had to face it, I had lost the sympathy of the crowd.

'I can't believe you've done this!' Sam was screaming, and all her despair was directed at me.

Looking at it in hindsight, I have to admit, there was no way that the party was going to be able to go back to the frivolous mood of insouciance that was in swing before my outburst. I guess Julian had much the same idea because the next thing I knew he was carrying me over his shoulder towards the exit.

I was finally in the arms of the man I loved, but it was not the way I'd planned – being thrown out of my own party.

Chapter 32

I hadn't been this close to a man in two years and what's more my hormones knew it

Flung over Julian's back with all the dignity of a sack of blighted Irish potatoes, I watched the remnants of the party close the door on me. I knew I was in trouble and I knew Julian didn't have a clue what was going on. What's more, if he had an ounce of grey matter, he wouldn't want to know. And if I had an ounce of shame or pride or whatever it is that stops you making a complete vagina of yourself, I would have shut up and played the meek one. But there we are. Like I always say – I didn't go to the Bar to say *die*.

'You don't understand, Julian – that's her! That was the bitch. Take me back!' I demanded. 'She was under *my* duvet for Christ's sake! Take me back. I want to finish the slut off.'

My little fists rained down impotently on his back. My words reverberated up and down the stairs. Julian struggled on as best a man can with nine stone of dead weight in stilettos over his shoulder. It was another one of those cringe-making memories to chalk up to the analyst's couch – when I can afford one.

Eventually the face of Nurse Cockerel from Flat Five loomed down on us.

'Miss Hornton. Miss Hornton. I want a word with you!' came her voice from above.

Julian didn't falter in his descent. Nurse Cockerel followed us, thumping down in her sensible shoes like a one-woman swat team, calling out in that indefatigable manner I'd become an expert at avoiding.

'Miss Hornton! I want a word!' she yelled out in her 'you're going to have an enema whether you like it or not' tone of voice. She'd been practising that tone for the last forty years on the sick and infirm of Guys Hospital. 'I'll be complaining, Miss Hornton. I warn you, I won't be taking this lying down.'

'Take a suppository, you ranting old bitch!' came the voice of Sam who suddenly appeared in the stairwell, stark-ovary-naked if you discount the gold paint. 'You've never taken anything lying down in your life. You stupid barking cow!'

Doors slammed. It was thought-provoking stuff.

By the time we reached the bottom, Julian was breathing heavily. He put me down and held my face between his hands the way I'd dreamed he would since he first helped me up – down in the cells of the Old Bailey. He was wearing the Armani scent again, but I could smell the machismo of his pheromones underneath. I hadn't been this close to a man for two years and my hormones knew it.

'Now, Miss Hornton,' he drawled in his telephone-sex voice. 'I can do one of two things with you. I can take you back to apologise to that poor girl you attacked—'

'But you don't under—' He put a restraining finger to my lips.

Oh this was too perfect. I swooned, dizzy with the anticipation of his next touch.

'Or,' he continued.

I looked solemnly up at him, like I used to look at my father before he gave me a rise in my pocket money.

'I can take you back to my place and make love to you,' he finished.

My place! I swooned some more, it sounded like the most exotic place I'd ever heard of. He may as well have suggested Pataya or Mustique. But he didn't even give me a chance to say yes please. He could read my mind. He kissed me.

One of those wet, full-lipped kisses that heroines get from Hollywood stars on films. I felt my legs give way, but he held me up.

He smelled the way a saviour should smell on a summer's night after rescuing his woman. This man was sex-on-legs as in S-O-L for all those who read the personal columns. I felt myself collapsing into him as his tongue excavated my throat. *This is incredible*, I was thinking, *I'm actually having one of those out-of-body experience thingammies.* But it was just the door behind me opening to admit another guest.

We did the honourable thing – hell it was about time I turned a new leaf – and we stepped aside. I was still swooning dreamily in Julian's arms like I was in one of those voodoo trances, but he must have opened an eye to check out our interloper because he pulled back from me and smiled at someone as if he recognised them. 'Hi!'

Oh my God! I screamed inside as I turned around. It was Giles. But I gathered myself together pretty damn smartish for some of that off-the-cuff sarcasm only a Loreto girl can truly carry off.

'Giles!' I smarmed. 'So good of you to come!'

Giles looked embarrassed. If my revenge upstairs had been an unmitigated failure, I was determined to get the upper hand here. Giles looked nervous, which was a hopeful start.

'I, well, I . . . was . . . er . . . invited.'

'Were you indeed? How silly of me to forget.' I made a mental note to string up Sam and Charles by their toenails and play Michael Jackson records to them full blast. 'Well I'm glad you came, Giles. In fact you'll find your daily up there.'

'My daily?' He looked lost. He rubbed a hand through his hair the way he did when he was studying.

I spoke through clenched teeth, still clutching Julian.

'Oh she's not your scrubber? Perhaps you call her your live-in? Your bit on the side? Your crumpet? Or maybe something more post-modern-feminist . . . like your *partner*?' My voice was getting increasingly louder. My sardonic tongue was thickening. Giles looked like he was about to cry. 'Oh don't tell me you call her your lover, Giles? Or let me guess – your fiancée? That's a bit sick-making, Giles. I'm disappointed. How seventies.'

Julian had extracted himself from my grasp and was attempting to open the door while simultaneously keeping me restrained. I was pushing him off like a defendant pushing off a Securicor guard. It was me in the dock now and I was bloody well going to say my piece.

'Well whatever you choose to call her,' I ranted, 'she's in there

195

waiting for you. I hope you'll both be very happy together once you get her wig sorted out.'

'Her wig?'

'Giles, you're just not on your toes tonight!' I shouted with more venom than either men had probably witnessed in their young lives.

Julian looked distinctly embarrassed – his head was sort of wobbling about as if he was in need of serious osteopathic surgery. I could see he was wondering if it was too late to say he'd never seen me before in his life.

Giles was red and flustered. 'I don't know what you mean, Evelyn. What wig?'

Julian seemed to gather himself together again and started using some of those biceps to manoeuvre me out the door. I hinged my foot and hand in the doorway.

'Her wig! You see I'm afraid I saw fit to scalp her when I saw her on my territory for the second time in my life. Pity I didn't do it two years ago!'

But Julian triumphed at that point, pulling me out the door like a rag doll.

'You're really in fine fighting form tonight aren't you?' he laughed later on in the car while putting some mileage between us and Notting Hill. 'I gathered back there that you and our learned friend knew each other better than I thought. Or was it just a chemical thing?'

I felt the red blush of shame creep up my neck. Had I really just been involved in a punch up with one of my own guests? Had I really just humiliated a fellow barrister on his way to avail himself of my hospitality? What was coming over me – next thing I know I'll start wearing cable-knit sweaters and burning Jags.

God, imagine if I behaved like that in an Arab country? Shit, I would have been publicly beaten, or had my right arm lopped off, or my ears or . . . but then if I lived in an Arab country they would have probably done it years ago.

I had done much to bring down the family name of the Horntons. The ashes of my grandmother would be blowing about in their pot. And as for Sister Conchilio well, I just dread to think. I had behaved as no Loreto girl should behave. This was not what my parents paid for when they packed me off to the last school in Australia that still had Deportment on the curriculum.

The bloke at British Rail was right, I was a bruiser. But for now I was sitting beside a man I'd dreamed of since I'd met him! What's more, this bloke has just laid bare his plan to unlock my chastity belt. If ever there was a time for letting sleeping dogs lie and leaving the past behind, this was it.

'I guess I really lost it!' I suggested.

Julian smiled. 'I guess you really did. But I'll tell you what, I wouldn't have missed it for the world!' he laughed. 'I guess I had you figured all wrong.'

How embarrassing – as we used to say when we were given the part of the donkey in the Christmas play at school.

'Oh God don't say that, Julian. Look this is very out of character. It's just that, well look . . . believe me there's a story behind all this. A long story and it's never going to make it to the bestseller list.'

'Is it part of your new image?' he asked.

'Excuse me?'

'Your haircut?' he expanded, running one of those long-fingered hands across my scalp like a blessing. 'That's quite a look you've got there.'

'Oh don't talk about it. It's sooo embarrassing. Can you believe it, I had to go to court in Hove like this today?'

He was laughing. 'Calm down. It's fine. I like it. It's kind of quirky . . . kind of boyish!'

'Not *très* grungy?'

'Tray what?'

'Nothing. You sure it's OK?'

'Seriously I love it.'

'Candida arranged it.'

'I bet she did,' he replied. I saw his jaw clench. That was it. I wanted to marry this man. Have his babies and . . . well, maybe no, not quite that, but Sam did! I wanted to collect his sperm in a dozen condoms. Speaking of which I hadn't brought a single condom with me. Thank God this was 1996. If this was sixties London I would have been up whatsit creek. As it was, I was pretty sure Julian was a man who knew his way round the rubber counter of Boots.

Weep all yea hopeful ovums of mine – weep!

★ ★ ★

Pretty soon we were on the Clerkenwell Road near chambers. The streets were utterly deserted. Giles had said it was one of the few places in London he'd feel safe walking down after midnight with a sign reading *free crack* on his back. In the daytime this street surged with the hell of nine-to-fivers, but now it looked like someone had let off one of those neutron bombs that kill the organic and leave the buildings intact.

If I was a director of thrillers I'd set my serious assaults and drive-by killings here – although actually there was no one to drive by and kill, no one to rape and pillage. Bit dead really. What the hell were we doing here?

I looked at Julian but his eyes didn't stray from the road. I could tell he was the strong silent type. If I was asleep now I realised I'd be having a wet dream. My pituitary glands were spitting out that oxytocin stuff that make your nipples erect like nobody's business. My uterus was leaping about like the Virgin Mary's did in the Beatitudes. There was no denying it, lust had me by the carotid artery.

In fact, I could be happy for the rest of my life, studying the way his jaw line flowed down into his neck and thinking about how his Adam's apple gave me an incredible awareness of my G-spot.

Chapter 33

I closed my eyes and inhaled him like a line of coke

When I first broke up with Giles – and isn't that a euphemism *broke up*? It was more like smashed to smithereens, or shattered into tiny fragments from where I was standing. I was still pulling the shards out of my heart two years later. But bit by bit the pieces were pulled out. The real damage was to my self-confidence as a sexual being.

Not that Giles was my first love – God no, that honour went to Joseph Mendez. His father was a surgeon at the Prince of Wales Hospital. Joseph was helping me with anatomy one day and my hymen didn't live to tell the tale.

The thing about sex and Catholicism is the confession afterwards. Not the bless me father for I have sinned part, no that's easy – three Hail Marys and an Our Father and it's over. I'm talking the *post coitus* confession. *Was that as good for you as it was for me? Did you come? Did I take you to heaven?*

The answer on each occasion was a resounding NO!

What did they expect? Writhing around on top of me, grinding themselves into me as if they were drilling for a kidney? I mean, I wasn't adverse to a little promiscuity – come on, I'm a modern girl. I don't believe a one-night stand has to mean for ever. But let's get real here, I was bored with them long before we got to the cigarette bit.

I tried to live up to their expectations – I knew I *should* enjoy having my inner being probed. On the advice of *Cosmopolitan* I

199

tried being inventive. I made love in doorways. I made love in minefields. I did it on satin sheets, waterbeds (yuk), in G-strings and in all the positions of the Karma Sutra. I tried surfers and body builders and professors. And remember – this was the first thing I couldn't pray to the Virgin Mary about. I was desperate.

There was an orgasm club and I wasn't in it. I read books, I asked my girlfriends and I spoke to sympathetic doctors. I even spoke to my mother.

'Mummy, have you ever had one of those orgasm thing-ammies?'

'Oh no. I've always enjoyed rude health. We never had time for yeast infections in my day. Better diets I suppose.'

'No, Mummy, an orgasm isn't an infection, as far as I can tell it's something to do with enjoying sex.'

'Oh sex. Yes, I remember that. Don't you just hate sperm stains on the sheets?'

'Well, Mummy,' I replied, 'actually you're meant to think I'm still a virgin – remember?'

Nothing could be done. The O Club had me blacklisted. What was I doing wrong?

And then along came Giles and opened the floodgates. Now I knew what it was they were writing into the agony columns about. Orgasm. Suddenly everything from clitoris to cellulite made sense.

But no sooner had I worked it out – three years of sexual fulfilment – and then wham-bam the dam went dry. And don't tell me that masturbation's the same! It's not, masturbation and men both start with *M* and I can't do one without thinking about the other. I'd just learnt to live with the drought and now for the first time in two years it looked like rain.

As Julian leant over to undo my seatbelt and kissed me, I was shaking.

'You're cold?' he said, tenderly blowing his warm breath onto my fingers.

'I'm fine.'

'You're sure?' he asked looking into my eyes.

'Do I have to answer that now?' I trembled.

Every word we exchanged was loaded with innuendo. This was heavy shit. Plato could have studied this repartee for years and still only discern a half of it. Then he kissed me again with those full lips and I closed my eyes and inhaled him like a line of coke. He carried me – kissing me – all the way to his door.

Julian lived in one of those loft apartments in Clerkenwell where the ceilings are rafted up to the heavens. It was minimal decoration/maximum alienation.

Standing in the long vast space I felt as small and as incomplete as I felt in church as a child, making my First Holy Communion.

We didn't go far beyond the door. We didn't need to – we didn't have time. He shut the door and undressed us both – while still kissing me. This man was proficiency incarnate. He should give up law and write one of those 'how to undress someone without taking your lips from theirs' blockbusters. I would buy every copy.

He unbuttoned, unzipped and pulled and tore until I stood in nothing but stockings and suspenders and he stood in nothing.

His muscled body was as warm and smooth as the polished floor. This was something I'd dreamed about since I first laid eyes on him. How could I have given up men? That Giles had a lot to answer for.

We looked at one another out of the corners of our eyes appraisingly – but still we didn't stop kissing. We smiled, we murmured and we moaned our way through every sexual cliché. But they were our sexual clichés – we made them worthy. Somehow he'd managed to put on a rubber along the way. I realised that after he held me up and leant me against the wall and I was guiding in his penis. What a boy scout!

I felt like Alice falling down the well, only I was falling into a wonderland of pleasure. My libido was doing nose dives and tail spins and crashing into my G-spot at a hundred miles an hour.

After the first time, we collapsed into one of those writhing heap things on the floor.

'Nice place,' I panted.

'Glad you like it,' he replied.

Were our conversational standards primitive or what? Looking back, our lines sounded like one of those bad commercials for Nescafé where all the communication is done with the eyes and wry smiles.

'Do you have piped water?' I asked with dry lips.

He laughed and stood up, leaving me splayed on the floor-boards in the doorway. Looking up as his buttocks disappeared down the corridor, I had to pinch myself to make sure I hadn't died and gone to heaven. The moments without him felt like an eternity so I struggled up from the floor and went to look for him.

I found him in the kitchen – just where I like my men. It was one of those stainless steel mortuary setups that give you migraines on sunny days. But it was a hot night and the cool surfaces glinted in the soft lighting like jewels. He passed me the water and wiped a recalcitrant hair from my eyes.

'That was pretty intense,' he said hugging me to his hairless chest.

'Mmmm,' I replied. He was rolling my nipples between his fingers – there wasn't a lot I could say. I was linguistically challenged by the ebb and flow of my libido.

Chapter 34

Should a girl put a man before her friendships just because he's found her G-spot?

I was still saying mmmmmmmmmmm ten minutes later on the kitchen bench and again twenty minutes later in the shower and again an hour later in the mezzanine bed that looked out over the city. By then we had the CD playing Marlene Dietrich and Julian was licking Taittinger from my pubic hair.

That night I got to know his loft and all its views biblically. By dawn I felt hungry for something more digestible than Julian and I pushed him from his post-coital meditations into the stainless steel of the kitchen.

It was while wallowing in the cloud of white sheets, satiated and blissful, that I saw the pile of condoms lying at the side of the bed. To think that inside those prophylactics swam more than a thousand potential lives that would never be given a chance.

It was kind of religious thinking about it like that. Maybe even murderous? There was a knot in the condom and it was that knot that gave me the first pang of guilt.

'Just tie a knot in it and run it into me!' Sam was always saying. Her voice echoed in my head. Next thing I knew my bloody Catholic guilt came swooping down on my harmless fun like an avenging angel. Despite our pact, I had no intention of preserving Julian's spunk for her. Or did I?

Sam and Charles had just about saved my life post-Giles. They had given me the space and friendship to go on living.

They'd fed me Panadol when I was sick, stuck pins in voodoo dolls of Giles when I was low – but most of all they made me realise that I was worth more than a cheating man. They made me value myself as only friends can.

I would never have got through Bar school without Charles sitting up into the early hours of the morning helping me study case after case, precedent after precedent. Sam brought us espresso by the bucket. If I was still in one piece with my sexuality functioning, it was largely them I had to thank. I owed them and what did I do? Ruin their semen-gathering party with a punch-up.

Sam was a friend in need. In that condom swam the seeds of her future happiness. Was I really about to flush them down the toilet? Wasn't it my Catholic duty to give those spermatozoon with their zygotic potential to Sam? The nuns hadn't morally programmed me to deal with this. What would Sister Conchilio say about wasting sperm? God, I regretted not taking that theology degree.

Julian appeared with an empty espresso cup and a large French coffee bowl.

'What are you up for? French or Italian?' he grinned.

The answer was standing before me with rippling pectorals and shining biceps. Yes – yes – yes! A thousand times yes! I'd flush my best friend down the toilet for this Adonis.

But was that right? Should I be putting Julian first merely because he'd touched my G-spot? Julian tapped the two cups lightly together. 'Hello! Earth to Heaven?'

'Sorry what was the question?'

'French or Italian?'

'Sorry – espresso yeah,' I replied, turning over, wrapped up in my inner debate.

In the end the choice was between Julian's sperm and my happiness – or Sam and Charles and their happiness. It all came down to potentials.

I could either tell Julian what Sam wanted – with the potential that he would think I was a weirdo-nut-case-freak or a cold-hearted sperm-gathering-witch.

Or I could flush the condoms down the lavatory and have Sam and Charles think my friendship was as semi-pelucid as the sperm.

★ ★ ★

Julian came back bearing a tray loaded with caffeine. Was there honestly any possibility that he would say, 'Gee swell what a great way for this otherwise wasted sperm to go?'

'Darling, you look tired. Am I keeping you up?' he asked, lying down beside me.

I threw my arms around him and rolled onto his hairless chest.

'No. Am I keeping you up?' I asked, running my hand from his weary penis up to his neck. 'Gosh, you have no hair at all,' I said absent-mindedly.

'I get it waxed,' he said matter-of-factly.

'I see,' I said, trying not to feel censorious. After all, it was his prerogative and a PC voice inside me told me it was wrong to be critical.

'I hate body hair,' he went on.

'Oh?' I said, trying to sound like I'd lost interest. This topic was digging in and I wanted out. Couldn't we go back to mmm? I mean, I was covered in the stuff. Hair! I spent a good deal of my leisure time plucking and shaving and bleaching my hairy torso and limbs – and still it grew.

'I just think it's like . . . *the* ultimate turn-off,' he persisted.

The ultimate turn-off? Was he talking above cellulite? I attempted to derail the body-hair conference from its assault on my self-confidence by moving on to a new conversation.

'Sam and Charles want a kid!' I said quietly as I snuggled into the hairlessness of his chest.

'I know. Sam told me last night. I think she's really cool. They're just so . . . together. I have other lesbian friends in that boat. You know, desperate for a kid. In fact I've drawn up the papers for donors disclaiming all responsibility and rights to their sperm. We were talking about it last night when you came in. I even told her I'd sleep with her. I mean, like I said, it's no skin off my nose.'

I sat up. 'No skin off your nose?' I repeated, not really seeing how his nose needed to be involved. I wasn't thinking clearly.

'Yeah. Well, hell, who am I kidding? I might need a womb myself some day. But she said she'd rather not go that far with a man. She showed me that turkey baster thing she's got.' He laughed. 'Yeah, those two are really good value.' He took a sip of his *café au lait*.

'Good value?' My womb had started to twist itself into a fist. Was he telling me that he would have been just as happy to go to bed with Sam as with me? Was she better value perhaps? Or had he only gone to bed with me because he wanted to do a good turn for Sam? And what did he mean he might need a womb someday?

Picture this, we'd been making love all night. It was brilliant. It was intimate and, for me at least, I thought we'd touched on the divine here and there. Now he was describing the possibility of sex with my best friend as being 'no skin off his nose'.

Julian shovelled into my misery with gusto. 'Yeah. I can see what she means though,' he said meditatively. 'I mean about not fucking a man. A lot of gays are like that. Not me personally. I'm not like that. Don't get me wrong or anything. I'm not exactly bi, but sex with a woman can be really cool too,' he laughed.

I pulled away from his chest. In a few moments I could see I might have to take direct action on it – like with a knife or something. I didn't want to go getting too attached to it.

Julian was warming to his theme now. 'A lot of gay men aren't as liberal as me though. I've got friends who say they'd rather sleep with a gorilla than a woman.'

I was sitting bolt upright by now – looking around for something very heavy or sharp. What was he telling me here? Was I meant to be complimented or what? Because he rated me as one up from a gorilla? OK, so I've got a little body hair – but I had conned myself into believing I was way up on the primate list? And there was another word popping in and out of his conversation that made me freeze. Gay!

'Your lack of discrimination does you justice,' I said tartly.

Julian was propped up on his European square pillows sipping his *café au lait*, wallowing in his open-door sex policy. 'Mmmm,' he grinned without a touch of shame. 'But you've got to admit it was fun. Maybe I even tried harder because it was with you,' he offered by way of a backhanded compliment.

How had I been such a fool? He might have a smooth chest

but metaphorically speaking it was as hairy as any chest that has ever sported a gold medallion. I had just shared the sacred orifices of my body with a male chauvinist gay!

I felt like Little Red Riding Hood lying naked with the wolf. My what a smooth chest you have . . . Oh, I have it waxed . . . all the better to humiliate you with!

I suppose I should have hit him, or thrown coffee at him, or drowned him in his own sperm, but I felt drained and used. Not even one up from a gorilla on the Richter scale of appeal. So I went quietly and purposefully out to the corridor to gather up my clothes. How had I been such an idiot? I went into the bathroom where – you guessed it – the seat was up.

In the end they all leave the loo seat up and put me down.

Well, not any more. What the hell was I thinking, putting Julian's ego before his sperm count anyhow? That was it. I was over men. As far as I was concerned the only thing about men worth bothering with was their sperm.

Once dressed I went to collect the seed of Julian's hairless loins. At least Sam would be happy.

As we said our goodbyes Julian tried to dig himself out.

'It's not that I didn't find you attractive, Evelyn. Don't think that. Hey, it was fun for us both wasn't it?' he chuckled. He was standing in the gentle rays of morning light coming through the open door.

I'd never wanted to castrate a man as much in my life. But I had my hands full with the condoms and was fighting back my tears. I was experiencing complete ego meltdown.

'Absolutely, Julian. I haven't enjoyed myself as much since my last smear test. You're not bad for a man! But listen, honestly, thanks for the sperm. I take it you have a clean bill of health . . . before I offer your seed to Sam?'

He was standing there with a honeycomb bath robe around him to keep out the early morning chills. While I'd been preparing my exit he'd been oiling his chest with baby oil. How had I actually found this parody of manhood attractive?

'Sure, I showed her last night. I've got the Aids test results here in my wallet,' he replied.

'You carry them around with you do you, Jules?' I snarled. What a SNAG (sensitive new-age gay)!

'I think it's so much better that everyone feels confident, don't you?' he asked without a trace of irony.

'Nice choice of words, Julian. You've done my confidence the world of good. Happy waxing. Maybe I'll *use* you again!'

Chapter 35

The liberty of the subject –
and all that shit!

I was standing on St Johns Street at five o'clock in the morning waiting for a taxi. It was as inhuman as Julian's loft apartment. I walked down to the Strand where the homeless were sleeping like Roman sentinels in every doorway. What an address eh? The Victorians would have been jealous.

'Hey, spare some change?' a cardboard box called out to me. Maybe that's what Sam should have done – stood on street corners with her turkey baster and called out to genetically suitable men.

'Spare some sperm?'

The streets looked grey and worn out like they'd had a hard night. *You're too old for this London,* I thought. Too old for this lifestyle. I was twenty-five next week and even I was feeling tired. Tired of the inhumanity of this careworn world, tired of this city that huddled behind cardboard boxes and scaffolding. I felt like crying.

But who was I fooling? What did I have to cry about? What had Julian actually done? Offered to help out a couple of girls who wanted some sperm when thousands wouldn't? Was that such a sin? No, that was modern love. Didn't that deserve a pat on the back?

Maybe it was me. Maybe I just invested too much in what was only ever going to be a one-night stand. After all, I had *wanted* to sleep with him. God, I'd have sold my soul to writhe

209

away a night with Julian. Had he really done anything so bad?

The answer was most definitely yes! He had done what I swore I would never let another man do to me. He'd made me feel second best. One up from a gorilla but definitely a few rungs down from a man. Almost anything was better than that.

I took a silent cab ride back to the civilisation of Notting Hill. There was a sense there that the show was over. The garbage truck was making its rounds. A few stray odds and sods of humanity wandered carelessly across empty streets on their way home. The dawn light was all pink and smoky which made me feel like I was walking into a dream. I had invested too much in Julian. And now I'd lost it all.

The girls were on the balcony wrapped in their duvet. I guess no one had slept last night. 'Hello!' I shouted out, willing the nurse from upstairs to call the police. I was tired of taking life on the chin.

They were strangely silent, but I didn't have my keys so I shouted up to them again. 'Can you let me in?'

They remained mute but Sam stood up and went inside. Charles looked down on me like I was some sort of abject stranger. This wasn't one of the thousand and one moods of hers I was familiar with. They must be *really* annoyed about last night, I thought sheepishly. But I knew I had the potential to make it up in the soggy little bags I was clutching.

Sam was still in her gold body paint. I put my arms out to hug her.

'Don't hug me, you'll get gold all over your suit,' she said with about as much energy as a famine victim.

Looking around our flat it looked like those people with the placards outside Victoria last week were right. The end of the world had finally come. And I'd spent it fucking a SNAG. Our spacious, high-ceilinged flat looked like Chelsea Kensington Council had designated it as the new dumping ground. Glasses, bottles and disgusting-looking leftover bits of food on paper plates vied with streamers, shoes, overturned ashtrays, and a few leftover people asleep in a corner.

There were even a few sequinned G-strings flung over the backs of the chairs. A champagne bottle stuck rudely out of one of the vulva seats said it all. Our little nest had been desecrated. There wasn't a cleaner this side of the Thames that would touch this mess now.

'So, Sam, how's it going? I said as I kicked off my shoes and went over to the sink to get a glass of water. 'Shit, what a mess. We'll be cleaning this lot up for the next week – hey?' I said, trying to sound light-hearted.

Sam shrugged and made a little resigned expression.

'Listen, Sam, I'm sorry about the punch-up. Truly, I feel r-e-a-l-l-y embarrassed. I just didn't think it would escalate like that. Really, I just saw Goldilocks and I had this blind impulse to throw my drink in her face. I didn't want to get into a fight. Seriously, I thought I'd throw my Pimms at her and that would be it like . . . like it! I'm . . . um . . . sorry?'

But Sam was not responding. She was wearing the brave smile she wore when Charles or I broke a piece of her Bohemian crystal. This called for radical action.

'Look, I got the sperm!'

I held up the oozy condoms proudly like they were pheasants I'd just shot.

That seemed to bring her round.

'Oh, Evelyn, you shouldn't have,' she cooed as she snatched them from me. 'Oh no, you should have really. You're brilliant, I love you, I love you, I love you!' She gave me a golden hug. 'The angels will sing your name. And forget about the punch-up. That's not the problem. But we've got something pretty dreadful to tell you actually. Something awful happened last night . . .'

She squeezed my arm. My father had squeezed my arm when Gran died. I looked at the golden imprint she'd left on my skin. What did this mean – something awful? Someone had died? Not Charles. She was quiet but definitely alive out there on the balcony. Wasn't she? I panicked.

'What's happened, what's happened?' I screeched.

Charles came walking in still gold from last night. 'So how was it?'

'Look, honey,' Sam cried out, jumping up and down with the condoms. 'Evvy's got the sperm. Quick, quick. We've got to hurry. Look, Evvy, don't worry, we'll talk about this later. Get the baster would you, Charles!'

Charles was still wrapped in the duvet. She ruffled my hair. 'So the great white hunter returns?'

'What's happened, Charles? What's going on? Sam squeezed my arm like someone's died and you're both acting weird. Is there something I should know?'

Sam's voice broke the silence.

'Are you bringing the baster, Charles? Hurry up I'm ready. Evvy, this is great, it's still warm.'

Charles went over to the kitchen.

'No one's dead. But we've got some stuff to talk about. Stuff that went down after you left. After your brawl.'

'Oh God! Nurse Cockerel upstairs didn't call the police did she? Oh shit! I'm so, so sorry.'

'No, not the police, not Nurse Cockerel. Look, I'll just go help Sam. Back in a minute. Relax all right?'

I went to my room to change. My pilot-case stood forlornly in the middle of the bed waiting for its next call. I suddenly remembered Candida. Maybe there wouldn't be any calls. I was going to have to face her Monday and own up to having lost the case. I was prepared to hazard a guess that she would react about as well as Mr Roberts had to the verdict.

Maybe I should start looking for new chambers? It wouldn't be easy. I hardly had a client list to speak of – unless you count Keith of Shepherds Bush who was almost certainly a repeat offender. I guess he'd send me the odd referral. Burglaries, car theft, casual drive-by killings. But could I count on Keith's loyalty?

I couldn't believe I was thinking like this.

I flicked the case open and pulled out the jumble of papers and my wig tin. The gown was so crumpled I'd need to dry-clean it. When I pulled it out, photographs sprayed all over the floor. As I gathered them up, I only half looked at the smiling faces of Giles and me in front of all our familiar haunts. Most of them came from a long weekend I'd spent in London with him – before the fall – when life was still simple and bonny and blithe. Tears welled up behind my eyes, but I stopped them. And then, just as I was putting them away, I saw it – the photograph of her!

Goldilocks – the bitch from hell. How insensitive could he be? I wished I'd tackled him last night as well. She was sitting on

Giles' sofa, laughing her vapid head off – no doubt about it. Oh she looked so smug with those tiny A-cups of hers. What in God's name was he thinking of sending me this?

No angles? Wasn't that what Worston said? The man was a veritable twenty-degree angle of a knife sticking into my heart.

Charles stuck her head round the door. 'I'm making Sam some camomile tea. Want some? She's going to stay in bed with her legs up – to . . . you know . . . keep the sperm in.'

'Love some,' I said, shoving the photographs back into my case. 'I'll give you a hand.'

I followed her into the kitchen and washed up some cups. The cupboards were empty, the sink was full.

'We'll have to wash up the glasses. Oddbins are going to pick them up at eleven,' she said, half to me half to the kettle.

'So what happened last night?' I asked. 'I'm really, really sorry you know. Like I told Sam, I didn't think it would go that far.'

'Don't apologise to me, apologise to Caroline.'

Caroline? Ouch, she had a name? That stung. But it struck me as disloyal of Charles to use it even if she did have one. We had always called her Goldilocks. She was the bitch – sleeping under my duvet. Sleeping with my man. Goldilocks – the intruder.

'Caroline?' I said archly. 'Is that the bitch's name?'

'Yes, Caroline – that's her name.' Then Charles turned to face me – and I could tell she was angry. 'What makes you such a judge? Where the hell do you get off? Defining the morality of someone you've never even met?'

Oh this was rich. 'Where'd you read that, Charles . . . on the back of a cornflake packet?' I snarled. 'Don't tell me you're going to give me all that shit about the liberty of the subject?'

'Oh I don't know, Evelyn.' The kettle whistled. She turned off the gas and poured the water into the pot. Afterwards she looked me straight in the eye as if she would like to slap me. 'You're so brilliant, you work it out! You call yourself a barrister? Well, have you ever heard of misreading the evidence?'

I felt that somewhere along the line my attempt at making amends had taken a turn for the worse. 'What's going on, Charles, you've lost me?'

Charles threw her arms around me and held me tight.

'Oh, don't listen to me. It's none of my business. You've got

Julian now. I shouldn't have said anything.'

'Julian's gay,' I muttered.

'Oh Christ . . . Evvy . . . I'm so sorry. Shit . . . but you . . . the condoms?'

'He's gay, not impotent. He *can* do it with a woman you see. Christ – he can do it with gorillas in a pinch. The man's an icon of indiscriminate sexuality.'

'Oh shit!' Charles exclaimed.

'So what's this stuff about – she whose name cannot be spoken and not reading the evidence,' I pressed.

And then she said something that felt like a tattoo being stencilled on my conscience.

'She's Giles' sister.'

Chapter 36

I was overdosing on Catholic class-A drugs! This was a mega-guilt with a serious street-sin value!

It took a while to assimilate what I'd been told. 'His sister?' I kept repeating like it was some sort of Buddhist chant that would eventually bring me enlightenment if I said it enough times.

His sister? How had I got that so wrong? I tried to remember my two brief visits to his family's home in Gloucestershire. A vague image of a grand piano with photographs of the family strewn on the top. It had just never occurred to me that he'd have his sister in his bed.

Apparently Giles and his sister had had a heart to heart with Sam and Charles after I'd made my dramatic exit. She knew who I was when I threw the drink in her face. I guess she'd seen my face in photographs too.

'His sister? But why?' I asked again and again. Incapable of comprehending the reality after two years of delusion.

'Why what? Why was she his sister?'

'Well, why didn't he tell me?' I pleaded.

'You hardly gave him a chance. You moved address – you disappeared off the continent. Face it, Evelyn, you overreacted.'

'Shut up!' I shouted with my hands over my ears. I felt like I was going to explode into a Molotov cocktail of confusion.

I wasn't going to take the guilt that easily. 'He fucking snuck around for weeks. Lying and avoiding me. I thought he had thrush or something. I thought he might be impotent. I went to the STD clinic. I had that steel cock thing shoved up me for Christ's sake! Why did he make me feel like that? Why couldn't he tell me? What's so strange about sisters? They weren't . . .'

'Incestuous you mean? No they weren't. Did it ever occur to you that *she* might not have wanted him to tell you? You've got such a one-track mind. Can't you see, Evelyn? You misread the evidence – you're a fucking barrister for Christ's sake. Haven't you heard of the presumption of innocence and, yeah, all that shit about liberty of the subject?'

'You keep saying that. So I'm a fucking barrister? Does that make me an expert on why people lie to me? Does it, does it? Because that's what he did, apart from anything else, he lied to me.'

'He didn't lie to you – he exercised his right to stay silent for fuck's sake!'

'Same thing.'

'No it's not and, anyway, it was her right not to say or do anything that might incriminate her. She was a junky.'

'A what?'

Charles looked tired. She sat down on my bed where I'd been lying immobile since the first wave of shock subsided.

'A heroin addict. She's what you might call the black sheep of the family. Apparently she arrived on his doorstep out of the blue the night before you were due down for the weekend. It must have been the first time he cancelled one of your weekends together. She'd been in Thailand for two years. She was sick when she arrived. Very sick.

'She didn't want the rest of her family to know you see. It was all a kind of tragedy by the sounds of it. Real centre-spread stuff. Her boyfriend had been arrested for drugs. He was a Thai national and since then he's been executed.'

'To death you mean?' I gulped. I had been sticking pins in a voodoo doll of a girl whose boyfriend had been executed?

'Executed. Anyway, so Giles let her sleep in his bed. She was three months pregnant, strung out and having a breakdown – all in his bed. The fact is, Evvy, she'd just had the abortion the day you found her. Giles thought . . . well, you're a Catholic you know and with your finals, he wanted you to do well. He was going to tell you once she'd sorted herself out and you'd got through your exams. Cold turkey wasn't one of the things you'd discussed in your relationship apparently. Fuck, Evelyn, you got it all wrong. He's a really sweet guy, Evvy.'

Charles was angry, her voice was tight – in turns appealing and sarcastic. I couldn't cope with what she was telling me let alone the way she was telling me. It felt like I was being read a riot act.

'I got it wrong?' I stammered. 'You mean, I spent two years recovering from a man that *didn't* cheat on me?'

'Shit, Evelyn, he's not a viral infection. He loved you – he told me he proposed to you? You didn't exactly give him a chance did you?'

I felt like I was drowning. What had I done? Could it be true that I had acted in such a high-handed and righteous way with a man who was helping his drug-fucked sister get on her feet?

I was overdosing on Catholic class-A drugs. This was mega-guilt with a serious street-sin value. Had I actually been jealous of a girl whose boyfriend was being executed? Their baby a junky before it was even born – an abortion? And me running around like a chook with its head cut off, sticking pins in effigies? God, I really showed Yahweh a thing or two about righteous anger. 'Oh, Charles, what do I do?' I cried in desperation. I lost it. I broke down and blubbered inconsolably.

Charles threw her arms around me. 'Oh, Evvy, you poor thing. Have I been cruel?'

I nodded – my face streaming with tears. She laughed and kissed my forehead. 'Don't worry, we'll sort it out somehow. If we have to we'll take it to the Court of Appeal and get your conviction quashed!'

I laughed into my tears.

'Charles?' My voice was small.

'Yes?'

'I'm afraid.'

'It's OK, we've got two of the finest legal minds in London working on this one. Let's have some sleep and then we'll launch your appeal. You know – "If it pleases, my lord, I thought 'e was 'aving an affair, like, and so I just cleared out. I know I should've given 'im a chance, but I was young, my lord. I hadn't even made it to Bar school yet. Give me a chance, my lord!" He won't be able to resist.' She smiled at me as she pulled the duvet over my head.

'I've got to go see Sam now. I'll wake you in a few hours. Who knows maybe you've got her pregnant!'

She blew me a kiss the way my mother used to when I was infectious. I'd never felt so small . . . or so guilty.

'And, Evvy,' she whispered. 'Remember, whatever happens, you've got us. We're always here for you.'

Chapter 37

Islington Mourning

It was midday by the time Oddbins picked up the glasses.
Charles woke me up brandishing a pair of sunglasses and an
espresso.

'Here you'll need these!' she said, passing a pair of Agnes B
glasses across the bed. 'Sam told me to buy them – she figured
you deserved them.'

She was in her hangover frock – a shocking red creation by
Gucci.

'What's the outfit in aid of? It's not Mardi Gras is it?'

'No it's bloody red – the way I feel!' she explained, slumping
on the bed. She looked stunning . . . too stunning. She was
giving me the DTs just looking at her. I put on the sunglasses.

'Shake your bones, girl, we're off to the Court of Appeal,' she
announced, throwing open my wardrobe. 'Wear black because
you're in mourning and tight because you want results!' she
ordered, pointing at my stuff like a dominatrix.

Pulp were singing, 'We're all sorted for Es and whizz,' the
psychedelic rhythms pelting into my head. Charles sat on the
end of my bed and started applying her orange lipstick with a
compact. 'Sam's staying in bed so none of it falls out!' she
stated.

My head felt as if it was suspended above a ravine. I couldn't
quite focus on what was going on. 'Court of Appeal? But it's
Saturday. And what's falling out of what?'

'The sperm!'

My head hit reality with a thud. Of course it was the baby thing. Julian's sperm. Oh God. I put my head under the duvet. 'It isn't a quantity thing with sperm though, is it? I thought it was quality?'

'Yeah sure, and it's the quality sperm she doesn't want to fall out. Darling, I found this lipstick in the bin in the bathroom. It's a brilliant colour, is it yours?'

I took a look at the stick. 'Oh sure! I wore it when I went to court on ecstasy – it's got bad associations. Keep it.'

She laughed. 'I warned you about drugs before breakfast. But enough of that, we've got an appeal to launch, girl, so it's up and at 'em.'

I poked my head out and found myself staring at dozens of photographs of Giles with his arms around me – stuck all over the room. They were the ones he'd just sent me.

Charles grinned. 'Like my collage? I did it while you were asleep.'

Significantly they all had eyes, unlike the ones I kept after we broke up – every eyeball rammed through with a pin.

'It's called a positive affirmation,' she laughed.

'I can't face him, Charles. I can't.' I put my head back under the duvet for emphasis.

'You can and you will. We've put up with you and your moods and your *all men are bastards* theme for two years. I want it sorted and I want it sorted *now!*'

She tore the duvet off me. 'I've got a girlfriend trying to get pregnant and a case at the Inner London Crown defending some bloke who's been accused of eating another bloke's dog . . . And no I don't want to talk about it.'

She pulled the duvet back over my head as if to suffocate me.

'I just want a nice serene flat to come back to when it's over. And if you're very good I'll tell you all about what I did for you yesterday.'

I sat up – curiosity had the better of me. 'What did you do for me?' I asked.

'A favour.'

This sounded ominous. 'What kind of favour?'

'Oh . . . nothing much. Let's just say something that's been troubling you has been . . . sorted.'

'*Sorted*?' I yelled, now seriously alarmed. Sorted was what Albert told me I was when he sold me the ecstasy. I had made a vow never to be 'sorted' ever again. It was like one of the cornerstones of my lifestyle – no more sorted!

'Can you just shut up and trust me? Believe me, you'll be eternally grateful. Call it a reward for being our proxy donor. But I'm not going to tell you anything until you sort things out with Giles. And that, my dear, is that.' She smiled so sweetly I thought her mouth would take off.

'Please, Charles. He's hardly going to want to see me now is he? I feel so awful, I can't,' I pleaded.

'Well, at the very least, you're going to apologise to Caroline about last night. I liked her and you will too. They still live together in that same place in Islington with friends and I've got it all worked out. We'll take flowers – you'll go down on bended knees and then we can go to the Orb for lunch – and a spot of Islington Man and Islington Woman. Cheer ourselves up with a few too many frozen margaritas! Heavenly. It's a perfect day. Now up. Get your tot in the shower. Now!'

'Blessed are the peacemakers,' I mumbled sarcastically as I stumbled to the bathroom.

After emptying the contents of the medicine cabinet into our systems and rejecting most of my wardrobe – bar one little black dress so tight and so clingy I was worried I looked like a piece of optic fibre – we went forth to plead the unpleadable. I harassed Charles a bit more about what or who she had *sorted*.

'Pleeeeaaaase, Charles. You know I hate surprises.'

But she remained tight-lipped. 'All in good time, my dear one,' she repeated mysteriously. But I couldn't help a growing sense of trepidation welling up inside me.

It was Charles' idea to buy the flowers. It was my idea to buy white roses. It was a mistake to buy so many. The florist outside the Piers Gough closed up after we struggled out with them. Standing there like two whores with our dresses up around our armpits, our sunglasses and our roses, we stopped the traffic.

'You shooting a movie or somefing?' the cabby asked as he pulled into the kerb.

'Yes,' Charles cried out in her best Belgravia voice. 'That's us, the film crew, and we're late.'

We had to abandon some of the roses in order to squeeze into the cab and even then it was like being in a mobile hothouse. The traffic was horrendous.

The Kurdish Freedom Party were having their annual rally in Hyde Park – the same day as the Highland music festival was holding its Annual Bagpipe Competition and the whole jamboree had spilled over onto the streets bordering the park.

The tempers of Pipers and Kurds alike were frazzled by the time we came upon them. We passed a dozen or so small altercations while we crept along in the traffic on Bayswater Road. Our cab driver intimated it was liberal immigration policies which were to blame.

'Absolutely, we should never have let those Scottish pipers in,' joked Charles. But her humour was not to our driver's taste – he slammed the adjoining window, mumbling something about fuckin'-movie-lefty-luvvies.

By the time we got to Kings Cross it felt like we were in a falucca drifting down the Nile without a breeze. I think it crossed everyone's mind, including the driver's, that maybe we'd never get to Islington. The flowers began dropping their petals as if weeping.

Some Arabs had broken down in the traffic outside Kings Cross and they'd decided to push their car to its destination in their shower sandals. Their white jellabahs looked like sails. About three hundred drivers were leaning on their horns. Thankfully our driver was above joining in.

After a while he decided to give us another chance and opened his window for company. 'Sooner they [the IRA] start bombing London again, the better... sort out this bloody traffic,' the driver muttered. Charles and I were too hot to think about the moral implications of the remark, so we agreed.

My head pounded, not with a hangover so much as the guilt. Guilt is the prime motivational force of all morally sound life forms! Gran often reminded us.

Underpinning all the guilt was a longing to undo the damage I had done. I had loved a man who put down the loo seat, who knew my dress size, who laughed at all my jokes (including the ones even I knew weren't funny!). And then I'd turned around and shown him I trusted him about as much as British beef.

What the hell was I going to say to get myself off? Mr Roberts of Hove had a watertight case compared to mine.

By this stage the pollen in the roses was making my eyes stream and compounding the general distress of my hangover and my fears. The tight black dress was sticking to my thin frame like a clingfilm shroud. I couldn't remember when I last ate. Oh yes I could, it was yesterday in Brighton with Mr Worston – it seemed weeks away. I longed for my well-fed past.

I peered through the roses at Charles.

'What am I going to say?'

'Try sorry?' Charles offered distractedly. She was painting her nails.

'Just say whatever comes into your head – it can't be worse than what you've said already.' She blew on her nails to dry them.

She was right of course but we didn't speak after that, it was too hot – even our breath came out sweating. It reminded me of summer in Australia when it was so hot, my school hat would melt into my hair and my shoes would stick to the bitumen of the quadrangle. It was worse for our poor nuns who wore the full black purda. None of this shin-high frock business for our girls. They had solid, woollen, full-length serge vocations and they were perpetually praying that a few of us would too.

'Vocations,' we used to sing. 'Nuns do it, priests do it, monks and cardinals and even Popes do it. Let's do it – let's have a vocation!' One day we played a practical joke. A group of us told the nuns that we had vocations. We managed not to laugh as we solemnly lied our way into a tight corner.

Our nuns were over the moon. We were chosen for special duties – setting the altar, ironing the vestments, polishing the monstrance. Sometimes, when we were called on for special duties, the nuns even referred to us as The Vocations. We pretended we were an all-female black American soul group.

Over the ensuing weeks the burden of our deception began to weigh heavily. After a while we felt compelled to admit our sin to the priest in the confessional, but he was quite phlegmatic.

'The Lord works in mysterious ways,' he laughed.

Then some of us started to have doubts. Maybe we really did have vocations? And if we did have a vocation and we ignored it, what would happen?

★ ★ ★

Caroline answered the door of the house. It was the same house I'd found her asleep in two years ago – and had run away from as if it were the base camp for the Black Death.

'Oh, it's you again,' she exclaimed, as if I was an unemployed youth selling dishcloths.

The cab driver and Charles were unloading the flowers.

'I've come to say sorry,' I explained in my most remorseful voice.

'Sure OK, well let's leave it at that.' She shut the door.

'What's happened?' asked Charles, as she carried the last flower bundle up the steps.

'I said sorry and she said, well let's leave it at that, and slammed the door.'

'Oh. Well, let me try.'

Charles rang the bell. She knocked on the door, she called out. My dress was riding up my midriff while around me wilted a hundred white roses. I was doing a dying swan. This was my finale. Maybe it would be better for me to do an Ophelia – slash my wrists and float down Islington on a barge of roses. There were worse ways to be remembered – such as the girl in the waist-high dress who'd thrown over a man who put down the loo seat.

Caroline spoke to us through the door with the chain on.

'Look, I don't feel in the mood for this. As far as I'm concerned, Giles is better off without you. Besides, he's not here. Now if you won't take your flowers and leave, I'll call the police.'

Charles squeezed her nose through the gap. 'Caroline? Hi . . . it's me . . . Charles – the golden girl . . . friend of Sam's? Look give her a chance, hey? She's been a jerk, but she knows that – look she just got the wrong angle on it all. She knows that now . . . imagine how she feels? At least take the flowers?'

'Yes take the flowers at least,' I pleaded. I was over these flowers.

'I'm serious,' she snapped. 'Giles and I have done a lot of talking. We're going to buy a house together. The last thing he wants is to be entrapped by *you* again.'

Hang on a minute, this wasn't the script I'd agreed to read. *Entrapped*? Excuse me! God I was thinking more along the lines of a vocation. I was thinking of giving up my life for him – wearing a purda-type thing. Maybe even taking time out to have a kid or two when we could afford a nanny.

'Isn't that up to Giles?' I asked.

'Well, he's not here to speak for himself, but if he were I know what he'd say. Fuck off.' She slammed the door.

Chapter 38

Facing the music – when they're not playing your tune!

When that door slammed, I suspected it was fate trying to say, 'enough is enough'. The gavel of life had come down on the bench. Sentence had been passed. Fate had slammed the door on our plan.

As Gran would say, 'Face the music, Evelyn – they're not playing your song.' The carnival was over – the time had come to grab my anorak and leave.

We were still standing on the door three minutes later. I saw the curtain twitch. Great, so maybe she'd call the police and I'd be dragged out in a blaze of glory, *verbals* and sniffer dogs. The sun was blazing on my back. Even my nail varnish was melting.

'So!' said Charles finally.

'So I guess that's it. I feel ridiculous,' I sighed, with one of those resigned smiles I usually reserved for two in the morning when I knew there was nothing worth staying up for on television.

'You're kidding?' Charles was clearly not in the mood to say *die*. She had her stun-'em dress and kick-'em-in-the-balls heels so I guess I could see her point. She wasn't dressed for resignation and, looking my own outfit up and down, nor was I. I looked like a member of Henry V's army at Agincourt or a berserker that had rubbed mud all over his body and swallowed a field of *amanita muscaria*. I was ready for battle.

A new feeling came over me. A feeling I'd seen on middle-aged woman in pubs around Victoria as they played the fruit machines. Women who knew Lady Luck wasn't smiling on them and said, 'What the fuck – I'm going to kick arse anyway.' A look that spoke volumes about women and fate. A look that said 'no Lady high-and-mighty Luck is going to tell me my luck's out'. A look that said they were going to pull on that one-armed bandit until Lady Luck bloody well changed her mind.

'Well, what else?' I asked, hoping Charles had the plan.

'What a bitch!' she exclaimed.

'I thought you liked her,' I retaliated teasingly.

'I thought I did too, but I sure as hell don't now. What a cow! Think about it, Evvy. Regardless of her problems and how bad they were, it doesn't change the fact that it was because of her that you and Giles broke up. Let's look at the facts. Drug habit or no drug habit, she damn well tore asunder what no woman should.'

This was a change of tack. A change that unburdened me of a fair share of my guilt. 'I get it. So you think *she's* feeling guilty now?' Guilt was an emotion I knew well. Maybe I could relate to Goldilocks after all.

'Maybe, although I suspect it's more a case of – when you're on a good thing stick to it. She still hasn't got her life together. Last night I saw her as the injured party. I mean, let's face it, you had been kind of hard on the two of them. But in the cruel light of day a few things have occurred to me.

'First up – apparently the family still don't accept her. I gather the narcotics problem isn't exactly ancient history. For starters she's still on methadone. And she's hardly supporting herself on what she makes as a temp in Sam's office. Sam felt really bad – like you might have thought the whole thing was a setup but Sam had no idea who she was. I mean, it wasn't as if she was wearing her name tag saying Goldilocks. She must have invited Giles who, by the way, is still supplementing her income. So she's sitting pretty while Giles has no one else in his life to interfere. If I was of a cynical nature I would be wondering if it's really in her interest to see you two make up?'

The realisation that I had an enemy behind that door – that the viper was still in my garden – fell on me like hot mud.

'So you're saying fuck the liberty of the subject?'

'Fuck it.'

'Well, we can't stand here all day,' I reminded her. I was beginning to feel like one of those boil-in-the-bag meals.

'No you're right, we need to freshen up before we put phase two into action. The Orb!' she said decisively as if it was a call to arms. 'It's time for frozen margaritas.'

Chapter 39

I may be an orgasmic woman with a promising career and healthy interpersonal relationships but I still felt like utter crap

The walk up the hill to the Orb was more than we'd bargained on. It was a Saturday market day and the crowds, returning after a morning wandering through the antique and bric-a-brac of Camden Passage, looked troubled by our presence. I'd seen that look of pure disapproval before – on the judge in Hove and it sat better on him in his sky-blue glasses.

We passed Joe Orton's house on Noel Road. The flat where he was murdered by his gay lover. I suddenly related to Kenneth. A spot of murder seemed highly appealing. It certainly didn't bring down the tone of the area. In fact it was a pretty seedy address once – if anything, Kenneth's bloody crime had increased the area's cachet. Proving that crime can pay – at least as far as the property market's concerned.

The street was neat and prosperous – parked with BMWs and Porsches. *Fabulous Georgian stucco: four bedrooms, two bathrooms – genuine celebrity murder site. Bedroom two opens onto patio where Joe Orton was slaughtered by his lover with a hammer.*

I was thinking of murder. OK, I know it's a cardinal sin but blame is an easier emotion to satisfy than guilt. The murder of Goldilocks – even Charles was back to calling her that now – had a nice ring to it. After all I could plan the perfect crime with *my* legal knowledge – something sophisticated and professional like smashing down her door with an axe and clumsily slaying her in the hallway – but I knew it would interfere with taking silk.

231

We sensed we didn't look like respectability personified by the looks passers-by gave us as we wheezed past, dragging our bundles of roses up the hill. Our faces were melting down our necks, our perfume had evaporated into the heat, the flowers were losing their petals and the thorns were digging into us and ruining our manicures. We made a decision to dump them.

We had to do it surreptitiously, to avoid the approbation of these community-proud citizens. This was Islington after all and there wasn't a Portabin in sight. So we dropped them on the pavement and walked on as if we'd never seen those white roses before in our lives.

It felt kind of sad. We'd had such high hopes for those blooms when we'd bought them – they were our banner in this brave quest to right the wrongs of two years. Now they were just expensive compost.

We were liquidised women by the time we perched ourselves up against the bar of the Orb – jellied women. The seedy, semi-beautiful young people of politics, journalism and law were gathered around knocking back their hangovers with double-espresso, nibbling rocket salad and shooting the political shit. It was clear from the outset that our barman didn't like us.

'Do you want those frozen margaritas with ice or without ice?' he added disinterestedly.

'Is that a trick question?' I replied.

He looked at us like we'd just crawled out of the Home Counties and drove a Volvo. He looked like he'd just crawled out of a Soho nightclub and strapped his lovers to their beds with leather thongs. He was wearing a lot of badges advertising Gay Pride and a T-shirt that read, Leather Equals Love. We weren't his phenotype customer.

'I'll give you time to think about it,' he said with a tone of menace. He didn't turn around when we screamed with laughter like girls at a Chippendales' party.

He didn't come back either for what seemed like a millennium to my dry mouth. I felt like I'd been chewing on cigarette butts all night and I needed my drink – with or without ice. We called him over.

'Excuse me, excuse me!' we squealed, like teenage girls of no political content.

He looked decidedly annoyed.

'So have you made your minds up?'

'Without ice please,' we chirped, attempting to dazzle him with our sunny smiles.

'So, two frozen margaritas without ice?' he repeated.

'Could we make that four?' Charles enquired.

'Four?' He looked like he wanted to strike us.

'Yeah, we're thirsty,' I explained.

He walked off. We giggled. The bar was full of Islington men and women dressed in their distressed chic.

'God,' said Charles, surveying them. 'I've either been against or represented almost everyone in this place. Which reminds me of that little favour I did for you.'

'What favour?' I insisted. I had all but forgotten that Charles had *sorted* me. Things were worse than I thought.

Our barman came back. 'We don't do frozen margaritas without ice,' he stated firmly.

'Oh, what a shame,' Charles pouted. 'Isn't that a shame, Evvy?' she asked in an American Deep-South accent.

I agreed that it was a shame and then demanded, 'What favour?'

'OK then, so make it four frozen margaritas with ice then,' Charles replied. It seemed a fairly straightforward solution to a couple of girls who'd had three hours' sleep.

Our barman glared as he spoke with exaggerated patience. 'So, let me get this right. Now you want to change your order . . . to four frozen margaritas *with* ice?'

'Or your testicles on a plate,' I heard Charles mutter. 'We thought there was no choice?' she stated pointedly.

'OK,' he sighed. 'Well, they'll be a few more minutes. I'll have to find your other order and change it.' His top lip rose at the corner and trembled – then he turned and huffed off.

'Why couldn't he just say straight out that he loathes us as no other? Maybe we're giving off the wrong pheromones or something?' Charles suggested, sniffing around my midriff. A few of the designer rag brigade sitting opposite smiled approvingly.

'Maybe that was why Goldilocks rejected us? Why the florist overcharged me? Why Julian decided he was gay?' I added.

'I think we upset him,' Charles offered. 'But I thought he was joking about the no ice thing. I thought he was trying to be like . . . amusing. How the hell did he think he was going to make something frozen without ice in it anyway?'

'I couldn't say but I'm going to check out the bogs and when I get back I want to know what this favour was!'

In the mirror I found the clue to our unpopularity. My make-up had melted into the sad mask of a retired stage actress from the twenties. It was time to cash in all my Calvin Klein frequent-shopper points and get that Mind-Body-Spirit Weekend Luxury Break. I needed luxury and pampering like I'd never needed it before. I needed truckloads of frozen margaritas – with or without ice – and I needed Giles.

Oh how had I ever got myself into this mess? One minute I was enjoying multiple orgasms with a man who put down the seat on the toilet and now here I was sleeping with a gay man who'd have been just as happy with a gorilla!

There was also the distressing Candida factor. She wanted to set me up with a reputation as a dyke around the Temple. In fact, she'd already given me the haircut to match! Now I had the face of an ageing bit-part actress and a girlfriend who's *sorted* me! What had Charles done – what was this favour? How had things gone so horribly wrong? Even barmen hate me.

I tried to talk myself up. After all I was an independent woman of the late twentieth century. I'd been breast-fed on Germaine Greer and Gloria Steinam for Christ's sake. I could quote from Naomi Wolf. I was politically aware. I was postorgasmic. I could draw a map to my G-spot. I had a black-belt in kick-boxing. I couldn't imagine not having the vote.

My career was everything to me. OK, so I might have to go without a seat on public transport – but I wouldn't have it any other way. The idea that I might need a man to make me whole was laughable. (Although I wasn't laughing.)

I tried to hum 'I will Survive' over the noise of the handdryer, but there was no getting away from it. I had a hole in my heart and a gap in my hormonal structure that wouldn't go away. I may be an orgasmic woman with a promising career and healthy interpersonal relationships with my genitals – but I felt like utter crap. What a schmuck, what a lousy, low down life form. I'd been *sorted* all right!

But I was also a realist. 'Com'on, girl,' I said to my reflection in the mirror. 'Get real. Your future is the future of all women. Standing on your own two feet. And the first duty of a new-age woman of the late twentieth century is to face up to life, put on your make-up, knock back your margaritas, pay your bill. And go on a course of Prozac.'

Chapter 40

Did I tell you about the thigh-high patent boots and the Chanel micro-mini?

'So let me get this straight,' I repeated stiffly. 'You went to my chambers yesterday and spoke to my head clerk, Warren, representing yourself as Candida's lesbian lover?' My voice got louder as the enormity of Charles' confession dawned on me.

'That's it!' Charles smiled shamelessly. 'Evvy – it was better than the RSC. I'm *definitely* in the wrong profession. You should have seen me. I had on that little Vivienne Westwood bustier – you know the one I attached tassels to the nipples to for last year's Christmas bash?'

'I know the one . . .' I gulped.

'And the thigh-high patent boots and the Chanel micro-mini?'

'Go on,' I heard myself say as I swallowed my third margarita and put my hand up to summon the waiter for refills.

'I love that skirt. I wish Sam hadn't washed the jacket in the machine. I really think Prussian blue's my colour . . . you know with my hair colour it's positively sinful—'

'Will you just get to the point.' I insisted, sitting on my hands to stop them flying around her throat.

'Where was I? Your clerk Warren is so sweet. He's much more civilised than my head clerk. Henry's a fat pig – always eating and belching. The clerk's room reeks of his burps.'

'The *punch* line, Charlotte. I want the *punch* line!' I demanded – laying heavy emphasis on the word punch.

'Sorry, I'm winding you up, but the suspense is making me orgasmic – you're going to love me when I tell you what happened.'

Why did I feel she was misguided as to the mood of her audience? I smiled bravely and nodded for her to continue. I didn't trust the English language to do justice to my emotions. Our drinks arrived – we both knocked them back.

'So there was Warren in his little room. He was all alone. Not that I'd have cared if he wasn't – my disguise was impenetrable. "Now Warren," I said to him, sitting on the desk. I used that Deep-South drawl of mine – I thought he'd find the whole thing more believable if I was American. "Do you think you could give this to Candida," I asked. "Only p-lease don't tell her you saw me, sweety," I crooned.'

She had called Warren *sweety*? My eyes rolled up into my head. I felt that I was going to be asked to play the lead role in *Exorcist IV*.

'So then I said, "Warren, between you, me and the computer screen, Candy's not going to be happy that I came. But I think I can confide in you, Warren. You see Candy is so anally retentive. She's got the makings of a rectum ulcer that woman. I'm telling her all the time, Warren, "Candy darlin' – you don't wanna worry what people think!" I think you'll agree with me, Warren. I mean, excuse me for breathing, but it's 1996, darling! You don't wanna worry what no tight-assed old homophobe thinks! Don't you agree, Warren?" And then he—'

'And then he what?' I demanded, losing control.

'He just sort of swallowed and watched the fish swimming around on the screen-save. But shut up and let me finish. I'm getting to the good bit.'

'Well I'm glad we agree that that wasn't the good bit,' I muttered sarcastically.

'Will you stop moaning. I did this for you. Anyway, so then I said, "Just because she's a dyke don't mean she has to spend her life sneaking and hiding for the sake of a few tight-assed bigots, does it, Warren sweety?" I said.'

'So what did sweety say?' I asked, too drunk to care by now. I'd taken the precaution of drinking Charles' margarita too.

'He was kind of green by then – rocking back and forth in his chair.'

'I can relate to that,' I slurred, going green and swaying slightly.

'So then I launched in – and this is the best bit, Evvy – I said, "But you know what, Warren? I was kinda curious to see yar'll. You see, Candy's told me all about you." And this was the part when the tears welled up in my eyes. I was a diva, darling. I was made for the stage. I wish you could have been a fly on the wall. Warren offered me his handkerchief and I said, "Oh, Warren, she can make me feel so itty-bitty-small sometimes. Always telling me about all her high and mighty friends and her high and mighty cases. Just to make me feel, you know, inferior like. Especially the way she's so hot for that Evelyn."'

'You said what?' I cried out, not believing my ears. 'Oh no, you didn't mention me?' I pleaded.

'Shut up and listen, I'm coming to the best bit now. So he looked really appalled, right? His face was sort of wobbling around his neck like it was waiting for cosmetic surgery, but he was obviously buying the whole charade. So I told him how Candida had a crush on you and that you'd knocked her back and that now she was determined to pay you back. I said that even though I was jealous, I felt sorry for you. By this stage he was nodding his head solemnly, agreeing that it must be hard for me and leafing through the magazine I'd given him.'

'The magazine?' I heard a small voice cry.

'Oh didn't I tell you about that? That was my *pièce de résistance*. It was a copy of *Skin Two*. I told him Candy always read it. I really hammed that bit up. I got all weepy and jealous as I pointed to a tall thin girl with a brown bob and big tits who bears an uncanny resemblance to you by the way. And I told him that Candida had told me it reminded her of you.' Charles put her head back and laughed outrageously. Our barman stormed over.

'Can I help you?' he asked grimly.

'As if,' Charles stammered gleefully. She was on a roll now – a drunken roll. And, judging by the way the barman was talking to the manager and pointing in our direction, I gauged that we were seconds from being flung out.

'An S&M mag? You gave Warren an S&M mag and told him to give it to Candida?' I repeated. 'I don't believe this,' I groaned. But the sad truth was I did.

'I should think it highly unlikely that he'll give it to her though. I really wouldn't think he'd mention it. When I left he was leafing through it under the desk.'

'I don't believe this. Do you know what you've done?' I screamed.

'Saved your tits that's what I did. It was Sam's idea . . .'

'Oh it would be.'

'We could tell you were really upset the other night. After you went to bed, we talked about what we could do to help you. It was Sam's idea. I didn't have to go to court, so I volunteered . . . I mean you basically told us your career was on the line.'

'It was,' I interrupted. 'That didn't mean I wanted you to give it a push!'

'Believe me. I was there – he bought the whole story from start to finish. Once his heart has recovered from the shock of it all only two things will remain in his mind. Well maybe three if you include my nipple tassels. One: Candida's a closet lesbian and two: she's trying to make your life hell because you rejected her.'

'But she's fucking Warren,' I reminded her.

'So? She's a two-faced bitch who used him. He'll probably have an Aids test. Mellow out will you! He bought it. I was there – he bought it hook, line and sinker.'

That was when we were politely but firmly asked to leave.

While making our indecorous exit we fell on top of a table of New Labour supporters and got our stilettos caught in the straps of their bags. They behaved as if they'd been caught in the crossfire of a gun battle.

Two of them hit the floor with their hands over their heads. Charles screamed with laughter and fell on top of them. The manager came over to pull her off. Realising the only real danger they were facing was from the alcoholic fumes from our breath, they became nasty and sarcastic. A pinched-face brunette with moles sneered at us, 'Haven't you heard of dignity?'

Dignity?

Charles and I looked at one another in mock horror.

'We're too young for dignity!' we squealed, laughing ourselves stupid.

Chapter 41

I'm coming in, bitch! – more or less . . .

We were lost.

'You've got to knock on that door and when she answers, you've got to say, move aside, bitch – I'm coming in to say SORRY,' Charles slurred as we circumnavigated Islington.

Even after several margaritas and still reeling from the shock of Charles' deeds of yesterday, I was doubtful about the success of her bold plan. I told her so.

'You're right. I didn't mean that literally . . . just, well, generally. You know, your mood should be *out of my wayish.*'

'Out of my wayish?'

'Well, maybe Giles will answer anyway. And then you should just like burst into tears and tell him the truth.'

'The truth?' This seemed like a vast and vague agenda.

'Yeah – tell him that you loved him so much you flew into a jealous rage. You've got all that passionate Catholic blood. Wipe some of it onto your sleeve.'

It was pretty late in the afternoon by now and there was no one on the streets to ask directions. Long spooky shadows spread out on the pavement, reminding me of an animation of the Passover I'd been shown at school. I had been cast out of the promised land because of one stupid mistake – and now there would be no forgiveness. Oh woe is me! I was living a tragedy – I felt in the mood for some Lee Harvey or Nick Cave or Charlie Watts even – suicide mood music, that was what was called for.

We were stumbling down Duncan Terrace round about where we had dumped our roses earlier. We were sliding into the gutter and tripping over bins and hose pipes when we saw Giles on the other side of the road. At first I thought I was hallucinating – but then I recognised the Armani jeans I'd given him three Christmases ago and decided they had seen better summers. Oh God, I never wanted to take him shopping so badly.

'Giles! Giles! Giles!' we screamed, thinking he was like going to be totally beside himself with excitement to see us.

But he didn't seem to want to know. He walked on – as if he was used to being mobbed by drunk girls with dresses up around their midriffs. Tall and yet with his head down, he had never looked so vulnerable – prime mugging material as my kick-boxing tutor would have said.

'Giles! Over here. Hi!' we squealed, undeterred.

He walked on.

On the other side of the road I saw someone else I recognised coming towards Giles, with his dog. He wasn't exhibiting the signs of a therapeutically correct individual. The fact was, he looked about as pleased to bump into his one time *persecutor* – the bloke in the wig that had tried to send him down a week ago – as I was when I saw Goldilocks last night.

I watched his approach and absorbed the body code. At that point, there was about thirty feet between Keith and Giles. Sometimes made me think that the way Keith was approaching Giles was not altogether harmless. Maybe it was the way his forehead glinted in the sun.

A few more seconds elapsed in which several things happened concurrently. The first thing was that I sobered up. I also remembered Keith's dog's name.

Then Charles saw that something was happening and shut up and stopped falling over. I realised that Giles didn't have a clue he was walking into the forehead of something he could live to regret. If *live* was the appropriate word. I guess it must have been post-menstrual tension that possessed me to wave a red rag of distraction at Keith.

'Have you ever seen such a stupid ugly dog?' I shouted out. I felt like one of those Hollywood movie moguls watching a block of screens on the wall, showing simultaneous wall-to-wall violence and mayhem.

Keith turned his attention to me.

Giles recognised there was danger.

Vomit was staring at Charles the way cats watch birds.

Charles was walking backwards on a grass lawn and became stuck in the turf with her heels.

And all this time the distance between the major protagonists was shortening. Pretty soon the violence was going to come off the wall and onto the street. It was Charles who got things moving when her legs gave way, giving Vomit all the encouragement he needed to charge.

Charles got her legs together fairly smartish and ran behind a Porsche. Keith sort of ran after Vomit. I'd never seen him run before – he looked like one of those comical bow-legged cowboys. But no one was laughing. By now Vomit was sniffing around the Porsche, confused.

Strangely I was not afraid. I was virtually robotic – that's because I was on Super-Oestrogen automatic pilot. Time stretched out like gum. Even though I knew fate was taking me on one of those U-bends before it flushed me into life's sewer, I was relaxed – noticing all the trivial details that made up this Tarantinoesque action drama – like Keith's tattoo which had all but disappeared into his sunburn and Vomit's bandanna scarf which was a canary-yellow leopard print.

I noticed how Giles looked like he had when I'd first met him. When I had accidentally kicked him in the stomach. Lost, helpless – eager to do good, but way out of his depth. This must have been how Boadicea felt when the Romans got in her hair. She turned to the Celtic men, but they had an urgent appointment elsewhere with a manicurist.

Ultimately it's the women who have to step in. Joan of Arc realised that – so did Eleanor of Aquitaine and Catherine Medici and all the legions of woman throughout history who have been surrounded by helpless men who wouldn't know danger if it drove at them like a Belfast lorry carrying Semtex.

I was woken from these musings by Keith. 'You talkin' about my dog, yar nutty bitch?' he yelled.

Surely it was a rhetorical question? There was no other dog on the street, but then maybe the mathematics of the situation had eluded Keith, so I answered him in the affirmative. Vomit by now was licking my feet and panting devotedly. A misplaced sense of loyalty that I doubt did my cause any good.

But as I said, things were happening all at once.

My reply was hardly out of my mouth when Keith lunged at me.

As he lunged, my Manolo Blahnik heel (two hundred pounds – always buy quality shoes) impacted – first with his chin and then with his groin.

Go at your aggressor with everything you've got from the start. 'Let him know the quality of your arsenal,' my kick-boxing tutor had urged. After all, as Gran said – you can't hit a man once he's down.

Keith landed in our wreath of abandoned roses. Splayed out like Leonardo da Vinci's anatomical man. He looked about as noble as he was ever going to look, lying amongst the bruised blooms with Vomit licking his face.

Everything was suddenly calm. Life went back to the one-screen version after that. A lawn mower started up in the background and two smartly dressed Italian women chatting away animatedly about their bargains gracefully sidestepped Keith as if he was an eccentric Englishman.

I still hadn't fully comprehended the enormity of what had happened. All at once I was in Giles' arms, inhaling those erotically familiar aromas I had taught myself to loathe. I think I was probably feeling drunk again.

'Oh hell! What have you done? God! You could have been killed,' he murmured, through tears and kisses.

I thought that was a bit much. I mean, I was the one with the black-belt in kick-boxing here! Keith was just a violent amateur who'd been born punch-drunk. Nonetheless it was rewarding to see the fruits of my training were still ripe.

'I'm fine,' I said, willing Giles never to put me down again as he wiped a bit of lipstick off my teeth.

'Did you two know one another – I mean you and your victim here,' asked Charles, still putting two and two together from the safety of the Porsche's hubcaps.

'Oh sorry. Keith Conan, meet Charles. Charles, Keith – my first Bailey brief,' I explained, watching the slow rise and fall of his chest.

'What a guy. Well, I'm glad someone was able to make use of all those flowers,' she laughed.

'I hope he'll be all right,' I sighed, as my natural state of guilt returned. But just then Keith groaned and the hand with KILL tattooed across the knuckles shoved the slathering dog away from his face. 'Leave it off, Vomit,' he growled as he opened one eye and looked up at me. 'Gees, luv, I really fort we 'ad something and all.'

'Oh God,' laughed Charles. 'Of course, he'll be fine.'

'Yeah right. Life's a bed o' roses for some,' he muttered sulkily. 'Shit, mate, you were meant to be defendin' me. You poxy lawyers. It's a conspiracy I reckon.'

We wandered off, leaving Keith rolling a cigarette.

'The flowers were for you,' I explained, looking into Giles' Med-blue eyes. 'Or Caroline, if she'd accepted them.'

'You've been to my place?'

'Yeah, but we got the feeling we weren't welcome,' I explained, dropping my lower lip.

'Well you're welcome now,' he smiled, his blond hair flopping into his eyes.

Later on, after Caroline had gone off in a sulk and Charles had gone home to check on Sam, Giles and I talked while Blur bantered on about love and life and coming of age under the influence of chemicals. I told him what I'd been doing over the last two years – hating him and reading books on castration mostly.

I told him about Sam and Charles (and no I didn't mention the sperm hunt) and the flat and my chambers and Candida and how she hated me and made me have this stupid haircut. And then I told him how I had caught her with Warren and how she'd threatened to expose me as a lesbian.

'A lesbian?' he declared incredulously as I lay snuggled into his chest.

'Yeah, because I live with Charles.'

'But you're . . .?'

'No I'm not,' I said firmly, elated by the suggestion in his voice that my sexuality was of moment to him.

'So, hang on a minute. You mean she was blackmailing you on an erroneous premise?' he asked, his voice black with anger.

'Yeah – Candida's big on erroneous zones,' I quipped.

'She could be debarred for that,' he exclaimed righteously.

That was Giles, always the innocent – no one had told him about the twentieth century yet.

'Yeah, but not before she had me thrown out of chambers, which I suspect was what she really wanted. I don't think it really mattered to her whether or not I was a dyke. She wanted me out and she saw my sexuality as a means to an end,' I explained. 'My head clerk's not big on women you see – let alone lesbians. At the very least my work would dry up.'

'But you're not a lesbian,' he insisted.

'Funny thing that,' I smiled. Then I looked up into his eyes with what I hoped was a look of desire.

He held my face in his hands and whispered, 'Maybe we should knock the rumour on the head for once and for all.'

'Charles already has,' I explained, giggling at the thought of Warren reading an S&M magazine.

'Not the way I'm about to,' he insisted as his hand found my breast.

I lay frozen, stretched out along his body, waiting for the world to end, or trumpets to start. Then he asked me about Julian. That I could have done without. Now was not the time for talk of other men's sperm.

'Oh that?' I floundered. 'Well, actually, yes I was doing a favour for a friend – girl stuff more or less. I'm sworn to secrecy you see – that's it, a secret pact.'

'Does that mean you slept with him then?' he tormented, his eyes sparkling. I think he wanted to back out of this one too.

'Com'on, Giles. Just because a bloke touches a girl's G-spot doesn't mean she has to tell him everything you know.'

He laughed. 'Darling, you're starting to sound like a feminist!'

'Am I?' I asked eagerly. 'Am I really?' I nuzzled back into his chest.

Gran would be pleased.

A selection of quality fiction from Headline

All Headline books are available at your local bookshop or newsagent, or can be ordered direct from the publisher. Just tick the titles you want and fill in the form below. Prices and availability subject to change without notice.

Headline Book Publishing, Cash Sales Department, Bookpoint, 39 Milton Park, Abingdon, OXON, OX14 4TD, UK. If you have a credit card you may order by telephone – 01235 400400.

Please enclose a cheque or postal order made payable to Bookpoint Ltd to the value of the cover price and allow the following for postage and packing:

UK & BFPO: £1.00 for the first book, 50p for the second book and 30p for each additional book ordered up to a maximum charge of £3.00.

OVERSEAS & EIRE: £2.00 for the first book, £1.00 for the second book and 50p for each additional book.

Name ....

Address ....

....

....

If you would prefer to pay by credit card, please complete:
Please debit my Visa/Access/Diner's Card/American Express (delete as applicable) card no:

Signature .... Expiry Date ....